THUG MATRIMONY

THUG
MATRIMONY

WAHIDA CLARK

KENSINGTON PUBLISHING CORP.

DAFINA BOOKS are published by

Kensington Publishing Corp.
850 Third Avenue
New York, NY 10022

ISBN-13: 978-0-7394-8159-2

Printed in the United States of America

ACKNOWLEDGMENTS

All praise is due to the Creator. I thank Him for always coming through for me in time, on time, all the time.

My husband, thank you for holding it down for a sista. We only have a few more months of this madness. To our daughters, Hasana and Wahida, I am very proud of both of you. Wahida, good lookin' out on the lyrics for Lil'E.

To the rest of the fam: my mom and dad of course. Love you both. Carla and Rob, glad you two are home safe from Iraq. Carla, you always have your family's back. Thank you for all of your sacrifices. To my bestest Aunt Ann, I love you. Aunt Sis, hang in there a little while longer. Aunt Ginger and Aunt Marva, you two have been writing me; and Aunt Ginger sending me money my entire bid. I love you as well. My cousin Jay Harris. Where are you? I miss you. My baby brother, Melvin, we gonna do this right this time, feel me? Love you and my nephews Tyrece & Damar.

My spiritual brothers and sisters. Can't wait to be in your midst to assist in doing our Father's work. Your dedication is inspirational. Gina, you took the torch from Kisha and are now holding it down. Words cannot express my appreciation. To Aisha Nobel Samataha, Hadiyah, Al Nisa, and Omar for driving my girls down to see me. And to the rest of the fam, you are appreciated and you know who you are.

Now for all those who was down with my personal grind: Sylvia Ryan Webster, thanks for always being there. Dee Favors, did we put in work or what? We thought it would never end! I know this has been an experience you'll never forget. Little Yalanda Carter, Sun Motley-Hill and Lashawn James, y'all are true team players. Watch out for the haters. Kisha Caldwell from the 'D,' you get double points: reader and hairdresser. Adriene Harrell, Barbara Hooker, Intelligent Tareef Allah, Angelia Ahladis, Courtney Moran: let's stick to our game plan and make it happen. Show me the money!! Adiam Berhane, I appreciate all the research. Antoinette Boxley and my bad little protege Armeca Gargani: think before you speak, thank you very much.

Supreme, keep ya head up.

Thanks to my cheerleaders and motivators: Reyna Daniels, Big G. Ganaway, Fish, Carolyn Jackson, Ms. Carter, Hope and Natalie Leath.

To the rest of the Alderson crew, Catherine White, the biggest Tramp and my hair braider Teresa Ramseur, Char Romane, Tanya McNeil, Kim Moffet and the whole Moffet clan out of Charlotte who ran to Wal-mart for my book and brought them out. That was love. And Nick Kiser, whatever! Sheila Waller, Tawanna Clark, Linda Gleaton, Regina Thompson, Vee, Von, Kisha Wade and Renay Coachman.

Angela James and Shontay, thanks for the office space (smile). Another one of my hairdressers, Sprinkles, Patty Dukes Gabriel and Marissa Massey: may your mothers rest in peace and to all prisoners whose loved ones passed away while they were incarcerated.

To my Spanish mamis who helped me with translating the Spanish parts: Ana Castillo, Rosalbo Villegas, Marcelina Machuca, Wanda Rodriques, Señora Cruz and Diana.

The peeps who I forgot to mention in *Payback Is a Mutha:* my adopted niece Ella 'Big El' Camp, big up on graduating, Kim McDowell and Michelle Smith.

To my fellow authors who keep it gully and sent me books and mail: Kwame Teague, K. Elliot, Joe Black, Rob Booker, Paul Johnson, Paula Edwards, Jaeyl Imes, Crystal Perkins-Stell, Brenda L. Thomas, Nikki Turner, Diane and everyone—be on the lookout for Seth 'Soul' Man Ferranti. You are always on your grind. Got me that King piece and I'm sure many more to come. I appreciate you and respect your hustle. T. Styles, Hickson, Sha, Jason Poole, C-Murder, Fajr Bint—it's a pleasure working with you.

A big, big shout-out to my Anthology contributors: *What's Really Hood? Vol. I.* Lashonda Teague, Mo Foxx, Shawn 'Jihad' Trump, Bonta and Victor Martin.

Thanks to my agents Marc Gerald and Earl Cox. My editors Selena James and Karen Thomas. I'll see you sistas soon.

Special thanks to all the book clubs, bookstores and vendors who are always on their grind. Can't forget Don Diva, Street Felon and *Essence.*

And saving the most important thanks for last: my readers. You are the best. I really do appreciate all of the love, support, fan mail and pictures. This one's for you.

Peace & Love,

Wahida

Wahida_Clark@hotmail.com
Wahidaclarkpresents.com

P.S. Project Pat, everybody is asking me if you kept your word and wore a FreeWahidaClark T-shirt on BET . . . Nope!

Prologue

It's my wedding day. I'm Angel Denise Smith but today I will officially become Mrs. Kaylin Santos. I am a corporate and entertainment attorney and I am marrying a retired drug dealer. He's a young brother who comes from a big family and who legally has a recycling business and a record label. He has a four-year-old son by his ex, named Malik, whom I love to death. You should hear him call me Red, the nickname his daddy calls me. He's a trip.

This has been a crazy day. For starters, last night I found out that I'm pregnant. My plan was to surprise my husband tonight on our honeymoon. But as fate would have it, I ate some salsa, guacamole, and spicy chips and two hours later my dream wedding gown, a hand-beaded mother-of-pearl, swarvoski-crystal Vera Wang, was being used as a vomit dispenser. I was devastated. Then what really pissed me off was when I sent for my husband to be, and these two uppity, bitch-ass wannabe wedding coordinators, who obviously forgot that I'm the one who signs their checks, had the nerve to tell me the bride is not supposed to see the groom or some ole off-the-wall bullshit like that. I went the fuck off! I told both of them hoes to "get ta stepping!" Shit, my husband to be, my baby, was the only one who could make it right and I needed him. Either that or call off the fucking wedding, because it was going to be my way or the highway. And just as sure as the sun does shine, my baby handled things. He made everything all right, well, actually more than all right. After he found out that I was pregnant, he was ecstatic. Then he told me how much he loved me, how beautiful I am and how I make him complete. Even when I began stressing over the fact that I was ready to practice law at our record label and wasn't sure about having a baby at this time, he made it all right again. He told me that the label wasn't going anywhere so I might as well enjoy the pregnancy. He said that we had enough money to do whatever the fuck we wanted. And for me not to sweat the small shit. I was, like, "I know that's right!"

Sensing that I was still stressing, he then asked me if I wanted him to get rid of all my tension. I purred, "Please do," and closed my eyes as he began to run his tongue over my pregnant nipples. I didn't give a damn about all the guests sitting downstairs waiting for our grand entrance. He then undressed me and spread my thighs so that he could look at my pregnant pussy. I could feel the juices trickle down as I watched my baby lick his lips while yanking off the Armani pants he was getting ready to walk down the aisle in. *Damn, this nigga is so fine*, I thought to myself. He began kissing the inside of my thighs and in four seconds flat, just like Lloyd Banks would say, "I'm on fire!" I grabbed that nigga's head trying to guide it to the spot, but he wouldn't allow it because he decided he wanted to tease. I thought I was gonna die! That's when he eased three fingers inside me and began working my juicy pussy, but as soon as he saw I was about to nut he slid them out and told me to finish myself off. I was in pure ecstasy as he watched me take myself to the stairway to heaven. As soon as my legs started shaking my nigga crawled all the way up inside me. He was fucking me so good that I was screaming. We both busted our nuts at the same time. And believe you me, all of my tension was gone!

After about ten minutes he reminded me that we had a wedding ceremony to perform and pictures to take. So we got up, showered together, and as soon as he got dressed he headed to get the photographer and our parents.

So now I have my dream wedding gown back on, vomit-free, and I'm sitting here at the vanity table looking in the mirror. Basically I'm just waiting on the photo session to commence. I have two group photos in front of me. The first one is of all the bridesmaids, and the picture is beautiful. We were having dinner at Kaylin's mother's house. Then my gaze goes over to my sho'nuff dawgs. I'm crying now because I'm looking at an eight-by-ten flick of me, and my girls Jaz, Tasha, and Kyra. We went to an Olan Mills studio to do this one, right before we all graduated. I can honestly say that those are my girls for life. We have all been through some shit, good times and some bad. Lots of bad (and if you haven't read *Thugs and the Women Who Love Them*, do so and you'll find out just how bad.) Anyway, I love these chicks.

Kyra is my cousin. Her mom and my mom are sisters. That ho was strung out on heroin, overdosed, the whole nine yards. You talkin' about a survivor. Her face should be by that word in the dictionary. She is still going to school to become a psychologist. She is enrolled in a graduate program at UCLA. She married Marvin, her nigga from back in the day. He got her strung out, did an eight-year bid upstate, came back for her, and they've been thick as thieves ever since. What makes me the happiest is that other than weed they both have been drug-free and have been blessed with a beautiful daughter named Aisha. They left Jersey and moved to Cali.

Then there's Jaz. That bitch is a whole mess. A fuckin' genius! Too smart for her own damn good. Can be dumb as hell sometimes too. Like the time she had that NBA nigga, not in her crib but all up in Faheem's spot. That bitch and the baller almost lost their lives. Come to think of it, that was also around the time when we found out she was working in a meth lab and had been doing so for almost a year. She was stackin' mad dough but livin' off Faheem's. They got married and even though Jaz didn't want any babies, Faheem wasn't tryna hear that shit. They ended up with a spoiled little girl named Kaeerah. Jaz went to jail over that meth shit and was looking at football numbers. But Faheem, that nigga, did some grimey shit and the next thing you know she beat the case. He's a real "G," stuck by her through it all. Now she's living in the ATL going to the Morehouse School of Medicine, which is the only part of the school that is coed. I hope she don't get into no shit, 'cause niggas are everywhere! Na mean!

Last but not least is my girl Tasha, the drama queen. She's another one who has been drug through the fire. But just like gold, she came out shining. She went from hoeing at the age of nine or thirteen (you gotta read *Every Thug Needs a Lady* to get all of those juicy details) to selling dope, to her hooking up with one drug dealer only to be snatched up by that same drug dealer's partna, Trae. That shit was crazy! She lost their first baby during some mad, mad drama that they was going through, but now she has twins and is pregnant with another one. She's one of them hoes that if you look at her wrong she gets pregnant. Anyway I love her and if she hadn't been snatched up by Trae I would never have met my Boo. That was weird the way that shit worked out. Trae and Kaylin are partners in crime. It's like they are brothers from another mother or spiritual twins, some shit like that. However, he is so good to her and for her, she is always happy and has changed and matured so beautifully. I can only thank God for everything He has done for all of us. She and Trae are the only ones outta the crew who didn't have a big wedding. They snuck off and got married in Jamaica or somewhere. They got money coming outta their asses and they too have moved to Cali. Tasha is a physical therapist and has her own rehab center. She gets to work on all of them big money-gettin' ballplayers.

That's right; there is nothing lazy about none of us. We may be hood, but we all know how to turn that shit on and off when needed. Now, that's what's up!

Now, me? My shit is so fucked up I don't even want to talk

about it. For example, like I said today is supposed to be the happiest day of my life, my wedding day. But somehow it turns into my wedding blues. I can't even bring myself to talk about it. So I'll let Wahida fill y'all in. That chick is wicked with the pen. We love you, Wahida! I'm out.

Chapter 1

"Fuck the groom! I'm here for the bride, she's my woman. Can you tell her Snake is here and he needs to talk to her?" As if on cue his boys came inside. There were five of them and every one of them was strapped.

"Snake? You're Keenan, her ex!" Trina glared in disbelief. He gave her this look that said *what the fuck you think?* When she got the message she made a mental note of all the niggas he had there for backup. "Aiight, then. Wait right here and I'll go get her."

"Yeah, you do that," he said to Trina's back as she walked away.

"Ooooohhh, shit! Ooooohhh, shit!" Trina kept mumbling as she wove around and in between the many hotel guests as she was trying to rush to the elevator. "Ooooohhh, shit! That nigga is alive and kicking!" She kept banging on the UP button as if that would make the elevator move quicker. She looked up to see what floor they were on, but only one of the elevators was moving. The other one appeared to be stuck on the eighteenth floor. She kept pressing the UP button. When it finally opened she pushed her way on without even giving the guests an opportunity to get off.

"Excuse you!" a young sister shouted at Trina as she mean-mugged her.

"Bitch, this is New York and you're excused!" Trina shot back.

"Trina, why you always gotta start some shit?" Jaz teased. "And what's up, who got your G-string all in a bunch?" Jaz was all hugged up on Faheem. They were the last two to step off the elevator.

Trina grabbed Jaz's arm. "Aw, shit. Come here, y'all. Y'all ain't gonna believe this shit! Guess who's here?" Jaz and Faheem just stared at her, both of them obviously not up for any guessing games. Sensing that, Trina yelled out, "Muthafuckin' Snake! That nigga is in the building!"

"Snake!" Jaz and Faheem said simultaneously. "Who the fuck is that!" Faheem needed to confirm. "Not Snake. You mean the pimp? I thought he was dead." Faheem had a puzzled look on his face.

"You and everybody else! It is on now!" Trina said, ready for some drama.

"You sure it's him?" Jaz was skeptical. "How do you know it's him?" she pressed. None of them noticed that they were just riding the elevators as if they had no destination. Surprisingly no one got on.

"It looks like him. He said it was him and he said for me to go get his girl."

"That's impossible." Jaz was shaking her head no. "What you been smokin'? You up here imagining things and shit."

"Imagining? I didn't imagine that he had five niggas with him and I know they're carrying some heat!"

"What?" That got Faheem on full alert. "Aw, hell no!" Faheem was looking at Trina to see if she was for real. Jaz could see Faheem's killer qualities kicking in.

"Faheem?" Jaz said as she squeezed his arm.

"Where's Kay?" he asked Trina, referring to Kaylin.

"I think in Angel's room."

"I need to go holla at him." He hit the button to the suite level. "Trina, go get Kyra. I'ma go tell Angel."

"Naw, you go get Kyra. I'ma go tell Angel. I'm not missing this!" Trina stood next to Faheem. "Later for Kyra. If I was you I'd go with the rest of us."

"Kyra is her cousin. She needs to be there." Jaz was getting agitated with Trina.

When the elevator doors opened they followed behind Faheem to Angel's suite. They heard laughter from behind the door. Faheem knocked as if he was the po-po.

Kyra opened the door. She had tears in her eyes. Everyone looked behind her and immediately knew why she had tears of joy cascading down her cheeks. Angel looked simply stunning. She was glowing as the photographer snapped pictures of her and Kaylin, then the bride by herself, then the bride and groom with all of the parents.

"Yo, Kay! I need to holla at you, man." Faheem didn't care about interrupting as he stepped inside the suite.

"Hold up." Kaylin kissed his moms on the cheek and walked her to the door.

When Kaylin came back to the bar area Faheem said, "Get your wife."

"Get me for what?" Angel was already right behind Faheem and immediately detected the tension in his voice.

"We got a problem."

"Damn. What now? We gonna start in exactly fifteen minutes," Kaylin said. "Whatever it is will have to wait until my day is over."

"Y'all got some unwanted guests and niggas is packin' that heat. I don't think that can wait. I suggest you get your squad ready," Faheem warned Kay.

"Them niggas stay ready. But I need to know who the fuck is tryna throw salt on my wedding and why I gotta get my squad in place."

"Me too," Angel chimed in.

"That nigga Snake."

"Snake?" Angel and Kaylin both said, confused.

* * *

In the meantime on the eighteenth floor . . .

Tasha was riding with one of her twin sons, Shaheem, on her hip, while glad to be spending some time with her little brother, Kevin. "I miss you, you little punk," she teased.

"I miss you too, you big punk." He looked at his sister in admiration.

"I worry about you all the time, Kevin."

"Don't do that, 'cause what's gonna happen is gonna happen." As soon as Kevin pressed the UP button the elevator doors opened and their eyes went to Trae lying on the floor bleeding.

Kevin mumbled, "What the fuck?"

"Oh my God! Trae!" She shoved Shaheem into Kevin's arms, who was just standing there. "Get my baby outta here. He can't see this!" she screamed. "Give me your cell phone. Oh my God!" She kept her eyes on Trae as she dialed 911. "Trae baby." She knelt down beside him as she felt his weak pulse. "Trae baby, don't do this to me. Don't you do this to me! I need an ambulance to the Hyatt Regency." She spoke firmly into the cell. "We're on the eighteenth floor in the elevator. My husband is bleeding, his pulse rate is probably about thirty-eight, his breathing is very shallow, and . . ." As she put her ear to his chest, she said, "I can't tell if there is bubbling in his lungs. I think I'm losing him!" she screamed into the phone. "He was shot in the chest and leg and I think the shoulder or arm, I can't tell, there's so much blood." She noticed that his gun was lying next to him. She ran her finger over the barrel and it was still warm. "Please hurry!" She ended the call while tearing a strip off the bottom of her dress. She tied it as tight as she could around his arm, went under the armpit up to the shoulder. Then she tore another piece off and tied it tight around his leg. "Trae, if you can hear me, I love you, baby, and you're a fighter. I need you to fight. Fight for me, baby. Fight for me and our boys. We need you, baby. I can't do this without you. Don't make me do this without you. Do you hear me, Trae?"

I hear you, baby. Trae was talking to her, but no sound or words were coming out of his mouth. He felt as if he were floating out in orbit.

"Stay with me, baby."

I'm with you.

Just then hotel security came off the elevator. "Holy shit!" He pressed the TALK button on his walkie-talkie and said, "They're here on the eighteenth floor in the B elevator. Blood is every-where."

The shooter obviously had pressed the emergency STOP but-ton. So hotel security got on with them, hitting the same button. "We're coming down to basement level now," he said as he hit the B2 button. "The ambulance is waiting, ma'am," he said to a crying Tasha, who had Trae's head resting in her lap. He had never seen a live and up-close gunshot victim before.

"Okay," she mumbled. "Please, baby, don't die on me," she whispered.

When the elevator doors opened, the paramedics rushed in-side. "Ma'am, we need you to step outside please." The older paramedic helped her up. "Is this your husband?" She nodded yes. "We need to get him stabilized. You said he was shot?" He noticed the tourniquets that she had made and was impressed.

"I think three times." She watched as they ripped his clothes off and set up an IV line, all with tremendous speed. She heard them say "One . . . two . . . three . . ." and he was on the gurney being loaded into the back of the ambulance. When Tasha tried to climb up onto the back with them the older paramedic shook his head no.

"What are you shaking your head no for? That is my husband and you best believe that I will be riding with him." Tasha was about to lose it.

"This is a high-trauma case, ma'am. We need to be alone with the victim," the older paramedic told her.

The two other paramedics were working on Trae as the fe-male paramedic tried to calm Tasha down. But she was holding on tight to the back of the ambulance door.

"You're wasting precious time, ma'am."

"Fuck you! That is my husband and I'm not leaving him!"

"Ma, what the hell happened?" Omar, Trae's cousin, apparently had been running. So was Kevin and two other guests, because they were right behind him.

"They shot him, Omar, and these muthafuckers are tryna tell me I can't ride with him. They got me fucked up! I'm riding!" She climbed up onto the back of the ambulance. She screamed, "Don't you touch me! Don't fuckin' touch me! I am going with my husband!" She was spookin' the older paramedic who was trying to grab her arm.

That's right, baby, Trae was saying.

"Kevin, I need my purse. Meet us at the hospital."

"Which one?" Omar looked at the older paramedic.

"Right down the street." And he closed the ambulance doors.

Omar took off to get his car. Kevin went to get Tasha's purse.

"Oh, God, please." She closed her eyes and prayed as they went to work on Trae. She hoped that when she opened her eyes this would have all been a nightmare.

"C'mon, people, we're losing him!" the older paramedic yelled, snapping Tasha out of her trance.

"Damn you, Trae, don't you do this! Don't you die on me!" she cried. "Fight, baby!"

I'm trying, baby. It burns. It feels so good when I don't fight. It feels like I'm floating.

"Fight for me and the boys. Don't forget we have another one on the way. I need you, baby. We all need you. You are my world," she said back as if she could hear his thoughts.

I love y'all more than anything. You are the best thing that ever happened to me. Y'all are what I live for, baby. But I did a lot of bad shit in the past so now I gotta reap all the bad shit that I've sown. I want you to stop crying. You know I don't like it when you cry. I love you forever.

"Trae, don't you do this! I need you to stay with me."

The heart monitor was getting slower, his vitals were dropping. She didn't want to believe that he was going downhill.

"This is too much of a blood loss!" the female paramedic said.

"Is he gonna make it? He's gonna make it, right?" Tasha was grasping for any ounce of hope.

"I can't promise you anything, ma'am. We're losing him fast."

Kaylin looked over at Angel. "What the fuck is going on, Red?"

Angel looked as if she was hyperventilating. But Kay didn't give a fuck. She was looking straight ahead; no words would come out of her mouth. *This ain't real. This can't be real.* Kay was talking to her. At least his lips were moving, but her ears felt like she was under water. She heard nothing.

Kay grabbed one of her shoulders and yelled, "Everybody get the fuck out! Now, goddammit!" Everyone scattered and the photographer grabbed all his equipment just like the piano player in the *Color Purple* did when Squeak slapped Sofia.

"Yo, nigga, what's up?" Faheem asked Kay. "We gonna do this or what?"

"Oh, fo' sho'!"

"Aiight, then." That's all Faheem needed to hear.

After everyone left, Kay turned to Angel. "Red, what the fuck is going on?"

"I don't know, baby." She was holding her chest as tears began streaming down. "I thought he was dead."

"What the fuck you crying for? Don't tell me you still got feelings for this nigga."

"I'm just as shocked as you are."

"You still got feelings for this nigga or what?" Kaylin pressed. Angel was still holding her chest as she sat down.

"Answer me, Angel!" he yelled, causing Trina and Kyra to jump away from the door. They had had an ear pressed hard against it.

"Why are you screaming, Kay?"

Kay obviously had snapped, because before you knew it, he had one hand around Angel's neck and he was holding her up in the air. "Do you still have feelings for him? Answer me, goddammit!" She wanted to but she couldn't because she couldn't breathe. He threw her back down onto the couch. "Ain't this a bitch?" He began kicking stuff around. Angel was crying harder and trying to catch her breath. "Ain't this a muthafuckin' bitch!" He went storming into the bedroom. As mad as he was she knew exactly where he was going, and what he was going to get and what he was going to do with it.

She ran behind him kicking herself for not making him leave those guns at the house. "Baby, don't do nothing irrational. He ain't worth it."

"Do you want to be with him?"

"No, I don't. And you know that. Kaylin, I need you to listen to me."

"It sure took you long enough to answer. Obviously there's sumthin still there being that you had to think about the shit." He was making sure that both of his gats were loaded.

Angel panicked even more. "Kaylin, baby, don't do this please."

"Why not? 'Cause you wanna be with this nigga?"

Angel hauled off and smacked the shit outta Kaylin. His lip began bleeding. "Nigga, will you listen to me? If you accuse me of wanting to be with that nigga one more time, I swear I'm walking outta your life forever."

He just glared at her. Kind of shocked from the slap while feelings of jealousy, anger that was off the meter, disappointment at the thought of her not wanting him anymore and at the thought of him losing her. *Damn, do she want to be with this nigga?* Picturing him showing up at their wedding and asking to speak to Angel enraged him even more. "That's what you want to do anyway! Go ahead and say it, so I can kill your ass too! 'Cause I'm definitely taking this nigga out today!"

She smacked him again. "Stop it, Kaylin. Listen to me. Why

can't you understand that I was caught off guard? The nigga I used to be in love with for years and was gonna marry disappeared. I wrote him off as being dead. Now all of a sudden he shows up and asks for me? Consider what I'm feeling for a minute, Kaylin. Come on now. Why the fuck you acting so damn insecure? This ain't you!"

"Oh, I'm getting ready to kill my insecurities right now." He tried to brush past her but she ran to the door, locked it, and threw her back up against it.

"Don't do this, baby. He's not worth it. Listen to me, Kaylin."

"He's worth it. How a nigga gonna show up at another nigga's wedding and ask to get with the bride? What kinda shit is that? Sounds like disrespect to me." He was foaming at the mouth.

Angel had never, ever seen him this mad before. "Do you hear yourself, Kay? You catching a murder charge is more important than me and the baby I'm carrying?"

"Move out of the way, Angel."

"No!" She pushed him. "Now it's your turn to answer me!" she screamed.

He grabbed her by her throat again and tossed her onto the bed. Before she could get herself together he was gone outta the room. When he opened the door, Faheem and the crew were right there. Faheem already had the game plan mapped out.

Chapter 2

When Kaylin stepped into the hallway, ready and waiting were his brother Kajuan, Bo, Marvin, and Angel's brother Mark.

"Who the fuck is Snake?" Kajuan wanted to know, his Puerto Rican accent very thick.

As they headed for the elevators with Kaylin in the lead he was firing off in Spanish who Snake was. When the elevators opened, they were met by Supreme, Kwame, Vicious, and two other dudes who were in Kaylin's crew.

Bo nodded to them and they jumped on a different elevator.

Fuck, Faheem said to himself as they rode the elevator down. The older couple getting off reminded him that it was broad daylight and they were in a very public place. "Yo, Kaylin. This ain't the place, nigga. You gonna have to take a rain check on rockin' son to sleep. That is unless you ready to take the Express bus upstate. Ain't no way all of us niggas won't draw unwanted attention. Plus, even if we are able to do this pussy, what about cleaning the shit up? What about security cameras? You feelin' me, lil' nigga?"

"He right, bro," Kajuan cosigned. "I know you heated right about now, but fuck him! You got the girl. The girl of your dreams is what you told me. Go ahead, get married and catch this nigga slippin' some other time." Kajuan gazed at his younger brother. "You got that, man?"

"I hear you," Kaylin mumbled.

"I know you can hear. But do you understand, nigga?" Faheem interjected.

"I got y'all."

The elevator doors opened up and the five of them stepped off. As they turned the corner the other elevator doors slid open while Supreme and the five niggas with him stepped off and followed right behind them, trying to keep up. Kaylin seemed to be walking ninety miles an hour. Their feet clicking loudly against the marble floors.

Kaylin saw a group of niggas with their backs turned. The group hearing the footsteps approaching turned around. As soon as Kaylin noticed the snakeskin eye patch all logic and reasoning flew out the window as he pulled out his burner, aimed, and let one off.

One of Snake's henchmen dived in front of him, knocked Snake down, and caught a bullet in his side. All parties drew their heat. Kajuan grabbed Kaylin. "Yo, man. Hold up." His gaze nor his heat left Snake.

"Everybody in here." Supreme opened the double doors to an empty ballroom. "There's too many niggas out here, yo."

Everyone followed, instantly clearing the hallway.

Snake's henchman (who caught the bullet) was trying to catch his breath. Luckily for him he had on a bulletproof vest.

After the last man entered the ballroom Kwame and Bo stood guard at the doors. With the blink of an eye everyone had their heat out and aimed at the next nigga.

"Y'all niggas outnumbered, yo." Mark smirked.

Bullet said, "Y'all niggas ain't got no armor."

"Pussy, this nigga's head ain't got no armor." Kaylin had two guns pointed at Snake. A red dot was on his forehead and the other red dot was on his neck.

"Chill out, nigga. I told the chick at the door, I just came to talk," Snake said with finesse. "I'm a lover, not a killer."

Kaylin's crew was now right up on Snake's crew.

"Put the burners away," Snake ordered, while staring at Kaylin. His crew reluctantly responded.

"This nigga shot me, man. You the only lover on this talk shit," Bullet yelled.

"Nigga, we in a fuckin' hotel ballroom. My man here made his point. And this obviously must be Kaylin." Snake's crew put their weapons away. Kaylin's crew kept the red dots on their targets.

"Can you put the heat away, my man?" he asked Kaylin.

Kaylin stuck one of the gats in his waist. He flipped real quick and began beating Snake with the butt, smashing his nose first, then repeatedly bashing in his face. Snake was able to grab his arm, causing Kaylin to drop the gun. Kaylin quickly pulled out the one in his waist and snarled, "Nigga, what? Go ahead and force me to merk your wack ass right here, right now."

Just then Angel was trying to get through the double doors, but Bo and Omar had them blocked.

"It's me. Trae was shot." She was trying not to be too loud.

Bo swung one of the doors open. "What did you say?"

"Trae was shot," she repeated.

"How many more niggas you got with you?" Kaylin asked Snake.

Through a bloody mouth, Snake said, "This it right here, man."

Bo left.

Angel couldn't really see Snake because he was bent over; however, his frame was the same. "Oh, God, let this be a nightmare," she prayed, blinking her eyes shut.

Snake looked up at her and reminded her that this wasn't a nightmare.

"Angel, tell this nigga you free to talk to whoever the fuck you want to."

Kaylin took a step back, refusing to take his eyes off Snake. He was ready to do them both.

Angel couldn't believe this nigga was actually here . . . on her wedding day. It just wasn't happening. The room was silent as she walked toward him. The closer to him she got, the angrier she became. Even though he was bloodied up he had the nerve to try and smile at her. She snatched one of the candleholders off one of the decorated ballroom dinner tables and smashed it across his head.

"You bitch-ass muthafucka!" she snapped. "What the fuck do you want? Why . . . are you here?" She hit him again.

"Red, I'ma ask you to calm down," Kaylin warned her.

"Nigga." *Whap*. She backhanded him. "That's for choking me. And the next time you put your hands on me you gonna wish you was dead. How the fuck you gonna jeopardize our baby, Kaylin? Have you lost your fuckin' mind?" Her eyes were red and she had transformed into another person.

"Red," Kaylin interjected.

"No! Y'all niggas got me fucked up!" She spat on Snake. "And you, nigga . . . you ask me to marry your bitch ass, then conveniently drop off the face of the planet . . . don't tell me shit, no phone call, no letter, not a trace. I waited for yo' bitch ass for a whole damned year while you was hiding like some pussy. While I was hoping and praying you'd come back, trying not to think the worst before finally accepting the fact that you were dead."

She started laughing as the tears flowed freely down her cheeks. She looked around the room. "Now this nigga gonna show up, on my fuckin' wedding day, mind you, as if everything is copasetic. Nigga . . ." She slapped him. "I don't want you. It's over. I've moved on." She kicked him in the nuts.

"Arrrgh," he screamed, balling up into a knot.

She then turned to a surprised Kaylin. The whole room was looking at her as if she had lost her mind.

"This is my fuckin' wedding day!" she screamed as she looked down at the blood on her hand, and the smudges on her gown made her even angrier. "Nigga, you are going to marry me . . . sometime today. Do you hear me, Kaylin? Call the cleaners, get my dress cleaned again." She sobbed.

"Yo, get the fuck out!" Kaylin yelled. He was waving his gun at Snake and his crew. Bullet and the white boy went to help Snake up.

"Angel, tell this nigga who you really want to be with!" he taunted, while laughing at Kaylin. "Go ahead and tell him you want me. Tell him you will always love me and I'll never stop loving—"

"Keenan, shut the hell up! What I do want is for you to get the fuck outta here so that I can marry my husband! I hate you!" she screamed.

"I love you, baby. You know you don't mean what you just said. You know it. I know it. Why you tryna marry that nigga? I came back for you," he yelled as they dragged him out the side door.

Kaylin stared at Angel shaking his head. He stuffed his gat into his waistband and turned to walk away.

"Nigga, don't walk away from me. I didn't do anything," she pleaded, then grabbed him. "I want to get married today, Kaylin . . . right now. Okay, baby? Let's get married."

He yanked away from her. "I don't think so, Ma."

"What?" she yelled in disbelief. She picked up another one of the candleholders off the table and threw it at his back.

He stopped and turned around. All of Kaylin's crew quickly filed out of the ballroom, leaving them alone.

"You heard me. I'm not marrying you today. I gotta sort some things out."

"I know you ain't let that fake-ass pimp take you off your square like that." She sucked her teeth and then let out a loud, disgusted sigh. "I don't believe this shit!" She got up in his face. "What! You actually think I want that nigga? Huh, Kaylin? Is that what you're thinking? Go ahead and say it so I can bust you in your fuckin' mouth. Say it, nigga! You think I want him?"

Kaylin smirked as he turned to walk away. "Red, chill out. Like I said, ain't nobody getting married today."

"Nigga, fuck you," Angel spat. "You punk muthafucka." She hurried and got in front of him, blocking his path.

"Red, you better go 'head. I ain't in the fuckin' mood. My man got shot. It ain't just about you today. And I damn sure ain't feelin' you all up in my face talking to me like I'm some fuckin' busta."

"That's what the fuck you are if you are gonna let that nigga come between us. All the shit we've been through. All the shit you took me through and now you're accusing me of wanting some other nigga who I said to hell with a long time ago? You're questioning my love for you all of a sudden? I should be questioning your love for me, nigga, seeing how quick you are to bitch up and flip the script on me."

"I never gave you a reason to even question my love." He stormed out of the ballroom, leaving her standing there in the middle of the floor.

When Kaylin stepped out of the ballroom Kajuan and Bo were waiting on him.

"That's fucked up, yo," Kajuan told him. "How you gonna not marry Shorty? What the fuck is the matter with you?"

"Nigga, I'ma ask you to mind your business. Now ain't the time."

"You kiddin' me, right? You're not gonna marry Red?"

"I said no, man. Not until I kill that fuckin' fake pimp-ass faggot."

"That's fucked up." Bo shot Kaylin a look of disgust.

"Let me go check on Shorty," Kajuan said.

When he went inside the ballroom Angel was sitting at the table with her head down, crying.

"Yo, sis," Kajuan called out to her.

"Leave me alone. I'ma be all right. Just leave me alone, okay?" He handed her a handkerchief and she pushed it away. "Please, just leave me alone. I'll be fine."

Kajuan stood there gazing at the beautiful bride to be. Despite her disheveled hair, smudges on her gown, and puffy eyes, she was still beautiful and glowing. He made a mental note to find out what was wrong with his brother. He had to be on some other shit. What? He didn't know but needed to find out.

"Aiight, sis, if you need me, just call my moms. My brother's ego is crushed. He'll eventually put it back together again and come to his senses."

"Fuck your punk-ass brother and his ego. Now, can you just leave me alone please?"

"Aiight. You got that. I'ma give you your space." He backed out of the double doors and headed up to the suite.

Kaylin was washing up and changing clothes. "What the fuck happened to Trae? Where was he?" he yelled.

"I just hung up. He said he got shot three, four times. He was in the operating room and that's all the info he had."

"Fuck!" Kaylin spat as he looked for some keys, forgetting that they took a limo to the hotel. "We gotta get to the hospital."

"We're just waiting on you. There's a car for us already out front," Bo told him.

"Let's roll, then," Kaylin answered, ready to go.

Chapter 3

Angel honestly and truly couldn't believe this shit. Words couldn't explain what she was feeling. They say everything happens for a reason, and she was looking for the lesson in this whole scenario and didn't see shit. She had no understanding.

She could see if it was her fault. But it wasn't. She didn't invite Keenan to the fuckin' wedding. The nigga was dead as far as she was concerned. So she moved on. Her feelings for him were long gone. Of course she was shocked when she was told that he was on the premises. What the fuck would Kaylin expect? Hell, so was he. Here a nigga shows up whom she was gonna marry, and who she thought was dead, and she wasn't supposed to be shocked?

Kaylin obviously was losing his mind. She'd never, ever saw him act like that. He instantly transformed into a totally different person. She didn't know who that man was who flipped the script on her. He acted as if he didn't know her and like she wanted to run and jump in the nigga's arms. She didn't want Snake. She had who she wanted. Kaylin. Shit, she loved the nigga to a fault. But know what? Her attitude was, fuck it! If he don't know that by now the nigga was blind.

But right now she was tired. Tired, tired, tired. Tired of niggas putting their hands on her. Tired of having to prove her love to these niggas. How about that shit?

What about when he decided to do his little disappearing act? What did she do? She waited for his ass. Not only waited for his ass, but held on to his money, oversaw his recycling business and record label, which she had to learn as she went along. They both were new to her. Then when Kaylin finally resurfaced, she jeopardized her freedom and her career by remaining in a relationship with a convicted felon. She moved into his house, kept it up for him, and took *his* son, not their son, to visit him every week. And he had the nerve to question her love? And on top of that she was carrying his seed?

Hell to the nah! She was so tired of these niggas she didn't know what to do. And her mouth. She never cussed this much in her entire lifetime!

Just then Angel's mother busted through the double doors.

"There you are. Oh, my baby. Look at you," she cried as she rushed over to Angel.

"Ma . . ." Angel sobbed, unable to get any more words out.

"It'll be okay, baby." Her mother was on her knees hugging and trying to soothe her daughter. "Go ahead, let it all out." Angel was crying uncontrollably. They remained hugged up for at least ten minutes.

"Mommy . . . it . . . it wasn't even my fault. He . . . he . . . just walked . . . Oh G-God . . . walked out on me." Angel still couldn't believe it.

"Why did he walk away, baby? You're not telling me enough."

"Be . . . because Keenan came ask . . . asking for me," she got out, in between sobs.

"Keenan?" Mrs. Smith inquired. "Chile, what on earth are you talking about? But I thought . . ." Mrs. Smith covered her mouth. She was now in shock.

"Yeah, Mom. Me too. The nigga is alive and kicking, Mommy. He was here. I saw him."

"Oh my God. Where is he now?"

"He left. Kaylin beat him up and he left."

Angel's mother stood up, hands on her hips. "Where is that boy Kaylin?"

"He left," Angel groaned.

"Well, where did he go, Angel?"

"To the hospital. Trae got shot. Oh, shit!"

Angel gasped. *Tasha!* "Mommy, I can't believe I'm sitting here drowning in my tears, and Tasha! O my God!" Angel stood up. "Mommy, I gotta go check on Tasha."

"Trae got shot?" Mrs. Smith was still stuck on that. "Who shot him? Well, where are the police? Is he all right? Oh my Jesus! Y'all children need help. This is just too much for me."

"For me too, Mom. Please. I need you, Mommy. To tell the wedding coordinators the wedding is off. Tell them to dismiss everyone with style. Tell them Kaylin will pay them extra. I'll go and explain everything to Reverend Run, then I gotta get to the hospital." *Tasha, I am so sorry, girl.*

Mrs. Smith and the wedding coordinators had a heck of a time explaining that the wedding and the reception were off. It was almost two hours before they saw the last guest out the door.

Angel apologized to Reverend Run and did her best to explain the main details of what happened. He was very compassionate as he listened, then insisted that he take her to the hospital. He told her that everyone could always use some prayer. He waited in the lobby while she went to go change out of her wedding gown and take a quick shower. She threw on the outfit she was to wear on the private jet to Hawaii, a pair of Seven jeans, a top, and crocodile loafers. Looking in the mirror, she saw her eyes were red and swollen, and so was her nose. Her neck was red from where Kaylin choked her.

"No more!" she said into the mirror. "No more!"

* * *

When they arrived at the hospital, Trae's father was in the lobby with the twins, Kareem and Shaheem.

"Mr. Macklin." Angel embraced the older version of Trae. "You already know Reverend Run." The two men shook hands. The reverend assured him that Trae was in the Lord's hands.

Angel kissed the twins. "How is he?" Her heart went out to the twins. "Trae is like a brother to me, Mr. Macklin. I would never forgive myself if . . ." Angel didn't want to say it and burst out crying instead.

"Baby girl, you know that hard-headed, stubborn boy is going to be all right. I bet you he scared the bullets away. Get on up there while you got the chance. They are ready to put us out. Too many of us up there." He handed her his visiting pass.

Even though Mr. Macklin was trying to sound strong, she could see the worry lines around his eyes.

Angel said a prayer as she and the reverend rode the elevator to the ICU. What did God want her to get out of today's events? she wondered as she stole a glance over at the reverend. Nothing but bad things had happened this day.

As she mentally tried to figure it all out, the elevator doors came open. The first person she saw was Kaylin. He was staring out the window. Angel's stomach knotted up with butterflies at the sight of him. *I hate that I love that nigga so much*, she thought to herself. Sitting in the chairs against the wall were Omar, Kajuan, Mrs. Macklin, Kyra, Marvin, Jaz, and Faheem. No wonder they were trying to put them out. The whole family was there. Reverend Run headed over toward Kaylin.

Before Angel could ask where Tasha was, she spotted her coming out of the bathroom blowing her nose. She had someone's jacket on over her bridesmaid's dress. The dress had dried blood all over the front of it.

When she looked up and saw Angel she broke down crying. Angel went over, hugged her, and led her back into the bathroom. Angel, seeing how distraught her girl was, knew that she had to be strong for her.

"Angel . . . what . . . I don't want to . . . live without him," Tasha barely got out between sobs.

"You won't have to. You know that nigga is a fighter," Angel assured her.

"Then what's taking them so long? I'm going crazy." She ran both of her hands through her hair and turned in a circle. "They won't even tell me anything, Angel. I can't take it."

"They're doing all they can, Tasha. He's a fighter. We got the money for the best doctors, so I promise you that nigga will be aiiight. You know he is not leaving you and his boys. His family is everything to him. Am I right?" Tasha nodded yes. "I know I am. We just have to have a little more patience."

"Roz." Trina was knocking on the bathroom door. She eased it open, looking from Tasha to Angel, and decided to hand Angel a large travel bag.

"Look at you, Ma. Let's see what we got in here." Angel opened the bag and pulled out a baby-blue and white Baby Phat sweatsuit, underwear, and a pair of white Baby Phat sneakers. There was also a toothbrush, lotion, washcloth, and a towel. At the bottom of the bag were magazines: *KING*, *FEDS*, *Don Diva*, and *Essence*. She took everything out of the bag except for the magazines.

Angel wet the washcloth with warm water and dabbed Tasha's face. She then helped her out of the suit jacket and peeled off the bloody bridesmaid's dress. She gently washed Tasha off before helping her get into the clean clothes. She then brushed her hair and put it into a ponytail.

"Tasha, I never imagined that a wedding day could turn into such a disaster. Today was supposed to be a happy day for everybody. I am so sorry, Tasha. If I could go back and do things different, I swear I would."

Tasha gave Angel a hug. "We'll get through this . . . I hope."

Angel broke down and cried. "Shit!" she cursed, mad that she caved in. "I'm sorry, girl. And yes, we will get through this." She tried to stop crying. "I can get married some other time. I'm sorry. Here I am supposed to be here for you and I'm crying on your shoulder." She smiled.

"Wait a minute. What do you mean 'you can get married some other time'? Y'all didn't get married? Then what were y'all doing all this time?" Tasha was honestly confused.

"Oh God, Tasha. I thought you knew!" Angel covered her mouth as if she just leaked the biggest secret.

"Knew what, Angel?"

"Keenan came to the wedding wanting to speak to me. Of course Kaylin went ballistic and beat his ass. He would have killed him if it wasn't for it being the wrong place and time," Angel rattled off before starting to cry hard, like a kid who just got a major ass whipping. "He . . . Tasha . . . he wa . . . walked out. He said he did . . . didn't want to marry me. Tasha, I swear it wasn't my fault."

"Keenan? Snake?" Tasha's mouth was wide open. Angel nodded yes. "I thought he—"

"We all did." Angel was tired of saying it.

"That slimy bastard! How does he look? What did you do?" Tasha was pacing back and forth, not believing what she was hearing. "Damn, that had to be crazy. What a fuckin' creep!" she spat.

"It was creepy. I don't think I'll ever be the same again. I hope I don't start having nightmares."

"Fuck! What does he look like?"

"The nigga hasn't aged a bit. He looks exactly the same except for the eye patch. It took everything I had not to freak out. If I had a gun I would have put out his other eye. I was so damned scared and mad."

"I don't believe Kaylin. Y'all really didn't get married?"

"Nooo," Angel sniveled. "He even choked me. Accused me of wanting to be with the nigga and everything."

"Oh, hell no! Fuck that! I told him he better not ever put his hands on you." Tasha stormed out of the bathroom, temporarily forgetting about Trae.

Angel was running behind her. "Tasha, I got him." She grabbed her hand. "I got that nigga, trust me."

Tasha yanked away. "I know, but I still need to check his ass. He got shit twisted. Kaylin! Kaylin!" She yelled as everyone turned to look at the disheveled sistas.

"Mrs. Macklin." The nurse on duty interrupted at the nick of time. This is Dr. Chen. He's filling in for Dr. Harabi." Dr. Chen was a tiny, frail Chinese man. He was bald on top, wore huge frames, and had protruding front teeth.

"Mrs. Macklin. I'm Dr. Chen." He gave a slight bow and then led her off to the side. Everyone in the waiting area was now standing up, anguish evident all over their faces.

Trae's mother was now up and standing next to Tasha. They were holding hands.

"Dr. Chen, this is my husband's mother. And these people standing around are all extended family." She was now squeezing her mother-in-law's hand. Her voice began to tremble. "Whatever you have to say concerning my husband please say it in front of everyone."

"Very well, Mrs. Macklin. The surgery was a success for the most part. We were able to dislodge all four bullets. However, the bullet that lodged in his chest and then hit his spine has triggered a comalike state. He . . ."

Tasha fainted.

Chapter 4

Seventy-two hours later, Trae was still in a coma. Everyone was going back and forth to the hospital. Tasha was the only one who wouldn't leave. She stayed by his side night and day. The family was bringing her meals, changes of clothes, and books to read. The twins, she would meet in the lobby every day, thanks to Trae's parents.

Angel couldn't understand how she did it. She didn't think Tasha ever went to sleep. Between keeping an eye on Trae, dealing with the detectives that came by daily, sometimes two and three times a day, the kids, Trae's crew, and even Reverend Run, who came by two more times, Angel saw Tasha in a whole new light. On top of that she was keeping Angel's spirits up. Angel had gone home to get a change of clothes and had been camped out at the hospital ever since.

Angel was balled up on the small love seat seated in the far corner of Trae's private hospital room. For privacy Mt. Sinai was the place to be. The room had a large bathroom, a sitting area, and if it wasn't for his hospital bed and all of the monitors you wouldn't know that you were in a hospital. It was freezing and Angel had the covers over her head and was trying to go back to sleep, that is until she heard Omar and Bo come in. They were talking low but Angel knew what she had heard.

"I want these muthafuckas found and I want them done just the way they did my husband. What do I have to pay?"

"Ma, you killin' me. How you gonna insult me like that?" Omar wanted to know.

"I'm not trying to insult you. I just want these niggas taken care of before Trae gets well." Her voice cracked. "I know he's coming out of this, Omar. I know he is."

"Ma, we got you, yo. It's just taking a little more time than we anticipated," Bo assured her. "But things are moving. It's all gravy."

Angel continued to listen as they explained that they finally got their hands on both of the surveillance tapes at the hotel. The one of Trae on the elevators, Kaylin firing on Snake, and all of them filing into the ballroom. Their people were going over them. The tapes were twenty-five grand a piece and Omar told Tasha they would keep her posted.

There's a price for everything, Angel thought to herself.

When the nurse entered, Omar and Bo left. Angel remained balled up as Tasha and the nurse made small talk. She figured that she was checking all of the equipment that was hooked up to Trae.

As soon as the nurse left, Tasha began talking to Trae. She made sure that every time she would be alone with him she would have a conversation with him. Angel peeked from under the covers and saw Tasha planting a kiss on his forehead.

"Hey, baby. I'm sure you just heard the nurse say that your vitals are fine and your wounds are healing. I miss you sooo much. Your sons miss you even more. Please come home to us real soon. Nana and Pop-pop are trying not to go crazy and they are doing such a good job with the boys.

"The apartment is ready. Who would ever have thought we would have needed it under these circumstances? We only lived in it together as a family for what, two, three days?" She giggled. "Now it looks like we'll be there for at least a month. The doctor said you won't be able to travel back to Cali for at least that long. You have to get good and strong. Glad you didn't sell it after all.

"Damn, baby, remember the first time I came over there? I remember it just like it was yesterday. You had hoes calling, putting them on speakerphone while trying to get me to spend the night?" She giggled at the memory. "Remember how I broke your blender making millions of strawberry shakes? What about the time that I was your patient and was supposed to be on bed rest? You also got your first shot of head right there in that apartment. Now a wife and two kids, one on the way, your bachelor/freak pad is now a family pad. Toys, cribs, bottles, the whole nine yards. Who would have thunk it?" She chuckled.

"Oh, your boy Jacob the Jeweler? He just got arrested in connection with a multistate drug and money-laundering ring. He's out on bond. But the feds hemmed him up at the Midtown Manhattan spot. You think I should give him my butterfly necklace back?" Psych!

"But for real, they seized five mil in cash, thirty pieces of jewelry, thirteen houses, thirty-five vehicles, and 270 million in numerous bank accounts. Is that crazy or what? Now, I'm not sure if it is all his, but the article said that his affiliation was with some gang called the Black Mafia Family. I bet some broke-ass government agents' wives will be rockin' some serious jewelry.

"On another note your Miami Squad won the championship last night. Your boy D-Wade got MVP, of course. The Glove finally got a ring. Big Daddy, Shaq Diesel came through. Zo, you know that's my nigga. Haslem, White Chocolate, Posey. They all came through. Riley pulled it off, just like you said he would. You would have been really proud.

"Your girl Angel is still here. I'ma make her ass go home today. You gotta hurry up and get well so you can talk some sense to Kaylin, or I'ma have to kick his ass. To walk out and not marry my girl? He got the game twisted. It's not like she's some fucking jump-off! You feel me? That was totally disrespectful and it wasn't her fault. On top of that she's carrying his seed.

Yeah. You didn't know that, did you? He choked her and every-thing. It wasn't her fault that Snake's ass showed up. Anyways, you need to put your man in check. That shit was foul."

Angel watched as Tasha took his hand and placed it on her stomach. As the tears rolled down her cheeks she was whispering in his ear.

Yeah. It's time for me to go home and face the music, Angel told herself.

Angel was livid as she dialed Kaylin's sister Tamara's number. She left the hospital with Tasha two nights ago and Kaylin still had not been home.

"Tamara, it's me. You still haven't heard from Kay?" Anguish was evident in her voice.

"Yeah. He didn't call you?"

"Tamara, no. If he had I wouldn't be asking you what was up."

"He's over at Malik's mom's house."

"He's what?" Angel had to make sure she heard right.

"He's over at Bianca's," Tamara stated matter-of-factly.

"It is almost one o'clock in the morning, Tamara. What the fuck is he doing over there? I've been looking high and low for this nigga and he's holed up at his baby mama's house? He hasn't even been answering his cell." She was acting as if it was Tamara's fault.

Sensing that, Tamara said, "I thought you knew!" Now Tamara felt guilty for telling her where he was.

"Thank you, girl." Angel tossed the phone onto the sofa. "Ain't this some shit!" She stood with her hands on both hips, deep in thought, trying to figure out what the fuck was going on. Getting angrier by the minute, she tried to control the negative thoughts that were causing her imagination to run rampant. As she paced back and forth, the visual of Kaylin wrapped around his baby mama caused her to move even faster. Before she knew it she was jumping into some jeans, a sweatshirt, and sneakers.

She picked up the phone and dialed the number for a taxi. She went to Kaylin's safe and grabbed his .22. She tucked it into her waistband. Taking fifty dollars out of her purse along with her driver's license, which she stuffed into her back pocket, she snatched up her keys and was out the front door where she waited on the porch until the cab came.

At 2:20 a.m. she was getting out in front of Bianca's home. She had a nice little house in Astoria, Queens. She paid the driver, jumped out, and walked briskly up the driveway. Kaylin's Mercedes station wagon was parked big as day. *This nigga ain't even trying to be discreet.* She patted where the .22 was. "Be easy, Angel. Be easy." Lifting her finger to ring the bell, she was startled when the door flung open.

Kaylin stood there behind the screen door wearing a black hoodie, the hood hanging loosely over his face. His eyes darted over the surrounding area. She noticed that his eyes were bloodshot and that he was obviously tired.

"What are you doing here, Red?" he snapped as he pushed open the screen door to let her in.

"What the fuck you mean what I'm doing here? It's three o'clock in the damn morning. I'm asking you the same damn thing! I came to take you home. Why the fuck do you think I'm here? My husband doesn't come home or call me in five days and then I hear through the grapevine that he's camping out at his baby's mama. Get your shit, Kaylin. You're coming home right now. We gotta straighten some shit out." Her voice rose.

"Red, it's after two in the morning. Folks are asleep." He closed the front door, walked right past her, and went to sit on the living room couch.

"So the fuck what? You fuckin' your baby's mama now?"

"Lower your voice, Red."

Bianca came running down the stairs, but stopped dead in her tracks when she saw Angel.

"No, that nigga ain't here yet. What you do? Call him and tell him I was here waiting on his ass?" Kaylin fired off at Bianca.

Bianca mumbled something under her breath and rolled her eyes. "I ain't got nothing but time, so I hope you told him to come on and get this ass whipping and to pack his shit."

"Why you always tripping, Kay? This ain't our shit. Why you gotta be such a bully, Kay?" Bianca looked over at Angel as if to say *please help!*

"What the fuck is going on, Bianca?" Angel snapped.

"Let me holla at you for a minute, please." She turned around and went back up the stairs.

Angel shot Kaylin a skeptical glance before following Bianca upstairs. Her head was poked out of her bedroom door as she motioned for Angel to come in.

"What the fuck is really going on, Bianca?"

"Girl, please talk to Kay. He is trippin' . . . hard. My man Vic spanked Malik, Malik told Kay, and now he's threatening to take Malik from me and threatening to beat Vic's ass. "Get that nigga out of my house. Angel, I swear to you, he only tapped his ass twice, with a freakin' oven mit. Malik didn't even cry, his bad ass just jumped on the phone, hit speed dial, and told his father. Now he won't leave. Please talk to him. You know how bad Malik's spoiled ass is. Between his father and grandmother the boy is rotten." She was obviously upset.

"Why would you let the next nigga hit on him anyway? You know he's gonna run and tell Kaylin. But I'll talk to him."

Angel was relieved that she didn't have to use the .22. "Girl, I thought you was fuckin' him. I was ready to fuck both of y'all up."

Bianca sucked her teeth and rolled her eyes. "Girl, please. Angel, just get him out of my house."

"Where is Malik?"

"At his grandmother's."

"Well, you know he is pissed off at me but I will see if I can talk to him."

Angel left Bianca in her bedroom and went back downstairs.

"What did she tell you?" Kaylin snapped.

"That you are blowing shit out of proportion. And I agree with her. You know Bianca is a good mother and you know how rotten Malik is. He needs a spanking sometimes. I spank him."

"You are his stepmother."

"And Vic is what? Isn't she getting ready to marry him? You just don't like him."

"That's different, Angel. You ain't supposed to be smacking on the next nigga's seed. Let's see if I wasn't a part of his life. This nigga got me fucked up. Damn right, I don't like his punk ass."

"Please, Kaylin. She wants you to leave. This *is* her house."

"She what? I paid for it."

"Let's go, Kaylin. Malik hasn't been abused. You been on some real crazy shit since the wedding and Trae and you're taking it out on everybody. Frankly, I'm sick of it. So let's go. Vic is not coming over here."

Kaylin jumped up off the couch and, taking three steps at a time, was up the stairs and banging on Bianca's bedroom door.

"Bianca. Call that nigga and tell him I'm waiting on him and if I gotta come looking for him he's gonna wish he was dead. Tell him he has until daybreak."

As he came down the stairs, Angel cringed when she saw that he had on his special steel-toe stomp-you-to-the-ground boots. When he flopped back down on the couch he grabbed the remote and said, "Angel, go home. I can't deal with you right now."

"Well, when do you plan on dealing with *us*, Kaylin? It ain't just me. It's *us*. I don't care how mad you are, we are going to deal with *us* right now!"

"Damn, Angel. What the fuck do you want from me? I told you I'm not ready to deal with you yet."

"I want you to come home, nigga. To straighten this shit out. I'm tired of negotiating with you, Kaylin."

"Ma, I ain't going home until I'm ready. Now take yo' ass home."

"I am going home but it's best to believe you'll be right with me. You can believe that. You gonna let that nigga fuck up our shit? I am not gonna have a bastard child. No. No. No. I did not come all this way with you to be treated like a fuckin' jump-off."

"I'm not going home, Red," he interjected.

"Your ass is coming home until after the baby is born. Your ass will be in the delivery room and your ass will be there to sign the birth certificate. After that, it's on you. If you wanna be a fuckin' sperm donor, cool. Do you, nigga? Because me and mines, we gonna be aiight. But for now we gonna do this shit my way. It's your turn to be there for me, like I've always been there for you. For now it's all about family. Our family. I'm not your baby's mama. I'm not wifey. Nigga, I'm the wife! And you know that there is nothing . . . nothing I won't do for you. However, I am officially tired. The old Angel is gone. And I refuse to allow you to fuck up my happiness. I'm tired of begging and pleading with you to do right by me. But you are going to do right by this baby. You are going to come home, we are going to continue to run *our* business, and you are gonna support me throughout this pregnancy, up to the signing of the birth certificate."

"Are you done delivering your sermon now?" Kaylin asked dryly. Angel shot him a *fuck with me if you want to* look. "Good. He ignored it; now take your ass home."

"Nigga, you heard loud and clear what I just said. I told you *we* are leaving together." She sat down on the couch next to him and folded her arms across her chest.

Kaylin sighed as he turned his attention to the muted TV screen.

Angel had dozed off but was awakened when she heard Bianca yelling for Kaylin to please stop as he dragged Vic down the basement stairs. Bianca closed the basement door and stood there crying. Angel jumped up, ran over to her, and walked her toward the kitchen, as far away from the noise as possible.

"All he did was tap Malik on his behind a couple of times. It wasn't even hard, Angel. Vic didn't mean any harm. Why does Kay have to take everything to the extreme? How is he going to tell me who I can and cannot see?"

"Girl, you know how Kaylin is about Malik." They both stood still as they heard the rumbling in the basement. Bianca looked like she was getting sick.

Finally, Kaylin came bursting through the basement door huffing and puffing. "Bianca, I want that nigga out of here, away from my son."

"He is not going anywhere!" she screamed. "You are not my guardian. I'm not going to continue to allow you to dictate who I can and cannot see. I was right there, Kay. He only tapped Malik and with an oven mit, Kay. I would never allow anyone to hurt my son, and you know that. You just don't like Vic."

"Aiight, then. Do you. But you won't do you around my son."

"He's my son too, Kay."

"Do you. But I bet you won't see Malik again until that nigga is out of my house."

Kaylin was on the way out the front door. Angel took off behind him.

Bianca ran down the basement stairs to check on her fiancé.

"Punk-ass nigga," Kaylin mumbled.

Chapter 5

The ride home from Bianca's house was very keyed up. But their first night together at home they seemed very detached, neither one acknowledging the other, acting as if they were strangers.

Angel indulged in a nice long, hot bubble bath and went straight to bed. She didn't care what he did as long as he was there.

The following morning she opened her eyes, looked at the alarm clock, and yawned. "Oh my God." It read 11:32 a.m. She yawned again, stretched her arms above her head, and sensed that she was once again alone in her bed. Reaching over and picking up the phone, she dialed Tasha.

"Hey," Angel said when she heard Tasha say hello.

"Hey back. Someone sounds as if they just woke up."

"I did. I haven't slept this late in a long time. I've been so stressed, I didn't realize how tired I was. How's my boy?"

"The same. No change . . . It could be worse." Tasha sighed as she tried to remain positive.

"Yeah, you're right about that. I'll be up there before the day is out. Do you need anything?"

"Yeah, I need for this nigga to wake up."

"He will, just hang tight." When Tasha didn't respond Angel said, "Trust me. He'll be up and about. Right?"

"Right."

"If you need anything just call me. But I will hit you up when I'm on my way up there."

"Okay. Here comes his doctor. Love you."

"Love you more." Angel ended the call and hit the speed-dial button.

"Game Over Records. Bobbi speaking. How may I direct your call?"

"Hey, girl. It's me."

"Miss Angel," Bobbi squealed. "Congratulations! Mr. Santos told everyone that you are expecting."

"Oh, did he?" She tried not to sound surprised.

"Yes. He is so proud. He even gave me a cigar. I asked him why can't I get a blunt? He told me to chill out." She giggled like a little schoolgirl.

Angel looked at the phone as if to say, *She can't be talking about the same nigga who walked out on my wedding and who's been acting like an asshole for the last five days. That nigga!* Angel was glad that she didn't have to do any explaining about the canceled wedding. *I'ma have to stick a pin in that larger-than-life ego and deflate that muthafucka.* Bobbi and the rest of the Game Over Records office crew were all at the wedding . . . the canceled wedding.

"Miss Angel, are you there?" Bobbi interrupted her thoughts.

"Yeah, girl, I'm here. What's happening around there?"

"The usual hustle and bustle. You want me to put you through to Mr. Santos?"

"Yes, please. I'll see you later on."

"Okay. Once again congratulations, Miss Angel."

Later on! Coming into the office later on. Ain't that some shit? I'm supposed to be in beautiful Hawaii, on the beach, butt naked, ridin' my husband's dick. Just thinking about it made her want to choke Kaylin.

"What's up?" the man she wanted to choke asked her.

"Why didn't you tell me you were going in? I would have come with you. Business is business."

"You were tired. You need the rest. We'll start fresh on Monday. I just came through to sneak up on these niggas."

"What's going on around there?" Angel loved being in the mix.

"Nothing that I can't handle. It's pretty light around here since we scheduled everything after our trip."

Trip? Honeymoon, nigga! "Well, I'll be in later on."

"Nah. No need, Ma. We on for Monday. Everyone already knows that Monday will be business as usual. Chill out. Get some rest."

Angel hung up. *All of a sudden he's concerned.* "Punk-ass nigga."

Later that evening after she left Tasha and Trae she stopped at the grocery store to do some much-needed shopping. After she put the groceries away she checked her voice mail: Kaylin's mother, Kyra, Malik, and Mrs. Smith all left messages. Malik was still at his grandmother's, so she called there first.

"Mama Santos, how are you?"

"I called you earlier. How are you? Did you and my son get this mess straightened out?"

"No, ma'am. Not yet."

"Well, y'all need to get it straightened out. Life is too short to be playing these games. I've never seen nothing like this before. Get it straightened out. I'm tired of him coming over here moping around. He doesn't even say anything. He's just in the way. I swear he is stubborn just like his father. It's ridiculous."

"I know, ma'am. Malik called over here. Since he has learned this phone number, he sure does use it."

"That boy better stay off my damn phone. His bad ass is supposed to be asleep."

Angel let out a chuckle. "Well, tell him Red returned his call."

"I will. After I beat his ass for playing on my phone."

"Good night, Mrs. Santos."

"Good night and get y'all's mess straightened out. Y'all have a baby on the way."

Don't I know it? Angel disconnected her and dialed her mother.

"Hey, Mom, I just got in. You should have dialed my cell phone. What's going on?"

Her mother let out a huge sigh.

"What's up, Mom?"

"Your sister. That chile is too damn grown. I swear, I'm hoping she gets accepted to a college far, far away. She is getting on my damn nerves. You ain't gonna believe this latest stunt. Carmen!" she yelled out. "Come get this phone and tell your sister what you told me."

Angel could hear her sister yelling in the background but couldn't make out what she was saying.

"You betta get this phone, chile, and tell your sister what you just told me! I swear I don't know what made me bring your sister into this world. I was damn near forty. Look at me. I am too old for this. I should have been through after I had you and Mark."

"Mom, don't talk like that."

"Hello," Carmen snapped.

"Carmen, what's going on? Why is Mommy trippin' like that?"

Carmen sucked her teeth. "Because I told her that I ran into Keenan and I told him that you were getting married and stuff. He asked me where and I told him, but how was I supposed to know he was gonna crash it and shit! I—"

"You better watch your damn mouth in my house, Carmen. You ain't grown, goddammit!" Mrs. Smith was yelling, cutting off Carmen's rambling.

"You did what?" Angel gasped over her mom's voice in the background—who was still cussing.

"Why is Mommy screaming like that? Damn. I said I didn't know he was gonna come. Let alone crash it."

Angel couldn't believe her ears. "Where were you when you ran into him?"

"He was at the club," she whispered into the phone.

"What the fuck you doin' at a club, Carmen? You're only seventeen!"

"Angel, you are not my mother. Mommy knew I went," she snapped.

"Where does he live, Carmen?"

"Who?"

"Keenan. Who else?"

"I don't know."

"You have his phone number?"

"Nope." She said it a little too quickly.

"Put Mommy on the phone." Angel was too rough.

"Maaaaa," she yelled. "Pick up the phone."

"I got it. Hang up, Carmen. You see that attitude, don't you?"

"Ma, why are you allowing her to go out to clubs?"

"She told me she was spending the night at Charlene's. But that's the kind of shit she pulls. I hope I can last around here for one more year without killing her."

"Mom. She has Keenan's address and phone number. She said she doesn't. But I can tell she's lying. Try and get it for me. What has gotten into her?"

"I don't know but it's taking everything I got to not grab this frying pan and beat it the hell out of her." Mrs. Smith was obviously exasperated.

"And, Mom, you got to keep a closer eye on her."

"I'm doing the best I can, Angel."

"I know you are but still . . ." Angel let out another sigh. "This is unbelievable. I gotta get down there and talk to her. Maybe I can do it this weekend. Don't tell her I'm coming."

"I won't. But good luck. She doesn't want to listen to anybody but them fast-ass girls she's always running with."

"Mommy, I love you and I'll talk to you later. Don't forget to get Keenan's address for me. I gotta go."

Angel was now visibly shaken. She dialed Kaylin's cell phone but hung up as soon as the voice mail kicked in.

She ended up sitting on the living room couch until one thirty in the morning, waiting for Kaylin, before deciding to shower and go to bed.

"Red." Kaylin was kissing her neck and trying to pull her nightgown up over her ass. She was disoriented but was quick to figure out that he was drunk as hell, and wanted some pussy.

"Kay . . . lin." She was trying to squirm her way from underneath him. "Stop . . . it." His hands were like those of an octopus. He tried to kiss her on the mouth. "Eeeew, Kaylin, you reek! You are so fucking drunk! Get the fuck off me." She gave him a hard shove and he rolled over onto his back.

"I can't get no pussy from my wife?" Kaylin slurred.

"Wife!" she yelled incredulously. "Nigga, don't get me started. Wife. Ain't no ring on this finger." She punched his arm. "And get them smelly-ass clothes off my clean comforter. Take your ass to the shower, Kaylin."

"C'mere, Red." He grabbed her leg and pulled her across the bed.

"Kaylin, stop." She kicked him in the chest with her free foot, but he didn't let her other ankle go. Her legs were parted and her pussy was staring him in the face. When she saw him lick his lips, she kicked him with her free foot and yanked the other one loose. He had his hand on her waist and had crawled in between her legs. "No, Kaylin . . . stop . . . You are too heavy." She squirmed once again out from under his grip, rolled over and off the bed.

"Red, why you doin' me like this?"

"Kaylin, you are drunk." She jumped up and grabbed her robe off the chaise and put it on. She grabbed the alarm clock and pointed to the time. "Nigga, it's after five in the morning." She threw it at him and it hit him in the stomach. He didn't even bother to move. "You stay out all night, don't call, then come in here pissy drunk and wanting some of this pussy? You won't get this until you marry me. Do you hear me? No wedding, no pussy! Comprende? Fuckin' asshole! Now get off my clean comforter!" She was pushing him, trying to roll him over. When she got him on his stomach, she pushed some more. The next roll landed him on the floor. "Get up, Kaylin." She got off the bed and kicked his thigh. "Go get in the shower."

"Red, I love you, baby. I'm sorry," he slurred.

"You're damn right. You *are* sorry. Now get the fuck up and get in the shower." She kicked him again. By the time she picked the pillows and comforter off the floor he was snoring.

Angel was so mad, she jumped into the bed and cried herself to sleep.

The next morning Angel got up, dressed, and ate breakfast while Kaylin was still asleep on the floor.

She headed out and ran several errands, the first being a trip to the furniture store, followed by the hospital to visit Tasha and Trae, and finally to Ewing, New Jersey, to see her mother and Carmen.

Angel had helped her mother get a single-level, three-bedroom home as soon as Kaylin was released from prison. It was a foreclosure that, with her mother's good credit and the money Angel gave her, was a smooth transaction. She had been determined to get her mother out of the projects.

She pulled into the driveway and beeped the horn, hoping and praying that she could talk some sense into Carmen, who was too smart for her own good. It seemed as if all of a sudden Carmen had turned into this rebellious teen. Something most teens do at thirteen or fourteen, not seventeen.

The front door was unlocked so Angel let herself in. Carmen

had the phone glued to her ear, and when she looked up and saw Angel she rolled her eyes, got up off the couch, went into her bedroom, and slammed the door.

"Ma," Angel yelled.

"I'm in here." Her mother sounded like she had been crying.

When Angel went into her mother's bedroom her mother was going through the contents of her flipped-upside-down pocketbook. Everything was spread out across the bed.

"Ma, what's the matter?"

"Girl, that demon chile in there must be smoking thcm crack rocks. Now, you know ain't nobody in here but me and her. I had the envelopes for the water, gas, and light bills. The bills are all here but the money is gone."

"What?"

"I swear on y'all's daddy's grave. She got me. I know she did."

"How much was it?"

"The water bill is one hundred and nineteen dollars and the gas and electric bill was one hundred and fifty-seven."

Angel set her pocketbook down and stormed out of her mother's bedroom.

She banged on Carmen's door several times and when she didn't get an answer she went and picked up the kitchen phone.

"I'm on the phone!" Carmen yelled. "Hang up the damn phone."

"Girrll, if you don't get your narrow ass off this phone and un-lock your bedroom door, I'ma kick the shit in. Now, Carmen!"

"I'll call you back in five minutes," Carmen told whoever was on the other end.

Carmen and Angel both slammed down the phone at the same time. Angel went back to Carmen's bedroom. Carmen had flung open the door and was standing there with her hands on her hips.

"Where is Mommy's bill money?" Angel pushed her so hard she fell back onto the bed. Angel slammed the door and locked it.

"Maaaaa," Carmen screamed when she saw that Angel was serious.

"Bitch, you wanna be grown? I'll beat your ass like you a grown woman. Now, where is Mommy's fucking money?" She grabbed her by her hair and wrapped it around her hand.

"Maaaaaaa!" Carmen screamed. "Mommy . . . Owwwwwww. You're hurting me!" She had both her hands on top of Angel's, trying to lessen the pain being brought on by her sister's grip. Her neck was snapped back and Carmen was literally doing the limbo, trying to lessen the pain. Tears were streaming down her cheeks.

"Where . . . Is . . . Mommy's money?" Angel asked through gritted teeth.

"Angel!" Mrs. Smith was banging on the door.

"Mom, I got this."

"She's hurting me, Mommy. Maaaaa!" Carmen yelled out. "Okay . . . okay. Wait. Wait. Owww. Pl . . . please."

Angel unraveled her hair and pushed her, causing her to slam up against the dresser.

"Oh my God," Carmen gasped. "My head. You crazy bitch!"

"I'ma show your ass crazy if you don't give me Mommy's money."

"It's under my mattress. Damn. I was gonna give it back," she cried.

"Get up and get it." Angel was standing there with her hands on her hips. "Now, damn it!"

Carmen scurried over to the mattress, slid her hand underneath it, and pulled out a wad of money. She threw it at Angel. "Here. Take it."

"Girl." Angel gritted her teeth. "Are you getting high?"

"No, I'm not getting high."

"Pick up that damn money, give it back to Mommy, and apologize. I'm coming back during the week to take your ass to Planned Parenthood and to get you a drug test."

"Why? You are not my mother," she whined.

"Shut the hell up. You better be here. If I have to look for you I'm putting a bald spot on top of that head. You better believe that."

"What day are you coming?"

"Don't worry about it! Just be here. And if you steal from Mommy again you might as well pack your shit. Now get up and give Mommy back her money!"

That night Kaylin didn't come home at all and Angel was furious. She stayed up until one thirty once again, waiting for him.

The following evening he came in and she was sitting in front of the TV eating a plateful of chicken parmigiana, spaghetti, and a huge spinach salad.

Without looking up at him she said, "I have my first prenatal visit on Monday morning, so make sure you are ready."

"What time?"

"Nine o'clock."

"Okay. Can I get a plate? It smells good."

"I only made enough for me." She continued to eat and watch TV as he stood there staring at her.

"So that's how we doin' it now?"

"Hell yeah, based upon your actions. You the one staying out for days at a time, creepin' in at four and five in the morning. The way I see it, you should have eaten wherever the fuck you been resting your head. I made sure shit was lovely for you, but you ain't got it like that no more. Your pride told you not to get married, remember? You want me to fix you a plate? But you ain't fuckin' with me like that no more, remember? But it's cool. I ain't trippin'. It don't even have to be about us anymore. This is about our baby."

"Fuck this bullshit!"

"Oh, it's bullshit now? Our thang has been reduced to bull-shit?" She shook her head in disgust. "Aiight, keep pushing me, nigga. I'ma have a surprise for that ass." She smirked.

"What the fuck is that supposed to mean?"

She was really getting under his skin and she knew it.

"Figure it out. Or better yet, keep doing everything that you're doing and you'll find out soon enough," she commented nonchalantly, pissing him off that much more.

Kaylin ran his hands through his hair and started to say some-thing but changed his mind. He headed upstairs instead. When he stepped inside the bedroom, he looked around in shock. He couldn't even form words. He just turned around and headed back down the stairs and out the front door.

Angel jumped up and ran to the door. "Kaylin!" He looked back at her. "Bring your ass home tonight by eleven!" She slammed the door, then picked up the phone and called him. She wanted to make sure that he heard her instructions. He answered on the first ring, knowing that it was her.

"Kaylin, did you hear me? I said you bet—"

"I heard you, Red. Damn. And yo, what you did to our bed-room got you that. I'ma give you that. That was real fuckin' bril-liant." He thought he hit the END button and tossed the cell over onto the passenger seat.

Angel started to scream on him, but when she heard the wind-shield wipers going she realized that he hadn't turned the phone off.

Kaylin tapped on the door before stepping inside. Tasha was curled up in a chair next to Trae's bed, watching television. She stared at Kaylin but didn't open her mouth.

"I know, I know. I'm such an asshole. Go ahead. Say it."

"You already did." She was still looking him over. "You look like shit, Kaylin. I'ma ask you to get it together. This is so not like you.

Even though I'm hating you right now, you actually have me worried."

"I promise you. I'ma get it together."

"Good. Because I am too tired to curse your ass out. But I'll eventually get with you. You got that coming."

She watched him as he looked Trae over. "Damn," he mumbled, eyes watering. There was a tube in his nose, his chest, and IVs in both arms. He didn't like seeing him like this.

"Trae, talk some sense to your boy because he's losing it. I'm going to get some fresh air. I'll be back."

Kaylin stood over Trae for a minute, then grabbed the chair that Tasha had been in and sat down. He bowed his head, while tapping the cell phone against his forehead.

"Trae, nigga, it's me. It's time to get your black ass up outta this hospital bed. I fucked up, yo. I fucked up big time and I'm falling deeper and deeper in the hole. My pride, man. My pride. You always told me that I had way too much and that it was gonna get me hemmed up one of these days. Well, my back is pinned against the wall.

"Aiight. I know, same ole impatient nigga. You want me to hurry and get to the point. Well, it's Red. I'm scared that she wants that fake-ass pimp. She got my heart but I'm not sure what she's gonna do with it. It's fucked up. I've been wildin' out. I've caused her to change to a whole 'nother person. She's a grimey bitch now! I'm serious, yo. I'm actually scared to go to sleep around her. She might kill me. I don't know who this person is. She's always talking all slick and shit and doin' crazy shit. I went home to the crib before I got here and she cooked this big-ass dinner. But guess what? She only cooked for her. The other night I went to get some pussy and she fought me like I was on some rapist shit. Yeah, I was a little drunk and yeah, I hadn't been staying at the house, but damn, I've been at Mommy's trying to sort this shit out. But the pussy still belongs to me and I ain't had none since the wedding day.

"I know I've been acting like a total ass, but that ain't all. This is the kicker! I goes upstairs in our bedroom and guess what she did? I don't know what the fuck she did with our king-sized bed, but it was gone. She got separate his and hers beds in the fucking master bedroom! Got it set up like a hotel room and shit. When I saw that, I said, 'I'll be damned!' Two full-sized beds. Now, you know I'ma tall nigga. How the fuck am I supposed to sleep in a full-sized bed?

"Nigga, I *know* I just didn't see you crack a smile. Whose side are you on? Shit, man. I'm losing this battle. I fucked up. I know it. I don't even know how to begin to fix it, yo. Like I told you the other day, she's my life. She's my soul mate. I need you to wake up to tell me what to do. Because, with this nigga back on the scene, I ain't feelin' the whole marriage thing. I'ma rock that nigga to sleep once and for all. You better believe that. This nigga is like a cancer or some shit that won't go away.

"So . . . I'm just trying to figure out how to apologize to Red. I did her dirty. Real dirty. I need you, my nigga. And I know yo ass is too evil to die, so snap outta this bull-shit ass coma. This shit is for pussies. What? You doin' this shit on purpose? Well, joke's over, playboy. I gotta go, man," he said, looking at his Rolex. "But I'll be back. My wife said I have to be home by eleven. This time if I don't do it, I really think she's going to kill me. I told you she got me spooked, dawg. I can tell she is fed up with my ass." He balled Trae's fist up and gave him a pound. "I'm out."

Angel hung up her phone, then picked it back up to call Tasha. "Hello."

"It's me." Angel's voice cracked.

"I know your voice. Your man just left. He looks so bad I couldn't even curse his ass out. I'm starting to feel a little sorry for the fool." When she didn't get a response from Angel she said, "Are you there?"

"I'm here. Why can't he tell me that?" She wiped the tears off her cheeks.

"Tell you what?"

"He told Trae that he fucked up and don't know how to make it right. He said he loves me and he's been staying at Mama Santos's."

"You heard all this?"

"Yeah. The dummy didn't turn off his phone."

Tasha chuckled. "You gonna say sumthin?"

"Hell no!" Angel immediately snapped back into bitch mode. "I'm not done torturing his ass!"

Tasha laughed. "Who are you?"

"I'm Angel Santos, bitch!"

Chapter 6

It was eight in the morning and Kaylin was seated on the couch waiting for Angel. They were on the way to her first prenatal visit.

"Red, c'mon. I fixed you sumthin to eat. Plus, we need to get going," he yelled upstairs.

He was still a little ticked because of the his and hers beds in the master bedroom. Then on top of that she had the nerve to say that the beds weren't comfortable and she ended up sleeping in the guest bedroom on the queen sized bed for the last two nights.

She finally came strolling down the steps. When he looked her over his anger softened up . . . a lot.

She posed in front of him, to tease him and remind him of what he was missing, with one hand resting on her hip, looking like a runway model. She was clad in a chocolate-brown Yves Saint Laurent suit. The short-sleeve jacket was accented by a sleeveless, big-collar oxford blouse. The skirt halted right above her knees, showing off those bare, smooth legs and sculpted calves that Kaylin loved to squeeze and caress. His gaze traveled down to the chocolate-brown Christian Louboutin stilettos.

"Are you supposed to be wearing those shoes?" he snapped.

"Oh, please, Kaylin. I'm not even showing yet. Well, a little. But the only thing getting bigger is my ass." She walked away from him, going into the kitchen.

She opened the refrigerator, grabbed a quart of orange juice, a banana nut muffin, and a pineapple yogurt. She placed everything in her lunch container and turned off the kitchen light. "Are you ready?"

"I fixed you breakfast," Kaylin told her, not wanting to believe that she didn't even acknowledge the gesture, let alone eat the meal he got up extra early to cook.

"Thanks, but I'm not hungry yet. I grabbed sumthin to snack on."

"Now, if I would have tried some shit like that, I'd be the dirtiest nigga in the world. Am I right?"

"Kaylin . . . never mind. Come here and let me fix your tie." She decided against going toe-to-toe with him on that issue. Because he was right. Plus, she was excited about her first prenatal visit. She had set her purse and the lunch container down on top of the coffee table and was adjusting his tie. "You look nice." This was the closest she had been to him since the night he was drunk and tried to take the pussy.

Her being so close up on him, where he could feel her and smell her, made him want to grab her, hug her, and kiss her. "What? You trying to choke a nigga?"

"No, not at this moment. Actually, you look too good to choke." The two days he spent chilling around the house did him good. On top of that he was wearing one of several Brioni suits. It was deep chocolate like her suit, white shirt, diamond cuff links, and matching tailor-made ostrich-skin shoes. "But we will stop at your barber's after my doctor's appointment. You need a shape-up. Now." She stood back and admired her handiwork. "We are ready to go."

*   *   *

Kaylin was seated in a chair in the corner as he intently watched Dr. Shelly T. McCombs give his wife her first prenatal exam. Angel's suit was draped across one of his thighs. He was telling himself that Angel was smart for getting a female obstetrician, because he wouldn't allow an old white man, or an old black man for that matter, digging all in his wife's coochie as he sat there and watched like a punk.

"Oh my," Dr. McCombs said as she probed around inside Angel. "According to the day that you said you were impregnated you are eight weeks. Everything feels fine in here." She pulled her fingers out, snatched off the rubber gloves, and trashed them. "You can rest your legs but remain lying down. I'll do the ultrasound so that Daddy over there can listen to the baby's heartbeat." She went over to the sink, washed her hands, and put on another pair of gloves.

Kaylin draped Angel's suit across the chair and came over to Angel. He grabbed her hand and caressed it as Dr. McCombs squeezed the cool gel on her stomach.

"Oh!" Angel giggled.

"Sorry about that. Forgot to warn you that it was going to be a little cool."

"A little?" Angel teased. "That was ice!"

"It was not!" Dr. McCombs reached over and turned on the machine. "Now let's find this little bugger. Plus, we'll find out exactly how far along you are."

Angel was still as Kaylin looked on. Faintly above the swooshing sounds they heard the heartbeat.

"Baby! Can you hear it?" Angel squealed.

"I hear my baby." He kissed her hand.

"Sounds good and strong. What do the proud parents want it to be?"

They both said, "Girl."

"I see. A good choice, and we'll be able to find out in a couple of months. Or would you guys rather wait?" Dr. McCombs teased.

"We want to know," Kaylin told her as Angel grinned, still tickled about hearing the baby's heartbeat.

Dr. McCombs dried off Angel's stomach and told her to get dressed. She and Kaylin then watched a ten-minute video on prenatal care and participated in a fifteen-minute counseling session. They walked out of the doctor's office hand in hand.

As Kaylin sat in the barber's chair, Angel was on the phone. She was able to set up a one-thirty luncheon with two Reggaeton artists, Papi Chulo and Suavecito Rico, along with their manager. The manager was trying to sign them up as a package deal, for whatever reason, and Angel needed to find out why.

Kaylin, as well as every other nigga, watched and drooled while she paced back and forth on those stilettos and wheeled and dealed.

As soon as she closed up her cell, a young kid walked over to her. Kaylin watched him through the mirror.

"Excuse me, ma'am. Can you please listen to my demo? I swear to you, it's fire!"

Angel glanced over at Kaylin, who nodded at her. "How old are you?"

"Sixteen."

"Sixteen! You look younger than that. Are you sure you're sixteen?"

"Yes, ma'am."

Angel smiled at his mannerisms. "What's your name?"

"Lupe Black."

"Lupe Black," Angel repeated.

Lupe Black whipped out a business card attached to his demo and handed it to her. "Hit me up anytime, ma'am."

"How did you know to give me your demo?"

"I heard you choppin' it up on the business tip and then I recognized Big Kay over there and put two and two together. I figured that you was Miss Kay and I always travel with my demo, so boom. I got at you. Thank you, ma'am."

"You're welcome."

He walked over to Kaylin and held out his fist to give Kaylin a pound. "The streets are feeling you, Big Money."

"Oh yeah?" Kaylin was surprised at this young cat and liked his style.

"Word."

"You still in school, shorty?"

"Yeah and no," he stated as he backed out of the barbershop and was gone.

Game Over Records was located on the tenth floor inside the new Time Warner Building on Columbus Circle. Kaylin was anxious for it to start paying for itself. Kaylin and Angel stepped onto the elevator looking and feeling like a million dollars. Hearing the baby's heartbeat was an adrenaline rush for both of them. Angel glanced at Kaylin behind her and noticed that crooked tie again.

"Hold this." She shoved her purse and now-empty lunch container into his hands and began adjusting his tie.

"You know I love you, right?" His comment, of course, caught her off guard. She brushed a few hairs off his ears and took her bag and the lunch container from him. He pressed up against her, his lips to her ear, and repeated, "You know I love you, right? I love you more than anything."

"Whatever, nigga. Don't even front. Ain't shit changed. Same shit, different day," she mumbled as she tried to lean away from him but couldn't.

He lightly kissed her ear, her cheek, and had moved down to her neck when the elevator opened. Kaylin wouldn't let her go, so they walked slowly off the elevator as if they were glued together. With each step Angel could feel his dick pressing up against her ass.

"Okay, you can let me go now," Angel told him as they entered the office of Game Over.

"Whatever, nigga," he mocked her.

"Oh, you got jokes now?"

"Whatever, nigga."

Everyone was trying not to look, but were looking at the couple who didn't get married last weekend. No one really knew what to expect . . . definitely, no one was expecting them to come into the office all hugged up like this. *All* bets were lost.

Still entangled, they stopped in front of Bobbi, who ran the receptionist desk and ran it well. Bobbi was Puerto Rican and black like Kaylin. She was about five seven, with carmel complexion and jet-black curly hair that was always cut short. Her eye shadow and lipstick always matched her blouse. Her small beady eyes smiled up at the couple.

"Hi, Bobbi," Angel said, taking the stack of messages she was handing to her.

"Hi, Miss Angel. Mr. Santos."

"Hey, guys." Dashae came over. She was their personal assistant. "Can I get you guys anything?" Dashae was almost six feet, dark as coal, smooth skin, and bright white teeth. Every day her locks were styled different. But today they hung past her shoulders.

"No, we're all right for now," Kaylin responded as he continued looking over Angel's shoulder as she separated the messages, making a pile for him, one for her, and putting the most urgent ones on top. Then there were those that he told her to arrange for a teleconference.

Bobbi was busy handling the switchboard as they finally walked away. Kaylin was still holding on tight to Angel's waist. He fished out his keys and unlocked his office door. As soon as they stepped inside he shut it and locked it.

"Kaylin, don't do this to me. You're not fuckin' with me no more like this, remember?"

"I'm sorry, baby." He was licking her neck, easing his hand down her skirt. "I miss you . . . I miss us," he whispered and gently rubbed her clit, causing her to surrender.

Back atop his chest, he began rubbing her stomach and planting firm but tender kisses on her neck.

Angel let out a moan. Something she had not done since that day . . . the wedding day. But now his lips had her feeling and getting caught up in the moment, melting in his arms.

"I love you, Red," he mumbled as he began unbuttoning her blouse.

His scent overtook her. The office smelled just like him. Where her color scheme was black and burgundy, his was black and forest green. Her knees got weak and that meant that it was time for her to go.

She wiggled out of his embrace when she heard him lock the door. "Why am I in here? Why are you locking the door?" she snapped.

Kaylin said, "I want to talk."

"Whatever, nigga. I bet you do."

Kaylin knew he was busted as he watched her hurry toward the door.

"Hold up." He grabbed her around the waist. With her back in his chest, he began. . . .

She tossed the lunch container and purse onto the sofa, barely missing. The messages rained all over the floor.

Easing her bra over her nipple, he began playing with it, rolling it between his thumb and middle finger, just the way she liked it. Hearing the way she was moaning brought a sly grin to his face, letting him know that he was on point. *Got her!* Sliding his hand up her thigh, he used his knee to spread her legs while he began rubbing her pussy through her wet panties.

"Baby," she cooed as she wiggled her ass against his hard dick while grinding against his hand. He slipped two fingers inside her panties and began massaging her clit. The shit he was doing to her made her pussy so wet, her entire body began to jerk. And the harder he pressed her clit, the louder she squealed, telling him the better it felt.

"Does this pussy still want Daddy?" he breathed in her ear, as she was on the verge of cumming.

She couldn't speak.

"Whose is it?"

"It's . . . all yours, Papi." She grunted y-yes as her juices squirted all over his hands.

As she caught her breath Kaylin took this opportunity to ease off her blouse and toss it onto the couch. He pushed a stack of papers over on his desk, picked her up, and sat her on top, sliding off her panties at the same time. He unzipped his zipper and she slid his pants and boxers down. He unsnapped her bra, and before he could get the straps over her shoulders good, he was sucking and biting on her nipples.

"Mmmmmmmmmm," Angel moaned as she gently pushed him back, squeezing and massaging his throbbing dick with both hands. She slid closer to the edge of the desk and roughly grabbed his ass and began with both hands.

"Damn, baby," he grunted. "That's the shit I'm talkin' 'bout. Ssss-shit."

"This is my dick." Angel squeezed harder. It was now her turn to take control.

"This dick . . . ssss . . . fuck, baby . . . just like that."

"It's Mami's, right, Papi?"

"D-damn . . . right." he stuttered as she gently massaged his nuts.

"Nigga, act like it." She released her magic grip, leaned back, and propped one of her stilettos up on the desk. She pulled his dick to her pussy and began rubbing the head up and down her hot, juicy pussy, teasing them both.

Kaylin was enjoying the view of seeing his big long dick being handled between her small French-manicured fingers.

"Ok-kay. This . . . feels soooooo damn good. Oh . . . yes!" she screamed as her body spazzed. She kept the dick on her clit, riding her orgasm higher and higher.

"Miss Angel, Dell Gindhart from Puma is on line four for you," Bobbi's voice belted out over the intercom.

"Fuck!" Kaylin spat.

"Oh, shit!" Angel gasped and shook as she tried to catch her breath. She had a smirk on her face as she gently pushed Kaylin back and slid down off the desk. *Two for me, zero for him. Now who's on point?* He was standing there with a rock-hard dick in his hands. She clumsily fastened her bra and snatched her shirt up off the couch. She wobbled over to Kaylin's desk to press the speakerphone button. Her knees were still weak from the two toe-curling, much-needed orgasms she had.

"Dell, hi, how are you? I have Mr. Santos here with me." Angel began fixing her clothes.

"Dell, what's good?" He rolled his eyes up in his head, wanting to tell his ass to call back after he busted his nut.

"Hey, guys, we just FedExed over some paperwork for New Day. Look it over and get back with me. It should be satisfactory to you guys, but either way talk to us. We really want to do business with your company and not just New Day. My people are liking your vision, Mr. Santos."

"Is that a good thing?" Kaylin joked, his eyes never leaving Angel. He was pissed that he had to put his dick away.

"You bet it is. Like I said, just have Ms. Smith look it over and we'll take it from there. Talk to you soon."

Angel disconnected the call and hit the front desk button.

"Yes, Miss Angel?"

"Bobbi, as soon as a FedEx from Puma arrives let me know. If

I'm not here let Mr. Santos know." Angel disconnected Bobbi, pumped her fist in the air, and squealed, "Y-y-yes!"

"Good job, baby." Kaylin had to give her her props. "Do you know what it means to have such a big company endorse a small label and a new artist? It's unheard of in this business. You are doing your thang and we're just getting started," he said in admiration.

Angel's heart was beating a mile a minute. If the contracts were to her specifications, that would be their first joint venture, possibly worth millions and the opening to many more deals. She planned on putting Puma back on the map and New Day on it. "I'ma bad bitch!"

"Yes, you are. And I'm the shit for having you on my team," he said as he grabbed her hands, pulling her close and massaging her ass. She was still trying to talk or rather celebrate as he covered her mouth with his, kissing her deep and long. Coming up for air, he whispered, "Let's finish where we left off."

"You want some of this phat, juicy, pregnant pussy, don't you?" she teased.

"Baby, you know there's nothing I want more, right now."

"You're going to keep on wanting it as long as I don't have my wedding ring." She pushed him away.

"Red." He looked as if he was just kicked in the nuts.

"Red, nothing."

"So, you just gonna let a nigga get blue balls?"

She laughed. "I ain't fuckin' with you like that, nigga. Shit, I'm horny too. but the issues that we didn't know we had, we need to tackle them and dead them muthafuckas. And I don't know why the fuck you thinking with your dick. Us fucking is not going to address our issues."

"I know, baby, but I don't even know where to began to make shit right between us. I know I fucked up."

"Yes, you did, nigga, but we don't have time to deal with that now. We have to meet with those artists in approximately forty-five minutes. And I need to freshen up."

"Damn, Red, that's fucked up. You can't just forgive a nigga?" He grabbed her.

"Umh. Maybe, I'll think about it. Matter of fact, hold that thought. We got a lot to work through." She broke free, grabbed her panties and the rest of her belongings, and headed for her own office.

Chapter 7

It was Friday at the offices of Game Over Records and Kaylin just walked into Angel's office and took a seat on the couch. She was going over a contract for two new Reggaeton artists, Papi Chulo and Suavecito Rico. She also had a phone glued to her left ear and their accountant, Tim Cohen, was standing next to her desk waiting patiently to get some signatures from her.

Her office was a little bigger than Kaylin's. She had a walk-in closet and a shower in the bathroom. The color scheme was gold and black and smelled like coconuts.

Kaylin leaned his head back and rested his eyes. MTV2 was muted on the large plasma flat screen while Wendy Williams, the HOT97 radio diva, gossip queen blazed in the background.

Dashae, the personal assistant, stuck her head inside the door. "Miss Angel, can I get you anything?"

Angel shook her head no as she swiveled around, turning her back to everyone, while still talking on the phone.

"Yeah. You can get her one of those pineapple smoothies that she likes and a Subway grilled chicken on wheat, mustard, lettuce, and tomatoes," Kaylin interjected.

"Got chu." Dashae left.

Angel swiveled back around and shot an evil glare at Kaylin.

He laid his head back and closed his eyes again.

When Angel ended her call, she took the checks from Tim Cohen, looked them over along with the attachments, before signing them. She then gave him a pen and the folder back for Kaylin. Tim went over to him, who double-checked them before adding his signature and passing the folder back to Tim. He left as quietly as he entered, shutting the door behind him.

"I ate already, Kaylin. Why did you order all of that food?" Angel snapped after she ended another call.

"What? You ate a muffin and a boiled egg. That is not a meal."

"Kaylin, I also had a quart of milk, a glass of carrot juice, and a Caesar salad!"

"Yo, just feed the baby, aiight? You are eating for two, remember?"

"No. You heard the doctor say that I didn't have to eat for two, Kaylin. That's your rule. Anyways, we have this same conversation almost every day. I'm not going to starve our baby."

"You damned right you ain't."

"Whatever, Kaylin, what's eating you today? You're getting on my nerves."

"Other than me not getting any pussy?"

"Yeah, other than that," Angel shot back with a laugh.

"That cat Lil'E. I want him. This cat is a beast and lethal as fuck with his tongue. He's been poppin' up on mix tapes that he's puttin' out himself.

"He's also been calling into radio stations freestylin' and shit, battling niggas and tearing them a new asshole. I want him on Game Over. And from what I hear he's not even signed yet."

"Well, what's stopping us?" Angel needed to know.

Kaylin chuckled. "I can't find him, neither can anyone else. No one knows what he looks like. It seems like he's hiding on purpose just to fuck with people and shit. I guess to make his worth go up."

"Well, it's obviously working. Look at you drooling at the mouth."

"Shit, turn up the radio, that's him now."

Angel turned it up as Bobbi barged in, "Boss man, Lil' E is on the radio."

Kaylin gave her the thumbs-up as they listened to Lil'E spit a bar and hang up. Kaylin couldn't believe the stations were allowing him to get through whenever he wanted.

"Oh, snap!" was all Angel could say when Lil'E finished. "Damn, baby. I see why you ready to send the posse out for him." Angel thought about what she just said. "Why won't you do that? If you want him that bad put somebody on him."

Kaylin sat there mulling her logic over for a few minutes. "I guess we could, huh?"

"I got you." Angel pressed the intercom button. "Bobbi, get Davina Ross of Ross, Ross and Davis on the line for me."

"Yes, ma'am," Bobbi answered.

"So, what do you think about Papi Chulo and Suavecito Rico being our first Reggaeton artists?" Kaylin wanted to know.

"Papi Chulo, I'm feelin'. Suavecito Rico, no!"

"What do you wanna do?"

"Scrap Suavecito Rico. I don't even like the name."

"What about their quote unquote package deal?"

"What about it? We still got three days to counteroffer or cancel. And I can tell that Papi Chulo will tell his agent to fuck off before he lets your offer pass him by. The cat is hungry."

"Aiight, then. If that's the move, handle it."

Bobbi stuck her head in Angel's door. "Miss Angel, Davina Ross said that she can squeeze you in today at three in her office or she can be over here tomorrow at eleven."

Angel looked at Kay and read his facial expression. "We'll be there at three."

For the next fifteen minutes they kicked it back and forth about what they were going to do with Papi Chulo, New Day, and the possibility of purchasing a record label in Canada and how Puma would fit in.

Dashae knocked on the door. "Come in," Angel said.

Dashae set the smoothie and Subway sandwich on the table. "Anything else?"

"No, thank you," Angel replied.

"What about you, Mr. Santos?"

"I'm straight, but tell Bobbi we'll be leaving at two thirty and I need tomorrow's meeting schedule on my desk before then."

"Baby, I'm coming back here after our meeting with Davina, so I'll get that for you. Thanks, Dashae." After Dashae closed the door Angel continued. "I'll be here until seven."

"What do you have to do tonight? And come eat your food." He stood up and went over to the table. He sipped her pineapple smoothie and set her grilled sandwich on the paper plate before pulling out a chair for her.

She rolled her eyes and reluctantly got up from behind her desk.

"What needs to be done tonight?" he asked again, motioning for her to sit down as he sliced her sandwich in half.

"Double over Papi's contract, let the manager know that Suavecito is a no go, look over the financials of the Canada acquisition . . . and I think that's it. It's only two hours, Kaylin."

"What about the budget for New Day's video shoot?"

"I put those numbers in your in-box this morning. Do we have enough press for them? I think they need more radio play, it's like they're teasing their fans," Angel told him.

"Shit, what artist couldn't use more press and radio play? I'm on it, though," Kaylin stated matter-of-factly.

"What's the A-and-R guy up to, Perry G? You like him?"

"It's only been three weeks, Red."

"Three weeks! All that jawing he was doing? All of them connections he's supposed to have? All the people he knows? I need to see some results!" Angel wasn't going for the bullshit.

"Damn, I've created a monster," Kaylin joked.

"I'll give him one more week. Then I think we should get someone else. I like Jet and Aja, the brother and sister team.

Them crackers at the label where they are ain't paying them shit." She paused to bite into her sandwich. "And, baby, stop being so charitable. I told you that nigga Perry G wasn't right."

"I feel you. Now eat up. I told you that hiring Perry G was a favor I owed. Since he failed his probationary period, my debt is paid. They knew he was a loser, that's why they dumped him off. We'll give shorty another week and if he don't produce we'll holla at that sister and brother team. Two heads are always better than one."

The investigation offices of Ross, Ross & Davis always delivered. Their specialty was criminal law and private investigations. Davina Ross went to law school with Angel and they always kept in contact with each other. So it was not a problem when Angel requested her firm's expertise. By the following Monday, Davina gave Angel a phone number for the mysterious Lil'E.

Since Kaylin, Angel, and Tim Cohen had to take an unexpected trip to Canada, to meet with the owners of the small independent label, Touch Records, and since Angel's mission was to look over their books and get a feel of the owners, she did that and left the following morning. Plus, she had the appointment with Planned Parenthood with Carmen. They assigned the meeting with Lil'E to the loud, obnoxious wannabe A&R bigshot Perry G. This was his test.

Perry G and his two flunkies barged into Junior's in Brooklyn as if they were the record label owners, not the employees. Perry G scanned the room and didn't see a rapper who would look like a Lil'E. He heard Lil'E rap on the airwaves and no one fit the description that he had conjured up in that big little head of his. So what he did was get a table and order him and his crew a hefty dinner. He did, however, feel he needed to place a call into the office.

"Game Over Records. This is Bobbi. How may I direct your call?"

"Yo, this is Perry G. Put me through to the boss man," he ordered.

"Mr. Santos is out of town. What is this in reference to?"

"If he's out of town, why do you want to know?" *Click*. The line went dead. "That bitch hung up on me," he yelled in disbelief as he dialed the office again.

"Game Over Records. This is Bobbi. How may I direct your call?"

"Why you hang up, yo?"

"To teach you some manners. Now, allow me take you to school. I am the gatekeeper. Ninety percent of the goings-on in this office comes through me. Now let's try this again. What is this call in reference to?"

Perry G sighed and explained that he needed to talk to Kaylin because they were at the spot to meet Lil'E but he never showed.

"Now, was that so hard?" She sucked her teeth. "Like I told you, the boss man is out of town. However, the boss lady is on standby. I know that she gave you her cell number, so I suggest that you use it. Have a good day." *Click*

"That bitch!" he yelled into the disconnected line. He pushed the speed-dial key for Angel.

"Hello."

"Miss Angel, this is Perry G. How you doin'?"

"What's up?"

"I'm at Junior's and that dude Lil'E never showed."

"He didn't?" Angel couldn't mask her surprise. When she spoke to him, he didn't sound like someone who wouldn't show up for a big opportunity like this. "How long have you been waiting?"

"For almost an hour," he lied.

"Aiight, sit tight. I'll call you back."

"Cool."

Angel hung up, pulled over on the side of the road, and yanked out her day planner to get Lil'E's number.

"Yeah," Lil'E answered on the first ring.

"Lil'E. This is Angel from Game Over. What's good? You said Junior's at four!"

"I'm here, yo." His raspy voice sounded excited. "I've been here. Nobody showed."

"Shit. Look around, see if you spot a high-yellow cat, flamboyant, he always has on a multicolored silk shirt and most likely has two young cats with him. One is dark-skinned and he—"

"Yeah. I see 'em. They just rolled in not too long ago." E burst into laughter. "Yo, he works for you?"

Angel laughed too. "Not really. But do me a favor, give me about forty minutes. Order whatever you want. You solo?"

"Of course."

"Cool, enjoy your meal but don't say anything to those three clowns. I'll take care of them when I get there. Can you handle that?"

"I got chu."

"That's what's up. Just tell the waitress you're waiting on Angel Santos." Angel immediately dialed Kaylin.

"Baby, what's good? You all right?" Kaylin asked his wife.

Angel sighed. "You're not going to believe this."

"What?" Kaylin asked in alarm. "Where are you?"

"I just got back into the city. I took Carmen to Planned Parenthood, got her an exam and some birth control pills. Thank God she isn't pregnant. But the drug test? That shit was a whole 'nother story. This little hooker had coke, weed, and E all up in her piss. I am so fucking mad at her, Kaylin, I could scream."

"Yo, how did you handle it?" When she didn't respond he snapped, "Red, you pregnant, Ma. You can't be brawling and shit! You risking the baby's life now! You gonna fuck around and I'ma lock your ass in the house and won't let you come out!" he seethed.

"Kaylin, calm down. I smacked her when we got back in the car, but we didn't fight. I told her I was too angry to deal with her right then. I dropped her off and I left. Okay?"

"Red, don't make me—"

"I heard you, Kaylin, damn. But check this out," Angel continued. "Your boy Perry G calls me up and says that he's been at Junior's for an hour and Lil'E didn't show up. So I calls him and I'm like what's good? You said Junior's at four, and guess what?"

"What?"

"Dude is sitting right there in Junior's looking at Perry G and his flunkies. He said that they just got there. Just like we figured, he got a half-assed work ethic. That nigga was supposed to go to each patron and ask, 'Your name Lil'E' or sumthin?'"

"Aw, hell no. That nigga fuckin' with my money like that?"

"Baby, I told you he was all talk. But check it, I told him to order and sit tight, that I was on my way. And I'm getting ready to call Perry back and thank him for nothing."

"Yo, don't say shit about him being out of a gig. I want that nigga to show up at the office so I can put my foot in his ass."

"Do you, Kay. I'll call you as soon as I'm done with Lil'E."

"Yo, don't be flirting with that lil' rap nigga, neither."

"Whatever. Why not? You ain't fuckin' with me like that, remember? Besides, I need to find out if I still got it."

"Red, don't get fucked up."

"Whatever." *Click*

"What the fuck?" Kaylin called back. "Yo, Red, don't make me fuck ya up about that bullshit you spittin'." *Click* He hung up, furious.

Angel called Perry G and thanked him for showing up.

Kaylin's cell chimed as soon as he hung up with Angel. "Yo."

"Big money, this me, Pras."

"What's brewin' down in the MIA?" Kaylin asked his and Trae's homey from way back.

"Yo, nigga. I think this the break you been having a hard-on for. Check it. I'm hearing shit about some new player with a snakeskin patch on his eye."

"Word?" This news caused Kaylin to stand up.

"But the only reason I'm not sure if this is yo' man is you said the cat's name is Snake. But this cat said his name, and you ain't gonna believe this, son."

"Nigga, spit it out!"

"He said his name is K, yo." You could hear a pin drop. Pras broke the silence. "Man, this nigga is either crazy as fuck or you got the wrong cat. But check it, we still on it. But I figured you wanted an update. You know I got chu, just say when."

"Aiight, nigga. You know what it is."

"All day and all night." Pras was gone.

Kaylin hung up, saying, "What the fuck?"

When Angel walked into Junior's, she told the waitress that she was Angel Santos and that she had a party of one waiting on her. The waitress motioned for her to follow her. As usual Perry G stood out like a sore thumb.

"Excuse me. Just point me to my party please. I need to say sumthin to these gentlemen right here."

The waitress pointed to a small boy with a hoodie over his head. "Right there."

"Thank you." Angel flashed a smile at her.

When Perry G looked up and saw Angel standing in front of him he began to stutter. "M-M-Miss A-Angel. What are you doing here?" He tried to get himself together.

"I was hoping to meet Lil'E. But since he is a no show, I might as well get me sumthin to eat." She looked at the empty dishes. "If you guys are done now I'll take care of the tab."

"Yeah. Yeah, we're done." Perry G stood up and his sidekicks, an Omar Epps reject and an older cat who resembled Danny Glover, followed suit. Perry G wasn't about to pass up a free meal.

"Thanks for coming," she told them, wanting them to leave.

"No problem. It's my job," Perry said as he handed the bill to Angel. "I'll see you at the office tomorrow."

She smirked as she watched them leave. Angel headed over to

Lil'E. Her stomach growled as her tastebuds and senses smelled French fries and fried chicken.

When she arrived at the table Angel said to Lil'E, whose back was turned, "Excuse me. I'm Angel, are you—"

"I'm Lil'E." She tossed her hoodie back. Lil'E was a female . . . rockin' blond braids and blue eyes.

Chapter 8

"Oh, shit!" was all Angel could get out. Lil'E sat there with a smirk on her face.

"You're Lil'E?" Lil'E mocked because she knew Angel was shocked.

"Well, are you?" Angel couldn't help but smile. Lil'E nodded yes. "Get the fuck outta here!" Angel had to take a seat.

This was indeed a surprise. Angel motioned for the waitress. "Can I have two slices of pineapple cheesecake, a plate of fries, and a mocha cappuccino?" She looked over at Lil'E and asked, "You straight?"

"I'll have a vanilla cappuccino."

The waitress nodded, took Angel's menu, and disappeared.

"You know I'm still in shock, right?" Angel confessed.

"Yeah, but it's cool."

"My husband . . . I can't wait to see the look on his face when I tell him you're not only a female but a white chick." Angel was looking her over trying to figure out who she resembled. She did know that she was a tomboy. "Are you gay?"

Lil'E laughed. "Nah, I'm not gay. Even though I may act like a boy, I'm strictly dickly. That's why I'm in the predicament I'm in. I love dick . . . black dick at that." She figured since Angel was keeping it gully she might as well do the same. Plus, it felt good to talk to another woman, a seemingly strong, powerful, positive woman. Angel's vibe gave off the feelings of confidence and said, *I got it goin' on*. And Lil'E liked that feeling.

"Oookay," Angel said. Just then the waitress came and set Angel's cheesecake and fries in front of her as well as both cups of cappuccino. Angel was still looking Lil'E over. Her mind, going over the possibilities, was traveling a mile a minute. "You know who you look like?"

"I know who you're going to say." E's eyes rolled upward.

"Who?" Angel indulged in a mouthful of cheesecake.

"Nah. Go ahead. You tell me."

"Alicia Keyes. You get that often?"

"Yeah." E smirked.

"Why do you have that hoodie on, covering yourself up? You're beautiful! The hoodie makes you look crazy like my husband." She smiled.

"I saw your husband. He doesn't look crazy. He is fine!"

"Where did you see him?"

"Felon, FEDS, Don Diva. One of them. He was in a flick with Fat Joe and Angie Martinez."

"Well, you said you like black dick but that's one black dick that is off-limits."

Lil'E chuckled. "I was just testing you. I'm not grimey like that."

"Good. Then we should get along just fine. And I see you got a little sense of humor. Tell me sumthin about you. What is your real name?"

"Lily Penzera."

"Penzera. You're Italian?"

"Yeah. But according to my grandmother my mom was white and my dad's Italian."

"Where are they?"

"My mom passed away when I was fourteen. My dad was just a sperm donor. I've been living with my grandma out in Hoboken."

"How old are you?"

"Just turned eighteen yesterday."

"Oh. Happy belated."

"Thanks," she answered dryly.

"How long have you been blessin' the mic?"

"Since I was nine, ten."

"How did you get so . . . good?" Angel laughed because she didn't know what other word to use. "You are amazing. You got my husband and everybody else going crazy over you. Why don't you have a deal? I mean, I know cats have been coming at you left and right."

"I already have one," she said with much disdain. "And yeah, a lot of labels have been trying to sign me but I'm in a jam. My hands are tied."

"Who signed you?"

"Phillip Johnson over at Tyrant Music Limited."

"Oh my gosh! That creep?" Angel was shocked.

Phillip Johnson was the East Coast version of Suge Knight. But the difference was, not only was he a bully but he was down right grimey, and the whole industry knew it. What earned him a permanent spot on Angel's shit list was when he tricked those artists on lockdown to sign a contract. He promised them the world. One of them wrote several lyrics and hooks for his other artists and got nothing. The guy was riding the subway and living at his mother's. The other cat, a producer, upon his release went to the label, produced tracks for another artist that went platinum, and wasn't even on the album credits. Now he was working a construction job. And they both were still locked into a contract with Phillip Johnson.

"How did you get hooked up with him?"

"The typical story. He saw me battling at Jimmy's Uptown. You know the rest, promised me the world, wrapped in a big fat record contract. He gets the pussy, I get pregnant, he gives me the abortion money. When I refuse it, he does nothing with my contract. So here I am, pregnant, no record deal, hustlin' mix tapes to survive, and still living with my grandmom."

"Hold up, you fucked him when you were underaged?" Lil'E nodded yes. "And you're pregnant right now?" She nodded again. "You sure it's his?"

"He popped my cherry."

"What the fuck? Isn't the nigga married?"

"And? What the fuck is that supposed to mean? P.J. has a thing for white girls, young chicks, and strippers."

"I'll be damned." Angel was so disgusted she couldn't finish her other slice of cheesecake. She sat there drumming her fingers against the cappuccino mug, glancing at Lil'E and trying to make heads or tails of the info she just received. Lil'E cleared her throat and sat there nursing her cappuccino, both ladies deep in thought.

"So, do you have your original contract or at least a copy of it?"

"Yeah. That's about all I have, is a contract." E chuckled.

"So, then. Why are you here?"

"Here we go." E sighed. "Just come out and say it. Everyone else said it, 'Lily, you fucked up.' Along with 'I can't sign you up until that contract expires,' or 'Philip Johnson is big in this business,' or 'You're white' or 'You should have come to me first' or, my favorite, 'You're pregnant, come back after you have the baby!'"

"Are you finished?"

"I just wanted a chance, Ms. Santos. That's why I'm here. I told myself that it can't be a coincidence that y'all called me. But I can't kill my baby, Ms. Santos. I won't do that for all the money and record contracts in the world." She stood up and was ready to leave.

"Wait a minute, let me tell you sumthin. I don't think you did your homework. My husband and I have a background of nothing but risk taking, struggles, and you'll find that we always go after what we want. And at this point that would be you and your unborn child."

Angel motioned for her to sit down. "Young lady, I have a little sister your age. She's smart as hell and has all the chances in this world, but refuses to take advantage of at least one. And here you are asking for just one, and you're carrying a baby? I'm impressed. I'm pregnant and I'm more motivated than ever."

"Pregnant?" Lil'E was shocked.

"Know that being pregnant shouldn't stop shit, nor should being able to whip a bitch's ass stop you from getting into your best gear. We can still be all we aim to be. I know I am. If you are drug-free, loyal, can stay healthy, and can show me that you have an above-average work ethic, I'ma show you the heights that us pregnant women can reach. No matter if you're white, black, Chinese, Indian, whatever. There's enough money out there." Angel was checking for any signs of hesitation. When she couldn't find any, she asked, "So, what's good?"

"I ain't got shit to lose. So . . . I'ma follow the leader."

"No. As of today you either lead or walk side by side."

After Angel dropped Lil'E home and picked up her contract she swung by the hospital to check on Trae and Tasha.

That next morning, she was on her way to Tetersboro Airport in New Jersey to pick up Kaylin. He had finally wrapped up the Canada contract. Things had been moving so fast that they still hadn't sat down and had "the talk."

She stepped out of the Mercedes SUV to stretch her legs. She was parked in front of one of the private hangars. Game Over Records had their own. She grabbed her cell phone and placed a call to Davina Ross. She needed everything that was there dug up on Phillip Johnson and Tyrant Music Ltd.

Kaylin had explained to Angel over the phone that he could easily take a limo home; she didn't have to drive way out here to pick him up. But Angel insisted that she come. She couldn't wait to see the expression on his face when she told him about Lil'E, aka Lily Penzera. He had tried to get her to tell him about their meeting last night over the phone but she wouldn't.

She watched as the private jet made its landing and pulled up into the hangar. Her thoughts went to her sister, Carmen. She was losing her, she could feel it. She had to figure out something.

Then there was Kaylin, the love of her life. Why in the hell did he feel threatened by Keenan? She had no understanding of that. Hell, he told Trae that she had his heart, and she felt exactly the same, he had her heart, but they both seemed to be avoiding the chance to confront their issues, afraid that they would be driven further apart.

She couldn't help but smile as the jetway door eased up and Kaylin came down the stairs. He was swimming in a cream Sean John sweat suit and beige Timbs. She leaned back up against the hood of the car. He smiled as he hurried toward her, that one dimple smiling at her.

"Nigga, I didn't buy that sweat suit," she joked.

He dropped his bag and went to hug her and she tried to push him away. He moved her arms and put her in a bear hug.

"This is how you greet a nigga who ain't had no pussy in months?" He gave her a sloppy kiss on the cheek, then one on the lips, their tongues doing a dance on their own. Angel broke away from his lips when his hands began sliding up her dress and squeezing her ass. "I didn't buy this dress."

"Yes, you did." She quivered as he pressed her against his dick. This time she went to kiss him hungrily, as she did a slow wind on his dick.

"Mmmmm," Kaylin moaned. "Now, that's the shit Daddy misses."

"Nigga, you gonna keep on missing it, until I get my wedding." She pulled his hands away from her ass.

Kaylin stood there once again with a massive hard-on. "Red, that's fucked up! That shit right there gonna get you fucked up! Stop playin'."

"Nah, you stop the damn playin'."

"You so fuckin' petty."

She rolled her eyes and left him standing there and snatched open the passenger door. "Kaylin, come on. You have a ten-thirty meeting and you know traffic is gonna be crazy." She jumped in and shut the door.

Kaylin was still standing there pissed off. He finally picked up his bag, yanked open the back door, and tossed it in the backseat.

She hated leaving Kaylin stuck on hard. As bad as her pussy needed to be touched and stroked? Sheeit. He was the petty one. At that point, she and her hormones instantly got mad. *I should fuck him up, for fucking up.* Something had to give . . . and soon.

He eased into the front, adjusted the seat and everything else before pulling off. He was clearly pissed. They rode the first ten minutes in silence.

"Angel, I can't do this shit."

"What?"

"Play these fuckin' bullshit-ass games, that's what."

"Then man the fuck up and take on your responsibilities or don't fuckin' touch me anymore, and you damn sure don't have to worry about me touching you. We'll keep everything strictly business. But I mean it when I say, no wedding, no pussy."

"You wasn't saying that crazy bullshit before we got married."

"Helloooo," Angel sang. "We never fuckin' got married!" she screamed.

"You know what the fuck I'm talkin' about."

"Yeah, you know what the fuck I'm talkin' about. You allowed your ego to fuck everything up, even though I'm still married to you but you're not married to me. You're married to your pride. So . . . my bad, for believing in what I thought we shared." Angel's voice dripped with sarcasm.

"Well, that was my fuckin' bad!"

Silence filled the car.

Damn. What was supposed to be a happy morning turned into total chaos, Angel thought to herself. *Fuck him! I wasn't the one who left the altar.*

"Red. You know what? I'm through. Fuck it!" Kaylin snapped.

"Hummph, what the fuck is that supposed to mean?"

"I can show you better than I can tell you." He looked over at her. "Strictly business, right?"

"What? What the fuck is you sayin'? You *know* you don't even want to go there. So play with it. That's what I want you to do. Remember, what you do I can do better." Angel wanted to cry, but mustered up enough strength to not give him the satisfaction.

"You can't even push your foolish pride and your fucked-up ego aside for nothing, can you? If not for me, then at least for the baby." When he didn't respond, she said, "You fuckin' asshole!" The longer he remained quiet, the angrier she became. "You think you slick, nigga, but hell no. I was gonna say fuck you too. I'm out. I'm moving out. But fuck that, I think that's what you want me to do. Nah, Kay. I'm not letting you off the hook. You can forget that. You pulled me off my square, temporarily, and actually won this round. I'ma give you that. But you ain't getting out of your responsibilities with me or the baby. Like I said, till death do us part. Say what you want, do what the fuck you want to do. Now take me home."

"I'm not going to have enough time to take you home and be at the office by ten thirty."

"Fine. Let me out. I'll take a cab."

"We got work to do, Angel."

"I *know* you're gonna let me take a day off, Kaylin!" Tears were streaming down her face. "Stop the fucking car now, Kaylin."

"Red, do yo see a muthafuckin' cab anywhere?"

"I don't give a fuck. I'm sick of hearing and looking at you for one day. You sound stupid and selfish. I am really hating you right now and if I stay here any longer, I won't be responsible for what I'll do or say to you."

"Fuck," he mumbled as he hit the child safety locks and sped up. "I'm sorry."

"Sorry? Sorry about what, Kaylin?" She was crying hard.

"Sorry for getting you all upset."

In the middle of Angel's crying bout she started laughing. "I see that there is no hope for you. I might as well throw in the towel. After I have this baby, we're out. Fuck you, Kaylin. You egotistical, stupid . . . son of a bitch! I can't even find the words for you. Sorry for getting me upset. Is that all you're sorry for? What about everything else, Kaylin?"

It took her damn near an hour but she finally got her emotions and frame of mind together. He refused to open his mouth.

Finally she was able to switch to business mode and told him, "I listened to Lupe Black's demo and if he can dance and perform half as good as he sings, he's gonna give Chris Brown a run for his money."

"Word?"

"I am not lying."

"I thought he rapped!"

"Me too. He not only sings, that little boy croons. He even has a song on there in Spanish."

Kaylin had to let that all sink in. Then he finally said, "No shit."

"E." She turned to face him. "Lil'E is a she."

"Is a what?"

"You heard me. A she. A girl."

"Get the fuck outta here."

"Not only that, she's white!"

He burst out laughing, until he realized she was serious. "Red, you killin' me, Ma."

"That's exactly what I'm gonna do. Kill 'em. Shes a beautiful Caucasion. She resembles Alicia Keys. I'ma be her agent and get her endorsements out the ass. Watch. And guess who she signed a bullshit-ass contract with?"

"Who?"

"Phillip Johnson."

"Red. C'mon, Ma." He didn't know if she was playing with him or not.

"No shit. Phillip muthafuckin' Johnson. And I'ma tear that ass up."

"Red, you can't be all up in the nigga's face. I'll have to kill that nigga if he disrespects you."

"I'll keep it strictly business, Kaylin."

"I don't know about that."

"Kaylin, this is business. I can handle him. I need you to trust me on this. This project means a lot to me."

"I'll let you know. I gotta think about that some more."

She rolled her eyes at him. "Now that's my news, so what happened in Canada?"

"Haven't made up my mind yet. I got some more paperwork for you to go over. They actually got a gold mine over there but don't know what to do with it. They really just need some capital. I may become a silent partner. I told them that after me and you put our head together and go over the additional paperwork, we would get back at them."

For the next three weeks Kaylin was barely at the house. They dealt with each other at the office more than at home. Angel was spending more nights at home alone crying than she wanted too. She didn't like being there without Kaylin. So she spent lots of time at the office focused on the Puma deal, Canada, Lupe Black, Papi Chulo, and Lil'E.

Her hormones were going crazy and she was now showing.

Business was on the verge of exploding at Game Over Records. Kaylin had called a staff meeting to make sure that everyone was on track and in sync. The conference room was full as Kaylin looked around the table. Perry G was replaced by the twins from Sony. Jet and Asia, a pair of black/Asian twins, his in-house producer, Shahid, his public relations maven, Courtney Moran, Angel, Tim Cohen, Dee, and Q, who was over their street team and Kym Ohn, the marketing director. He gave instructions to each one and was now listening to their feedback.

"Ooops." Angel giggled. Everyone turned toward her since she had interrupted Kym.

"Sorry, Kym. Oh my!" She giggled again as she held her stomach. "Baby, she moved! The baby moved!" She stood up in her excitement and went over to Kaylin. He pulled her onto his lap and they both had their hands on her small, round belly.

Kym Ohn resumed where she left off, discussing marketing strategies.

"Oh, snap! There she goes!" Kaylin beamed. His hands now circling her entire stomach. They both had tuned out the meeting and were watching Angel's stomach.

"Amateurs," Dee mumbled, but she was joking. She had been through pregnancy twice.

"Oh my God. I have a living being growing inside me." Tears had begun flowing down Angel's cheeks.

"Can y'all excuse us?" Kaylin looked around at the smiling faces in the room. Tim gave him the thumbs-up as he was the last one out of the conference room. Still rubbing her stomach, he buried his head into her chest. She began playing and rubbing in his hair. They were both deep in thought until Kaylin began kissing her breasts and biting her nipples through her dress. "Tu chi-chis are swelling up nicely. I miss them," he whispered.

"So is my culo. I can no longer fit into any of my pants or jeans. Oooh!" She felt another flutter. "She is going to be an active little thing."

"Her mama is an active little thing."

"And? What are you trying to say?"

"I love you."

"I love you too."

"I don't want to lose you," Kaylin said with sincerity.

"You have a unique way of showing it."

"I know, baby, and I'm sorry. But you know I love you, right? Regardless of how stupid I've been acting, right?" He was kissing and sucking on her breasts.

"Kaylin, don't make me answer that right now. But I will say that I'm tired of this emotional roller coaster you've got me riding on. How long do you expect me to keep riding?"

He held her tight. "I'm sorry, baby. Can I come over tonight?"

"It's your house. Do whatever you want."

"I want to have a nice quiet romantic dinner where me and you can talk."

"Dinner? You cooking?"

"I want you to cook."

"Is that right?" She giggled. "Why can't you cook?"

"If I cook, you gotta give a nigga some pussy."

"Oh, do I? And if I cook, what do you have to give me?"

"Some dick." He squeezed her nipple.

"What if I don't want any dick?"

"Oh, you want some. You're my wife and I know my wife."

"Do you?"

"Yeah. You know I do. And right now you want me to kiss you." He grabbed her neck, pulled her close, and they kissed like they were long lost lovers. The way she was moaning and rubbing on his ears, he knew what she needed and wanted. He lifted her up and placed her on the conference table, propping one foot on the table, the other leg over his shoulder, before sitting back down. He ripped her thong in half.

"Kaylin," she squealed. But threw her head back when he inserted two fingers inside her pussy. When she felt his tongue up against her clit, she let out a moan, arched her back, and grabbed his head. "Oh, Kaylin," she moaned. "Hell yeah. Sss-r-right there." She rode his face as if it was her last ride. "Sssss, right there . . . baby. Oh, shit . . . right there." She felt his tongue snake in and out of her pussy before sliding back over her tongue. She now had his head and neck in a choke hold as her stomach did flips, her legs trembled, and the orgasm came on. "Oh, f-fuck," she screeched. "Ssson of a bitch," she yelled.

Kaylin had come up for air and had both of her legs spread-eagle, was massaging her ass and watching her pussy jump and her clit throb and beat. "What a beautiful sight," he whispered, then dove back into the pussy, putting down some more of his lethal-ass head game.

Courtney Moran was at the door getting ready to knock when Angel screamed out in ecstasy, "Suck this shit, Kaylin!" Courtney's face turned red as she made a U-turn and headed back to Kym Ohm's office. "Oh, shit!" Angel screamed again as the second orgasmic wave swept her over.

"Still think I don't know what my wife needs?" Kaylin teased, while standing up. He pulled out his long thick dick. "This is what yo' ass needs right now." He rubbed the head of his dick up and down her pussy, getting the head nice and wet before rubbing it up against her throbbing button.

"Kaylin . . . wait," she panted as she bit down on her bottom lip. Her pussy was extrasensitive and she needed a breather. "Sweet Jesus." He was rubbing faster against her clit and just before she was ready to bust another nut, he stopped. She opened her eyes, looked at him as if to say, *Nigga, if you don't stop playing!* When he put his dick back in his sweats she whined, "Kaylin."

"Now you see how it feels. It's a fucked-up feelin', ain't it? To get that close and can't get your shit off."

He pulled her up and began kissing her. She wrapped her legs around his waist and slid her hand into his sweats and pulled his pipe back out. She began stroking it. Lips pressed to his ears she whispered, "I know what my husband likes and wants and needs."

"Aww, don't even try it. You not gonna catch me slipping again."

"I got what you like. I definitely got what you want, Daddy," she said as she squeezed him harder.

"Do you?" He was now kissing her neck. "What does Daddy like? What does Daddy want? What does Daddy need?"

"You want me to stop?" She squeezed a little harder and massaged a little faster. "Answer me, Daddy."

"Shit!" Kaylin grunted.

"I want Daddy to put this rock-hard dick into this moist, tight, steamy, hot, pregnant pussy. We're waiting, Daddy," she whispered, then sucked on Kaylin's sweet lips. They both was now ready to fuck each other's brain out. "Fuck me Daddy." She was playing with the precum that was oozing out the head of his dick.

He grabbed his dick, looked down at her pussy, and gently laid her back. He spread her legs wide.

"Mr. Santos," Bobbi came over the loudspeaker. "Phillip Johnson and two police officers are here to see Miss Angel."

They looked at each other and wanted to scream.

"Fuck!" Kaylin couldn't believe his luck. His dick was harder than Chinese arithmetic.

Angel banged her head on the table several times. "Phillip muthafuckin' Johnson. That creep!"

Chapter 9

Kaylin grabbed both of Angel's hand and pulled her up. He gave her a quick kiss on those soft and beautiful lips. "I love you, girl."

"Are we going to talk tonight?" She gazed at him as he helped her off the conference table.

He nodded yeah. "You want me to go feel this nigga out first while you go freshen up or what?"

"I'd appreciate it."

"Aiight, then, go to your office and let me see what these fuckin' clowns are talking about. Niggas just rained on my damn parade." He went to a stash spot behind a picture frame to retrieve some heat, not giving a fuck that "New York's finest" were out there. Hell, he was licensed to carry as well. Plus, they could have been fake cops for all he knew. He dropped the burner down in his pants pocket, then slapped Angel on the ass. "Go ahead, wait for me in your office." He picked up the phone and dialed.

"Law offices of Murray and Stacy Richman. How may I help you?"

"This is Kaylin Santos of Game Over Records. I need to speak to Murray or Stacy."

"Neither one of them is in the office right now."

"Well, I need you to get in touch with one of them and let

them know that I have Phillip Johnson and two police officers in the waiting room of my place of business, asking to speak to my wife. I'm getting ready to go see what they want, but y'all muthafuckas need to be on standby. Make sure that they get that message. I didn't get your name."

"Meg," the receptionist replied.

"Aiight, Meg. Handle that for me." Kaylin hung up and headed for the front reception area.

When Kaylin arrived up front, Phillip was standing there trying to flirt with Bobbi, the receptionist. He was flanked by two of New York's finest, in full uniform. To Kaylin, Phillip looked like an older version of Mario Winans. He was the same complexion and he was shaved clean, including his eyebrows.

His tailor-made suit hung gracefully off his medium frame and his Stacy Adams shoes were shined to a gloss. The only jewelry he sported was a wedding band and a diamond cross in his left ear. In Kaylin's eyes, he looked nothing like the grimey reputation he wore.

"I'm Kaylin Santos. What can I do for you?"

"Hey, hey. I'm Phillip Johnson." He rushed over to Kaylin, extending his hand for a shake.

Kaylin gave him a pound, nodded toward the policemen, and asked, "What's up?"

"Just a little added security. I didn't know until the last minute that I was coming to a real place of business. Man, you doin' big things." He flashed a row of perfectly white teeth. "I didn't know you was rolling like this. A tenth floor office and looking like this? Player, you got some big people taking notice, and I just added myself to that list."

"Yeah, so what is this visit pertaining to?" Kaylin was still pissed. He was finally getting ready to get some pussy, to be interrupted by this nigga, rolling with a couple of pigs.

"There seems to be a misunderstanding pertaining to one of my artists, Lily Penzera, also known as Lil'E. I just wanted to pull your coattail personally, and nip any potential problems in the bud. You see, she is under contract with Tyrant Music Limited and now she says that she has signed on with you guys."

"You did right by requesting to see my wife. She is the one handling Lil'E. She's the one you need to be talking to."

"No disrespect but since you're here, I may as well talk to you, man to man, label owner to label owner."

Kaylin smirked. "Man, it ain't me that you should be trying to brownnose. It's my wife, Angel, you should be worried about. She's also a label owner and our attorney. Bobbi, ask Mrs. Santos if she's available to see Phillip Johnson now."

"Aiight, man," Phillip conceded. "We can do this your way."

Kaylin looked over at the policemen. "Can I get you guys anything?"

"No, no. We're fine," the spokesman of the two said.

"What about you, Mr. Johnson?"

"Call me Phillip. And no, I'm fine."

"Miss Angel said come on back, Mr. Santos."

"You guys make yourselves comfortable. If you need anything, Bobbi here will get it for you." Kaylin wanted to make it clear that only Phillip was going to see Angel.

The officers looked at Phillip, who adjusted his silk tie and assured them, "I'll be back. This won't take long."

"Cool," Kaylin said. "Follow me."

When they arrived in Angel's office she came from behind her massive desk to greet Phillip Johnson. "I'm Angel Santos." She shook his hand.

"Damn! And I'm Phillip Johnson. Shit, you sexy as a muthfucka." He looked her up and down. *Oh, this is going to be a piece of cake.* He turned to Kaylin. "Shit, Kaylin, that's wifey, you did that."

"Yeah, man, I get that a lot. Thank you, but you can stop being disrespectful in my house."

"No disrespect, no disrespect."

"Man, don't be fooled by that creature of beauty," he warned him.

Angel motioned for Phillip to sit in one of the chairs in front of her desk. Kaylin sat down on the love seat in the back. He wanted to watch his baby do her thing. He wasn't the only one watching her. Phillip's eyes were glued to her ass.

Angel sat down, took a sip of her pineapple smoothie. "What can I do for you, Mr. Johnson?"

"Phillip. Call me Phillip." His eyes were soaking in her breasts. "My artist, Lily Penzera, Lil'E, *seems* to think that she has signed a contract with you guys."

"Well, it *seems* she did."

Phillip let out a chuckle and got comfortable in his seat. "Well, that's all good. But she obviously left out a very small detail that she failed to share with you."

"And what would that be?"

"She's already under contract with Tyrant Music Limited. A very extended one at that." He watched closely for Angel's reaction.

"Phillip, I think she obviously left out a very small detail that she failed to share with you."

"And what could that possibly be?"

"That she was a minor when she signed your bull-shit ass contract."

"*Damn.*" Kaylin leaned over, scooting to the edge of the seat. Once he heard her cuss, he knew it was only a matter of a few more choice words and she'd be ready to fight.

Phillip was now adjusting his tie, as if it was choking him. And Angel was now watching for his reaction with a smug look on her face.

"I don't know where you got your information from or what all she told you, but that's not correct."

"Why isn't it? Have you looked at her original birth certificate, like I did? What? She showed you that fake-ass ID and you thought it was all good. You need to be careful of who you sign to your label and especially careful of where you stick your dick. Miss Penzera's contract with your company is null and void.

Now, if there isn't anything else, I have to get back to work. Baby, can you show Mr. Johnson out?"

Kaylin stood up.

Phillip turned to Kaylin. "Yo, man. You need to let her know that—"

"Hold up, my man. Don't tell me what the fuck I need to let my wife know. She's right there. If you got sumthin to say to her, say it. There she is."

"Naw, man. I'm saying—"

"You're saying what, Mr. Johnson?" Angel challenged.

"All right, fuck it. I came in here acting civilized, figuring we could handle this the easy way. But it's obvious y'all muthafuckas don't know who the fuck I am. I suggest y'all look me up and get back at me." He stood up.

"And I suggest you look us up. Because you obviously don't know who the fuck we are." She pointed at Kaylin. "That's Kaylin Santos. Ain't you street? You should know the streets, Mr. Big Time. And I'm Angel Santos. That bitch your mama told you to stay the fuck away from. 'Cause I'm not intimidated by you. And I suggest you drop this shit. Because if anything happens to Lily, anybody she knows, anybody we know, or anyone affiliated with our business, your pedophile ass is grass. Just tell me how you want it. You want to push up daisies or you'd rather take it up the ass?"

"Is that a threat?" He grinned.

"Shit, take it how you wanna take it. But, nigga, you must have forgot that you're married. Does *wifey* know about this little underage white girl carrying your baby? You ready to shell out about five g's a month in child support? Or are you ready to do time for statutory rape? I'll take your ass all the way down, if you even think about violating our empire in any way. Baby, can you show Mr. Johnson out please?" She turned her back toward them and picked up the phone.

Chapter 10

Angel was on the phone with Jaz, Kyra, and Tasha, something they hadn't done in a while. Tasha had initiated the conference call because she missed her girls something awful. They had been on the phone for the last thirty minutes.

"Tasha, me, and Faheem will be up to the hospital this weekend. I have to admit that you are so strong, I mean pregnant and all. Girl, you are such an inspiration to me." Jaz was choking up as everyone agreed with her.

"Angel, what are you doing?" Kyra asked her cousin. "I hear lots of banging and shit."

"I told you, I'm fixing dinner. Me and Kaylin are supposed to have our 'talk' tonight."

"What are we having?" Tasha wanted to know. "Make sure I get a plate, please, ma'am."

"I got you. You know I'ma hook my sister up," Angel stated matter-of-factly.

"So . . ." Tasha continued. "What are we having?"

Angel smiled. "Baked macaroni and cheese, stuffed Cornish hens, fresh string beans, tossed salad, and dinner rolls."

"Oh my God. I might have to come get me a plate tonight," Tasha teased. "What about dessert?"

"Now, that I don't know. Kaylin is bringing that home. I'm

just hoping that we can straighten this shit out tonight. It's been crazy around here. Y'all wouldn't even believe it if I told y'all."

"Oh yes, we would," they all chimed in.

"Hold on, y'all. Someone is trying to get through." Angel clicked over. "Hello."

"Hi, Red."

"Malik, what's up? I miss you," Angel squealed.

"I need to come over to spend the night."

"When?"

"Now."

"Now? What's so important?"

"I gotta surprise for you. I gotta show you sumthin." He giggled.

"What is it?" Angel prodded.

"Reeeed," he whined. "I told you it's a surprise. Can you come and get me now?"

"I'm in the middle of cooking dinner for your father."

"Well, can he come and get me?" Malik was not giving up.

"He's not here. Let me speak to your mother. Did she say you could come?"

"Uh-huh. Maaaaa! Pick up the phone," Malik yelled. "It's Red."

"Malik, if you don't clean up that mess you made, you won't be going anywhere but to your room and that PlayStation will be coming out," Angel heard Bianca yelling in the background.

"Red, come and get me," whispered Malik into the phone.

"I got you."

Bianca snatched the phone from Malik. "I swear, that boy is going to drive me to drink. He has a surprise for you and he's been talking about it all day. But I'm not coming back out. So he figured he'd get you to come and get him."

"I'm cooking but I'll call Kaylin and have him swing by and scoop him up."

"That's fine with me. And thanks again, Angel, for talking to Kaylin for me."

"Girl, you already thanked me a zillion times. It's all good. Tell Malik I'm getting ready to call his dad and to be ready."

"He's been ready for hours."

Angel laughed. "Okay, then." She clicked back over to her girls. "Ladies, I love you all but my stepson needs me. And can I get some e-mails from you queens sometimes? I mean, I hit y'all up and y'all don't even bother to respond."

"Whatever," Jaz snapped.

"She's talking about you." Tasha laughed.

"She knows it. I love y'all." Angel hung up and called Kaylin.

"'Sup?"

"It's me. We have an unexpected dinner guest for tonight and he needs the car to come by and pick him up."

"Car? I'm not no damned chauffeur. That lil' nigga!" Kaylin automatically knew who it was. "Man, how are we supposed to be fuckin' tonight with that lil' nigga running around?"

"Who said anything about fucking?"

"Red, yo. Don't start no bullshit." Kaylin was seeing his little plan crumble right before his eyes.

"We are supposed to have dinner and talk, honey, remember?"

"Don't honey me, Red. We were supposed to finish off what we started earlier," he snapped.

"Says who, Kaylin? Our issues aren't going to disappear just because the King wants to fuck." She heard him mumbling but couldn't make out the words. "If we are not going to get to the bottom of these issues we're having, then just drop Malik off and do what you've been doing. Staying the fuck away!" She hung up on him, threw the phone on the sofa, and began pacing the floor. Angry. Angry that she allowed him to piss her off once again. And to think that she almost gave him some pussy.

An hour and a half later she was putting the lid over the plate of food that she made for Tasha. She heard Kaylin pulling up into the driveway. She placed the container into the refrigerator. Giving the kitchen the once-over, she stuck the dinner rolls into the oven, took off her apron, and headed for the front door.

"Red! Red! It's me." Malik came barging in, running full speed. When he saw Angel he covered his mouth with his hand.

"Hey, Malik." Angel smiled. "You made it over, huh?"

"Sit down," he told her. "Close your eyes."

"Oh my, this must be some surprise," she said as she sat down on the couch and closed her eyes.

"Don't open them yet." She could hear him going into his book bag and then fumbling with something. "Okay. Open 'em."

She opened her eyes and he was in her face so close, she could smell candy and he was grinning a grin that was missing two front teeth.

"Malik!" Angel gasped. "What happened?"

Ignoring her, he shook one of those egg-shaped bubbles that come in those machines, when you buy bubble gum in order to win a prize. He opened it and inside were his two front teeth. "See, both of my teeth. Are you surprised?"

"Yes, I am. Very surprised. How did they come out?"

"I fell," he stated matter-of-factly.

"You fell, and knocked out two teeth! Did you cry?"

"Nope," he said proudly.

"Malik, go put your knapsack in your room, wash your face and hands, and get ready for dinner," Kaylin told him.

"Okay, Dad." He leaned over and kissed Angel on the cheek, stuffed the plastic case in his pocket, grabbed his knapsack, and took off running upstairs.

"Malik, walk!" she yelled after him.

Angel stood up acting as if Kaylin was invisible and headed back to the kitchen.

"Oh, I can't get no love?" he asked, admiring her jiggling ass as he followed behind her. He had a bottle of vintage grape wine, a dozen red and white roses, and two bakery boxes. "Red, I can't get no love?" he asked her again.

He set everything down on the table and went over and hugged her.

"Get off me, Kaylin." She tried to push him away. "Why don't you just go? Do what you've been doing."

"I'm sorry about earlier. I couldn't help it if all I could think about was getting some pussy. But damn, baby. I'm sexually frustrated. You can't keep doing this to me. Daddy misses you, Ma." He kissed her lips.

"Daddy sure has a strange way of showing it. Now turn me loose. I have sumthin in the oven."

"Can I stay for dinner?"

"Kaylin, just turn me loose. Do whatever you want. I'm sick of you."

"Here go me." Malik came barging into the kitchen, shaking his wet hands.

Angel pushed Kaylin off her and went to get the rolls out of the oven.

"Dad, did you wash your hands?"

"Did you wash yours?"

"Yes."

"You didn't dry them."

"Because I'm hungry, Dad."

"So am I. Come on, you blocker!"

"Blocker? What's that?" Malik giggled. "I'm not a blocker."

"Nothing."

During dinner, Angel basically ignored Kaylin. And he didn't mind, because he enjoyed watching and listening to the interaction between Angel and Malik. It was genuine. And he could tell that Malik loved Angel and Angel loved him, confirming that he couldn't let Angel get away. He couldn't lose her over some bullshit. He also had to face the fact that he'd been acting like a total asshole. He couldn't wait to make Snake suffer.

After dinner, he and Malik showered while Angel cleaned up the kitchen. After he tucked Malik in he ran Angel a nice hot bath filled with vanilla-scented bubbles. When he went down-stairs she was lying on the couch, watching TV.

"Red, c'mon, baby. I made you some bathwater." When she ignored him, he lifted her off the couch and carried her upstairs to the bathroom.

He undressed her slowly before lifting her up and gently plac-ing her in the bathwater. She let out a moan and closed her eyes. Kaylin lit the vanilla-scented candles, turned out the light, and stuck in her *Kindred* CD. He picked her clothes off the floor and left.

When he came back fifteen minutes later she had dozed off. He turned the hot water on to warm the bath back up. Squeez-ing her body wash onto her bath sponge, he stood her up and sponged her down, bathing her delicately. He rinsed her off and let the water out. Standing there with the oversized terry cloth towel spread open, he said, "Come on, baby."

She stepped out of the tub into the towel. He wrapped it around her, lifted her up, and carried her to the bedroom.

Angel looked around at the many candles flickering in the dark room.

"Relax," Kaylin told her as he unraveled the towel. He poured some oil onto his hands and then proceeded to smooth it over her entire body. He massaged every inch of her body, relieving her of any and all stress.

Angel was silent, except for constant sighs and moans. He turned her on her side as he massaged her back and shoulders. He then put extra oil in his hand and began lightly rubbing her stomach. She placed one hand over his and watched as he con-tinued making circular motions. When she started to doze off he began planting soft kisses on her back, shoulders, and neck.

Her eyes still closed, she sucked her teeth. "Kaylin, please." He continued to kiss her. "Kaylin, do you know what you're doing to me? To us? Do you even care?"

"Damn! How many times do you want me to say I'm sorry?"

She laughed. A laugh that said, *Get real*. "Kaylin, your mouth is always saying you're sorry but your actions have been saying sumthin totally different."

"Come on, Ma, let's go ahead and get married."

"Kaylin, stop. Don't insult my intelligence. All of a sudden you want to get married. You just want some pussy, treating me like some off-brand bitch." She shrugged him off her and got up.

"I'm serious. Let's get married."

"Fuck you, Kaylin." She grabbed a pillow and tossed it at him with a look of disgust, then went into the guest bedroom and slammed the door.

Kaylin looked at the clock: 1:38 a.m. "Fuck!" he mumbled. He turned on the light and found his phone book. Thumbing through it he snatched up the phone and dialed Reverend Run. As soon as he answered the phone he didn't even give the reverend a chance to say hello. "Yo, I know it's late but I need a miracle."

"Who is this?"

"Kay. I need to get married. Like right now."

"It's two in the morning."

"I know but this is an emergency. You know I walked out the last time."

"Walked out? That's an understatement."

"Whatever. I've been in turmoil ever since I pulled that stunt. I've been walking in hell, Rev. Save me. It's now or never. Do me this one, man. I need you."

Silence.

"I'll send a car for you. It'll be there in an hour."

Click. Reverend Run hung up on him. Kaylin made about eight more phone calls. By the time he got off the phone it was well after 2:00 a.m. He blew out all of the candles and went into the guest bedroom.

He snuggled up behind Angel. "Red, get up and get ready. The reverend and everyone else are on their way over. Baby, I need you to give me one more chance. Will you marry me?"

More silence. Then finally she said, "Kaylin, please. Leave. I'm tired. If you love me and if you're really sorry, let me go."

"Red, I can't live without you. You mean the whole world to me. I love you. My son loves you. I love our unborn child."

Silence.

"Baby, please. I know I fucked up. I was scared that you wanted that nigga."

Angel turned over and smacked him as hard as she could across his face. "Why?" she screamed. "What made you think I would want him, Kaylin? Huh? What could I have possibly done to make you think that?"

Kaylin hung his head and didn't respond.

"What the fuck were you thinking? That I've been faking my love for you all of these years? Huh?" She stood up. "You are so fucking . . . stupid!" She stormed out and went into the master bedroom.

"Fuck!" Kaylin spat as he got up and went after her. When he opened the bedroom door she was yanking her clothes out of the closet.

"Where are my suitcases?" she screamed.

"What the fuck are you doing?"

"Fuck you, Kaylin!"

"What did I do? You wanted me to apologize and tell you what the fuck was the matter and when I do, you pack your shit? What the fuck part of the game is this?"

She was now dumping out the heavy dresser drawers all over the bed.

"Red! Red!" he screamed. "Stop this crazy bullshit! Did you forget you was pregnant?"

"Naw, nigga, you the one who's crazy! Acting like a fucking bitch and taking me through all of these changes because you *thought* that I wanted to be with some nigga. Fuck you! You're a stupid muthafucka."

"Oh now you give a fuck? The question is, did you forget? Every fuckin' day you got me stressing. You don't give a fuck so, naw, fuck you! You been bitchin' and whinin' and complaining about a fucking wedding. Well, you're getting ready to have one. If I got to hog-tie your ass you're getting ready to marry me." They were now engaged in a full-fledged screaming match.

"Marry you? Fuck you, bitch!" Angel spat.

He leaped across the room, placed a hand around her neck, and pushed her down onto the bed. She bounced up and began swinging wildly at him. He pushed her back onto the bed. When she tried to bounce back up again he pushed her back down. When she tried it again he pushed her back down.

"Oh, we're gonna get married." He stood there and said it very calmlike.

She covered her face with both hands balled up into knots and started crying. "Let me go Kaylin, I want out."

Malik stood in the doorway. "Daddy."

Kaylin jumped up and went to Malik. "What are you doing up?" He shrugged his shoulders. "Come on, let me tuck you back in."

"I want Red to tuck me in." He yawned.

"Red is not feeling well. You can see her in the morning." He kissed his cheek as he carried him and put him back in the bed.

"Night, Dad."

"Good night." Kaylin closed his door.

When he went back into the bedroom, Angel was still balled up crying. He leaned over her. "Ma, tell me you don't love me and I'll pack your shit for you."

"I hate you, Kaylin," she cried out. "Just let me go."

"Tell me you don't love me no more."

"Kaylin. Just let me go, please."

"Hell to the nah. You wanted to get married, remember? So go get yourself together. You have about twenty minutes."

She bounced up and began swinging at him. He grabbed her and they fell onto the bed. "I hate you, Kaylin. Let me go. Get off me!" He had pinned both arms to the bed. Her robe was open and he began kissing her neck and breasts.

"I don't love you!" she cried out loud.

"Yes, you do." He was sucking on her breasts. "You don't mean that, do you?"

"Kaylin . . . stop it."

"I'll stop when I'm good and ready. This is my pussy."

"No, Kaylin. It's not. You allowed some punk-ass nigga to come between us. Look how one man got us acting, disrespecting each other. So no, not anymore."

He raised both hands over her head and she tried to knee him in the nuts but missed.

"Nice try, Ma."

"You're hurting my wrists, Kaylin."

"Then be still, calm down, and stop crying. 'Cause who got the upper hand?"

"Kaylin, stop playing!"

"I will, once you calm down."

"I'm calm. Now let me go."

"You sure about that?"

"Let me go."

"Aiight, when I let them go, you are going to get up quietly, and get yourself together. Is that clear?"

"You are not my father, Kaylin. Now get off me. I'm calm, damn," she yelled.

He let her wrists go but remained on top of her. She swiped the tears off her face, then tried to wiggle from under him. When she saw that she couldn't go anywhere she managed to flip onto her stomach.

"Calm the fuck down, don't lose my baby, Angel."

"Then get the fuck off me."

"Where you think you're going?"

"Kaylin, you said you were going to let me go. Now stop playing," she yelled out.

"What's the magic word?"

"Fuck you."

"Uh-uh. That's not it," he sang.

"Kaylin, stop it."

"What's the magic word?"

She didn't respond.

"I'm asking you one more time. What's the magic word?"

"Asshole."

"Aiight, have it your way." He grabbed both of her wrists and pinned them back together.

"Kaylin, stop!" she screamed. "You play too damned much!"

"I gave you your chance." Since her ass was already up in the air, he smacked it one time and used his knee to spread her legs. "I know how to shut your ass up."

"Kaylin!"

He slid one finger into her pussy and then another and he started working 'em.

"Kaylin, stop playing." Her voice trembled.

"Who's playing? Do this feel like I'm playing?" He began teasing her throbbing pearl tongue.

"Shit! Kaylin, stop it!"

He left the clit alone and went back inside her pussy with three fingers.

"Oh, sshhh . . . ," she moaned as she began throwing it at his fingers. "I hate you . . ." she whispered.

"Yeah. That's what I thought." He leaned over to get him a kiss, and her tongue parted his lips. Their tongues added fuel to an already raging fire.

"Mmmmm," she moaned.

"You still hate me?" He began teasing her clit once more. He was back flicking his fingers over her clit. She continued to purr. "Well, get ready to hate me even more because I'm getting ready to get me some of dis." Her pussy was throbbing and jumping as he turned her clit loose and then pulled out his dick.

"Kay . . . Unnnnghh," she groaned as he dug inside her. He grunted as he grabbed her by her hips and began to grind deep and slow. She raised her ass higher and tried to make her pussy squeeze and suck up his dick.

"F-fuck. Do that shit, baby. Work that pussy," Kaylin moaned, as he went in deeper.

"Damn baby . . . right there. Shit . . . that feels good. Right there, baby. Yesss. Right there . . ." she screamed as Kaylin worked it. "Shit, nigga . . . I love . . . you . . ." she crooned as she began to come. Kaylin was now in a zone smacking her ass. When he was ready to nut, he pulled out and shot all over her ass, before falling over onto his back. Angel crawled over to him, got in the sixty-nine position, and began bobbing up and down on his dick. Kaylin rubbed his cum all over her ass, blew on her clit, and went to sucking on her pussy.

Ding, dong. The doorbell rang as they both licked and sucked on each other feverishly, refusing to stop. Unable to stop.

Kaylin's dick was so thick and hard that Angel had to ride it. Coming up for air, she sat up, kept her back turned to him as she slid down on his dick. Kaylin watched her ass jiggle as she slid up and down, faster and faster. As he grabbed on to one of her hips and reached around for her inner piece, they went at it as if this would be their last fuck.

Angel was the first to start skeeting. Kaylin held on to both hips as he let go of what felt like buckets of cum.

Ding, dong.

"Who . . . is . . . that, baby?" Angel could barely get the words out.

"The reverend or Kajuan, or my mom, Omar. It could be Kendrick and Kendra or Tamara. I called them all up as witnesses to our marriage." He was still trying to catch his breath. "Fuck, I nutted hard."

"You know I'm not going to let you off this easy, right?"

"You killin' me, Ma." He sat up, wanting to taste her pussy juice on his lips and tongue. "Come here."

She crawled over to him and hungrily tasted her juices in his mouth.

Ding, dong. Ding, dong.

Neither one of them wanted to stop tasting the other.

Bbrrring.

Whoever was at the door was obviously now calling on the phone.

"We gonna get married, baby, or are we gonna fuck some more?" he asked as he played with her nipples.

"Nigga, both."

Kaylin was spent. "Well, you gonna have to suck my dick back to life."

Angel moaned as she climbed back into the sixty-nine position.

Chapter 11

After keeping everyone waiting, forty minutes later, Kaylin and Angel were standing in front of their guests. Kaylin was clad in a simple white-on-white ensemble shirt and tailor-made pants by Ralph Lauren tapered off by a pair of white-on-white Air Force Ones. Angel sported a simple white Prada dress and white Jimmy Choo stilettos, accented by a pregnant belly.

They stood hand in hand and were basking in the love they possessed for one another and of course from that overdue love-making session they had just indulged in.

"Boy, I first want you to apologize for having us out here at three o'clock in the morning. Then you had the nerve to keep us standing out there on your front porch for damn near a half hour. None of this would be happening if you hadn't acted the fool on your wedding day. Apologize to the good reverend first!" Mother Santos scolded.

Reverend Run raised both hands and said, "There's no need. It's all good. We're all here now and ready to proceed."

Kaylin knew that he needed to obey his mother. "Ma, Reverend Run, and family. I apologize for the inconvenience that my past actions have brought us to, but I truly thank each and every one of you for coming out when I really needed you the most. You all being here lets me know who really has my back.

Again, I offer my sincerest apologies. Kendrick, can you start taping?" Kaylin asked his cousin, who was there with his twin sister, Kendra.

"Man, we've been taping from the time we hit your doorstep. Everybody is gonna know how you called us at two in the morning, talking about getting married and needing witnesses. Then like your mom said, you leave us standing on the porch for almost thirty minutes," Kendrick snapped. "Plus, nobody would believe this shit if it wasn't on tape. Three in the damn morning," he vented. "Excuse my language, Rev."

"Man, cut me some slack. I would have done it for yo' punk ass. I know I'm the bad guy here. Y'all also know I had some issues that I've been trying to work through. So—"

"Muchachos!" Mother Santos cut in. "Cut it out. Y'all acting like y'all still them same little five-year-old knuckleheads I had to whip, with all this bickering y'all doing."

Tamara, Kendra, and Omar giggled. It definitely reminded them of the good ole days.

"Yeah. Cut the nigga some slack," Kajuan added. "This the same nigga who left this beautiful woman at the altar. So you know he ain't right," he cracked.

"Kajuan, cayate!" Mother Santos scolded him.

Kaylin hung his head in embarrassment as his mother, Kendra, and Tamara all circled around Angel and gave her a hug.

"Can we get on with this?" he finally asked in protest. "I'm sure the reverend would like to go home . . . sometime in the near future." Kaylin attempted to get the pressure off himself.

Angel finally spoke. "Before the reverend officiates this I need to say a few things. Thank you, ladies."

"Aww, man," Kaylin groaned.

"I know you didn't think you were getting off this easy?" She cut her eyes at Kaylin. "However," she continued, "we do thank everyone for making such a huge sacrifice on our behalf, especially you, Reverend." She then turned to Kaylin. "And as for you, I want you to get down on one knee and apologize to me in front of everyone, while the tape is rolling. I also want you to know that this isn't it. You owe me a wedding. I want my wedding, Kaylin. A full and complete wedding planned and put together by you. From the invitations to the place to the caterers. I'm not lifting a finger. I want you to go through everything I went through." There were snickers in the room from all of the guys. "And I am not wearing that same dress. I want a new dress for myself and my bridesmaids. Is that understood?" That got some amens and, "I know that's rights" from the ladies.

"Anything else, Your Highness?"

"And don't you dare forget my honeymoon!" The ladies in the room snickered while the men cringed.

"Anything else?" Kaylin was ready to get it over with.

"No, you can apologize now."

Kaylin adjusted his pants and got down on one knee. He took her hand, kissed it, and gently wrapped it in both of his. He looked into her eyes and began, "Baby, you mean the world to me. I love you more than anything. I need you in my life and I know it sounds corny but you complete me. And that's real talk. I apologize for making you suffer because of my insecurities. I apologize for not putting my ego in check and my pride aside. Baby, I need you in my life, forever. I swear that I am still the man you fell in love with. I want us to be a family. I want to be the best father for our baby and I need you to be a permanent part of Malik's life. He loves you and I love you even more for loving him and accepting him as your own. Will you forgive me?" Angel was fighting to choke back her tears and no words would come out. "Baby, will you forgive me?" She nodded yes while trying to swipe away the tears. "Will you marry me?" He pulled her close and he was now on his knees, hugging her and kissing her belly. "Answer me, baby. I know I hurt you and I probably don't deserve you, but I need you. Tell me you'll marry me," he pleaded.

"Baby . . ." She ran her fingers through his hair. Reverend Run handed her a handkerchief. "I need you to tell me that you'll let nothing or no one come between us."

"Ma, I swear I won't slip like that again. I will protect what we got and I swear I won't let nothing or no one come between us."

"Baby, tell me that you meant everything you just said to me."

"I meant every word that I just said. You know I meant it. I need you. Baby, will you marry me? Will you continue to be my wife?"

"Baby . . . yes." Her voice cracked.

Kaylin stood up, hugged her, and they began to kiss, neither one of them hearing what Reverend Run was saying. There wasn't a dry eye in the room.

"Umm, who has the rings?" Reverend Run asked.

"Right here." Omar stepped up and tapped them both on the shoulder.

They came up for air and both said, "I do" and went back to kissing.

"We already did that for y'all. We just need y'all to put the rings on, and then we normal folks can go home," Kendrick snapped.

They came up for air again. Angel was giggling as they both took their ring boxes and placed the rings on each other's fingers.

"I love you, baby . . . forever."

"I love you too . . . always." Angel grinned as she eyed her seven-carat diamond ring.

Kaylin, immediately got rid of the twin beds. Several days after the marriage ceremony and when they finally decided to leave the bedroom Angel and Kaylin were in the living room. Kaylin was on the couch, chilling and watching television, while Angel was sitting on the floor going through her bridal shower and wedding gifts. She had refused to open the wedding gifts, and had refused to put away any of the bridal shower gifts until he had slipped that ring onto her finger.

"Baby," Angel whined. "We are supposed to be doing this together. You aren't even paying attention."

"Yes, I am."

"No, you're not."

"Baby, yes, I am."

She waved him off as she looked all around her. Scattered around were Tiffany picture frames, champagne flutes, Manolo Blahnik candles, Teflon pots and pans, a Krups cappuccino maker, Cuisinart food processor, Manrico cashmere sheets, which she really liked. She had just seen them in a *Town & Country* magazine for forty-nine hundred dollars. There was a set of Frette terry cloth towels, crystal; gift certificates of all kinds, money, Egyptian cotton four-hundred-thread-count linen, and several bottles of chardonnay.

"Baby, if you're paying attention, then tell me who gave us gold. Gold bars, to be exact. Now, that's some gangsta shit. How much do you think these are worth?" She let out a whistle and passed them to Kaylin. She picked up both cards and read them out loud. "Best wishes to the groom and the bride. *Que tu sagra do matrimonio dura para siempre?*"

"That means may your sacred marriage last forever," Angel clarified.

"Let me see," Kaylin told her.

"This card is from Alexjandro Reyes." She handed it to him and opened the other one. "This one says exactly the same thing but is signed by Don Carlos. Who are—?"

Kaylin snatched the other card out of her hand. "Excuse you." She rolled her eyes at him. He was looking at the cards in deep thought. Looking at them as if they were written in code. "Baby who are they?" He didn't even hear her. "Baby." She was now standing in front of him. "Hellooo . . . Kaylin. What is up with you? Who are they?"

"Just some family I haven't heard from in a long time." He

stood up. "I gotta make a run. I'll be right back." He kissed her on the lips, then on the cheek. He snatched up his car keys and headed out the door.

Kaylin tapped lightly on the door before going inside. Tasha looked up at him and smiled.

"Damn, nigga, you was just up here a minute ago," she teased.

"I know you gonna let me."

"Whatever."

"Come here and give your brother-in-law a hug." She stood up and they embraced. Her stomach was about the same size as Angel's. "You all right?"

"It's strange how we adapt. Us humans are definitely creatures of habit. Being here now seems as if it's normal . . . natural. And the Creator is blessing me to stay positive. And since your boy gets such a huge kick out of taking care of me while I'm pregnant, I hope that he doesn't think because he missed out on a few months, I'm supposed to do this again."

Kaylin laughed. "Oh, you know how he do it. And you know that's exactly what he's going to be thinking. So you might as well get ready."

She punched Kaylin in the arm. "Whatever, negro. So, tell me how does it feel to be married? *Finally*."

"Oh, so now you got jokes?" It warmed his heart to see her smile. "For real, we were already married in spirit. We've been living together almost since day one, she had already accepted my son, we just wasn't married on paper. Which to me ain't all that important. But since it was important to her, I gave her that," he stated matter-of-factly.

"Oooh. You know I'm telling her what you just said," Tasha teased.

"You do that and I won't bring you up any more plates."

"Oh well, in that case . . ." She pretended to be thinking it over. "Well, where is my plate for today?" Her hands were on her hips.

"She hasn't cooked yet. But I got you."

"Aiight, then I got you too." She held out her hand and he shook it. "Deal?"

"It's a deal," he confirmed.

"All right, then. Let me let you holla at your boy." She was used to Kaylin coming and talking with Trae. She also welcomed the break. "I'll be back."

"Cool."

Kaylin went over and grabbed the chair, adjusting it to his usual position and spot before sitting down.

"Yo, nigga. You still playing like you asleep?" He looked Trae over. "Well, I'm beginning to understand why. Everything happens for a reason and I guess it's meant for me to do some things solo." He thought about what he just said and spat, "Nah, fuck that! Shit, I really could use your companionship right about now and Tasha needs you too, nigga. She's holdin' it down but I don't know how long she'll be able to hold up at this level.

"At any rate, and the reason I'm back so soon, check this out. Red was going through the wedding and bridal shower gifts and guess what? She came across these gold bars. Yeah, nigga. Gold bars. The same size and weight we jacked from that fat fuck we merked in Mexico. Yeah, nigga, you heard right. Our shit is stashed away deep and we agreed to keep it like that until the time was right. So? You guessed it. Them cats knew what was up all of these years. Yeah. The big kahunas." Kaylin smirked. "Them same kahunas whom we had to pay to get out of the game. Don Alexjandro and Don Carlos. The cards that came with the gold bars were signed by each of them. Now, why all of a sudden they pop up? That's the shit that got me shook. But I know why. And you do too. They want sumthin. Plain and simple. You know it's not retaliation because we did them a huge favor, and they still eating off the fruits of our labor. You smell me? So they want sumthin, man. How the fuck they gonna drop off them gifts at my wedding? They damn sure weren't there."

Kaylin leaned his head back and closed his eyes, as he tried to make sense of the whole scenario. He was so deep in thought that he didn't even feel Tasha's presence when she stepped back into the room.

"Everything okay?"

He looked up at her and cracked a smile. "Yeah, sis-in-law. Everything's okay." He stood up and stretched. "This nigga is lucky to have you. You know that, right?"

"Yeah, I know it."

"Red told you that we were gonna be gone for a couple of weeks, right?"

"Yeah, she told me. She said sumthin about a tour with Papi Chulo and the white chick, Lil'E. Angel is liking her job a little too much. I'm getting jealous." Tasha pretended to pout.

Kaylin laughed. "We mixing work with pleasure, that's all that is. And sort of like a prehoneymoon before the honeymoon. Nah mean? But check it. You're welcome to come. We could pack up my boy and all of this here shit." He waved his arms around the room. "I'll make it happen for you."

"I'm sure you will. It would be some *Weekend at Bernie's*–type shit, huh? Rolling him around on beaches and to clubs." They both started laughing. "Trae would kick our asses when he woke up and found that we did some shit like that. Hell to the nah." Tasha laughed

"Our asses? I'd blame that shit all on you!" Kaylin teased.

"Whatever, nigga, and I'm sure you would. Thanks, but no, thanks. We'll wait here until y'all get back."

"Aiight, then. But if you change your mind, let a brotha know." He went over to Trae, balled up his fist for him, and gave him a pound. Then he gave Tasha a hug and was gone.

* * *

The crew of Game Over Records were amped and ready for their fifteen-day working vacation. Everyone was excited about the newcomers Papi Chulo and the white chick who was a lyrical genius, Lil'E. They were anxious to rock the crowd and Kaylin and Angel were looking forward to their working vacation and prehoneymoon. Bobbi, Dashae, and Courtney put the tour together in two months. They worked night and day.

The first and most important stop was Ibiza, a hedonistic island off the coast of Spain and the epicenter of the European party circuit. All you do is party around the clock. And when you finally decide to get some sleep, it's during the day and you do that on the beach. Talkin' about a hot spot? Ibiza can't get any hotter with its nonstop partying and sitting right there, literally . . . on the equator line. Sizzle . . . sizzle . . . sizzling! People clambor there from all over the planet, making it a very cosmopolitan hot spot.

The music scene had hooked Kaylin with its many new artists, and the DJs coming there were doing groundbreaking things. Ibiza is so on fire that many of the hottest DJs come all the way over just to showcase one song. So Kaylin definitely wanted to make a lot of noise and showcase for Game Over. And he planned on doing just that, with the four shows he had lined up at Privilege, the largest club in the world.

This was night number four as Kaylin stood in the back of the club next to Peter Gatin, the former nightclub King of New York. He had reigned over the Limelight and the Palladium, but Kaylin remembered him from his old Tunnel days. Now Peter was over here looking to open a new club. He wanted to be king again.

They both stood there in awe as Lil'E had them and the crowd going bananas. Her raw energy was unbelievable . . . unreal. Even the people who didn't speak English were going nuts. Peter and Kaylin looked at each other and Kaylin knew right then and there that it was official . . . he had a star on his hands. He owed his wife big time for this one.

His spirits rose even higher as Papi Chulo received the same love. Papi showed him that Reggaeton was here to stay. Kaylin was amped. The crowd was already up on New Day. When they did their two singles, "Lovemakin' Music" and "What's Happenin' Streets," they sang along word for word.

"My man." Peter passed Kaylin his business card.

"Call me. Promise me that your crew can do the same thing they did here tonight at my grand opening?"

"You got that," Kaylin assured him and took the card. They gave each other a pound and Peter slipped off among the crowd.

All four nights were performed in front of a packed house. They then spent the next four nights performing at the smaller clubs: Space, Pacha, Eden, and DC10. Then it was off to Greece to cruise to Mykonos, where Kaylin looked forward to a much lighter schedule and some rest and relaxation, not only for him but the two pregnant women as well. Kaylin left Ibiza on a natural high.

They were now reveling in their downtime and the last two days of their working vacation and prehoneymoon. The expectation and goal were to make a lot of noise for Lil'E and Papi Chulo. They did both.

"Damn, I'm mad that we couldn't get Lupe Black on this here ticket." Kaylin was kicking himself.

"We'll get him on the next one," Angel assured Kaylin as they lay cuddled up.

Angel was half asleep as Kaylin spooned her. He was wide awake since he had slept most of the day; plus, he was still hyped up. His head rested on one hand as he leaned on his elbow. His other hand was rubbing Angel's belly. "Ma, you fallin' asleep on me or what?"

"I'm listening, baby, what's up?" she whispered sleepily.

He stopped rubbing her belly as he reached back onto the nightstand and snatched up a brochure. "Yo, Ma, listen to this.

Does this sum this joint up to the letter or what?" Kaylin began to read the brochure out loud. "Mykonos is now the most cosmopolitan island in the world, more famous than Capri, more fashionable than Hawaii. Picture in your mind's eye a deep blue sea, covered with white waves, and set in it a bare island bathed in sunlight. Add to—"

"Baby, please." She cut him off. "Why are you reading that to me? I see it, I see the island, it's lovely." Her eyes were still closed. "Mykonos is lovely, it's heavenly. Don't read anything else to me. Why are you still so excited? This is only the beginning."

"Exactly, Ma. And oh, what a start! Papi Chulo and Lil'E are gonna break platinum right out the gate, watch. I gotta get Scott Storch and Rick Rubin to hook up a coupla tracks on their albums. And there's a new chick, Mayra Veronica, Reggaeton all the way, we gotta get her on a track with both of them," he rattled off. "But check it, she'll be showing soon, we can't just let her disappear."

"She won't disappear. We release a single, run that, remix it, run that. She can still do interviews and print ads, getting herself and the fans ready for the album. And if we move fast, we can get back to Ibiza and do a quick video."

Kaylin mulled over what she had just said, and was feeling where she was coming from. Brilliant. His wife was fucking brilliant. A video shoot was a must because Ibiza had some blazin' natural beauty. His thoughts went back to the long-standing bar called Café del Mar, which was legendary for everyone to stand around and watch the sunset. It was the first one he and Angel experienced together and it blew both of them away.

Snapping out of his reverie, Kaylin said, "Yo, what endorsements do you have in mind for Lil'E?"

"Baby," she whined. "Can't we have this meeting in the morning? Aren't you tired?"

He bent his head and gently kissed her shoulder. "Nope. You can sleep all day, *again*, if you want to."

"Don't get smart, nigga, because that's exactly what I plan to do. Sleep all day."

They were staying at the Andronikos Hotel and if you looked up the word *tranquil* in the dictionary, a picture of the hotel would be next to it.

The drapes were pulled back and they had the bomb view of the sea, lying right there in the bed. One of the windows was open and the smell of the water was intoxicating. Angel really didn't want to leave the island of Mykonos.

Her eyes fluttered open as she tossed the brochure off the bed and lifted his hand off her stomach. He scooted over so that she could turn onto her back. He had this lazy grin on his face. "I'm not tired, baby. Talk to Daddy for just a few more minutes." He reached up and began to stroke her nipple with his thumb.

"You know I'ma get you back for this, don't you?"

"What? I ain't doing nothing. I just said talk to Daddy for a few more minutes, with your beautiful self." He loved that sultry look she had on her face when she was tired. "Now what's up with Lily? How is she coming along? How soon will we have to make sure that she chills out?"

"I think that this trip has given her a whole new outlook on who she is and where she wants to be. You know, I introduced her to that Reggaeton chick, Ivy Queen?"

"Word?"

"Yeah, and they clicked. She gave her a little heads-up on the industry. Kept it gully with her. Let her know that even though it's a man's industry, she can still do her. She can still prosper. She told her no matter what, don't let them take her rawness away and told her to make sure that she stays true to herself."

"Aww, man. That was all love right there. Real talk," Kaylin complimented Ivy Queen.

"It was and it blew Lily away. She couldn't stop talking about her."

"What else?"

"We're gonna have to let her continue to evolve into her own unique style. Let her be her. She's very versatile. I don't want her to be typecast, I want her to continue to do her."

"I hear you." Kaylin was in agreement. "She don't have to prove herself and be all hard, because the way she spits, her lyrics speak for themselves. And we peeped her work ethic."

"We did. Two mornings in a row she had morning sickness. Throwing up, tired, the whole nine. But come showtime, she stepped up to the plate. No crying, complaining, no excuses. She just got on her grind. Now to answer your last question. We need to arrange the video shoot and get that out of the way. That's going to be the most strenuous. She said being in the studio working on a single and the album is lightweight. So after that we need to make sure she takes it easy. Just interviews and stuff like that."

"Aiight, then. Sounds like a plan." Kaylin smiled at her.

"You got Papi straight?"

"Oh yeah. That nigga is hungry. He's ready to grind nonstop. And marketing is already talking to iTunes."

"Good. Now is this meeting adjourned?" she wanted to know.

"Endorsements," he reminded her.

"I pitched a couple of companies on her being a spokesperson for the Twix white chocolate bar, Reese's white chocolate cups, and Dove Bar ice cream. Oh, and I'm waiting on Vanilla Coke to get back with me. I got marketing working on putting sumthin together for Motorola ring tones and MAC cosmetics. I'm getting ready to get this little white chick paid. America is getting ready to fall in love with her," Angel stated with confidence. "So I'm excited just like you. How does it feel to be legal, nigga?"

"Feels great."

"I'm happy for you. But right now Mami would like to count some sheep. Anything else?"

"Can I get a little somethin' somethin' before you fall into that deep, deep comalike slumber?" He began running his hand up and down her thigh, knowing that he was getting ready to get what he wanted.

"A little somethin', huh?"

"Yeah, just a little somethin' to help you fall asleep." He leaned over and tenderly kissed her lips.

"I don't need help falling asleep."

"Yes, you do, you just don't know it." He kissed her again. "I'ma show you that you need help. Then in the morning you can thank Daddy."

"Whatever, Kaylin." She giggled as her arms creeped around his neck. He pulled her on top of him, reached over, and turned out the night-light.

Angel was seated in the back of the limo, sandals off, feet propped up on the seat. She was totally relaxed and had enjoyed the trip immensely. It was indeed one for the memory archives.

Kaylin was still getting the artists, luggage, and everything else together; she picked up her cell but wasn't ready to check voice mails or e-mails but instead dialed her mom and then said she would call Tasha.

As soon as her mother picked up, she sang, "Mommy, we're back. And I brought you back some trinkets that are gonna make you tell everyone that I'm the bestest child in the whole wide world," she teased.

"You are, baby. Believe me when I say it. You are," Mrs. Smith responded dryly.

"What's the matter, Mom? What did Carmen do this time?" She sighed. "Where is she?" Mrs. Smith didn't respond. "Ma, where is she?" Angel was now sitting up on the edge of the seat. "Is she all right, Ma?"

"I guess she is," she finally answered.

"What do you mean, you *guess* she is?"

"Well, she sent me money last week and called to see if I got it. She took off the same day that you did."

"Ma!" Angel yelled. "Why are you just telling me this? I told you how to get in touch with me in case of an emergency," she scolded her mother.

"Chile, please. I told you that I was tired of that girl. She is not going to give me a heart attack and put me in an early grave."

"Where is she, Ma?"

Mrs. Smith exhaled. "Somewhere with Keenan."

Angel could have sworn that her heart stopped beating and time stopped.

Chapter 12

Almost a half hour later, Kaylin jumped into the limo. "Damn. I hate unorganized muthafuckas!" He leaned over and kissed Angel hard on her cheek. Usually she would smack him when he did that, but her gaze remained fixed straight ahead.

"I know you do, baby, but still you gotta delegate. Just stay on top of those who you delegate the work to," she mumbled.

He looked her face over. "Yo, beautiful, what's the matter with you? What the fuck happened in the last forty-five minutes?"

"I called Mommy." Angel bit down hard on her bottom lip, trying not to flip out.

"And?"

"My sister."

"What she do?"

"She left home the same day we left."

"Damn. So where she at? You want me to go get her? Just say the word."

"Oh, that's the least of the drama. You're gonna love the rest."

The limo was finally pulling out of the airport.

"C'mon, Red, spit the shit out."

"She's hanging with Keenan."

"You killin' me, Ma."

"I'm killing myself. My mom said that she had the nerve to send some money and call to see if she got it."

"Where the fuck are they?"

"I don't know."

"Baby, this may be the break that I've been looking for. You gotta find out where she is."

"How am I supposed to do that? This nigga . . . he knows how I feel about my sister, he's fuckin' with me, Kaylin, don't you see it?" She finally could no longer fight back the tears. "That's my damn sister," she sobbed. "There's no telling what the fuck he has her doing."

"Sssh, baby, I'm sorry." He wrapped his arms around her and held her tight. "Don't cry, baby. It's just that I want this nigga so bad but he keeps slippin' and slidin' right through my damn fingers. Nobody has been able to get a real solid lead on him. But if I gotta use your sister, then so be it. You understand?" She nodded yes. "Baby, *I am* going to put this muthafucka to sleep," he stated with conviction.

"I know him, Kaylin. And I know he's saying the same thing about you. Oh God," she groaned, as reality instantly hit her. "I don't know what I would do if sumthin happened to her . . . or you, Kaylin." She placed a hand over her mouth as the tears cascaded down her cheeks.

"Baby, it's gonna be all right. I just gotta move smart." He wiped her tears away.

"I don't believe this shit." She looked over at Kaylin.

"Oh, he's gonna get handled, baby. I need you to chill out. And your sister, is she trying to get your attention or what?"

"I don't know." Angel sighed heavily. "I don't know what the fuck is her problem."

"Let me make a few phone calls. Do you have a picture of her?"

"No, not a recent one," she sniffed. "Why?"

"I need to get it to my peeps."

"You know where he is?" she snapped. "When were you going to tell me?"

"I heard he was down in Miami. But they haven't been able to give me anything more definitive."

She rolled her eyes at him, then picked up her phone and dialed her mother.

"Hey, Mommy, it's me. I need a recent picture of Carmen. Can you get that ready for me? I'll be down to see you tomorrow."

"If I'm not here I'll leave it on the kitchen table. I'm thinking about changing the locks. What do you think?"

"If that's what you feel you gotta do, Mommy, then do it. I need to know where Carmen is. How did she send you the money?"

"She wired it to me."

"Where did it come from?"

"Right here in Jersey."

Angel sucked her teeth. "That bastard knows that he isn't anywhere near Jersey. He had someone else send it." She was talking out loud to herself. "Anyway, it's important that we find out where she is," she said with urgency. "We'll talk more tomorrow. Love you, Mom."

"Love you too, baby. And listen, don't stress about your sister. Because I damn sure ain't."

No sooner had they got settled into the house than the phone started ringing. Angel was already coming out of her clothes and heading for the Jacuzzi.

"I got it!" Kaylin yelled as he picked up the phone. "Hello."

"Hi, Dad," Malik said with excitement.

"Malik, what's up? We missed you."

"Can I come over?"

Kaylin looked at his watch. "It's almost ten o'clock, why aren't you in bed?"

"'Cause I was waiting on you."

"Why didn't you call me on the cell phone? We just got in the house."

"Dad, I did. You didn't pick it up. Red didn't neither."

"My bad. They must have been off. I'll come and get you in the morning, is that cool?"

"Aww, Dad," he said in defeat.

"It's late, little man. First thing tomorrow, call me, and I'll come scoop you up. Aiight?"

"Whatever," he mumbled under his breath.

"What? Watch your mouth, Malik!"

"Okay, Dad. Did you bring me sumthin back?"

"Yeah." Kaylin was trying not to laugh.

"Did Red?"

"Yeah, little man. Have you been on your best behavior?"

"Yes, Dad," he said dryly.

"I'm going to ask your mother when I come over there. You brushed your teeth?"

"Yes, Dad."

"Aiight, then. I think it's time for you to go to bed."

"Can I speak to Red, please?"

"What for?"

"I want to come over tonight."

"Malik. What did I just say?"

"In the morning," he whined.

"All right, then. Good night."

"Night, Dad."

Kaylin hung up the phone shaking his head, thinking how Malik never ceased to amaze him.

Kaylin decided to go into his playroom, down in the basement. He had a full entertainment center, a flat-screen plasma TV, a mini-bar, a couple of weight benches, a full bathroom with a Jacuzzi, a laundry room, and a refrigerator. Plus, he could blaze up the purple haze without Angel complaining about it making her nauseated.

Snake.

His face popped up in his mind as he looked around his second sanctuary and dimmed the lights. He took off his sweat suit jacket, pulled off his T-shirt, and got in position to do some push-ups. Up . . . down . . . up . . . down . . . he pushed, faster and faster. *Snake.*

He thought about how it was going to feel to put a couple of bullets into his head, and a smile lit up his eyes. He pushed up . . . down . . . up . . . down.

Losing count, but coming to a halt when he felt the beginning of a burn, he stood up, wiped his face with his T-shirt. Going over to the bar, he poured himself a glass of Hennessey, blazed up a blunt, and grabbed a pool stick.

Snake. That muthafucka got mad jokes, he thought to himself. He threw the Henny back and knocked the rest of the blunt off. By the time he cleared everything off the table except for the eight ball, he was feeling nice. Laying the pool stick on the table, he took off the rest of his clothes and went to indulge in a nice hot shower.

As the hot water massaged his head, neck, shoulders, and back he strategized on how he could quickly put Snake to sleep. Soaping up once and then rinsing off, he stepped out, lit another blunt, took a couple of pulls, and put it out. He brushed his teeth and rinsed with some mouthwash. Since there were no towels in the bathroom he left the basement dripping wet and butterball naked.

When he walked into the bedroom, it was dimly lit with a red light. Angel had on a caramel see-through negligee that was held closed with a small ribbon across her chest. She had on a pair of caramel stilettos and was leaned back on the bed playing in her pussy.

Kaylin licked his lips as his dick slowly began to rise. "Yo, hold up, Daddy's here. Let Daddy handle that pussy."

"I didn't think you wanted it, as long as you were talking," she purred, but didn't stop trying to get herself off.

Kaylin began stroking himself as he walked over to the bed.

"Oooh, that's what I'm talking about." Angel panted as his

dick was staring her in the face. She leaned up, getting into position, and took his dick with her free hand. She raised the three
fingers she pulled from her pussy and gently painted Kaylin's lips
with her juices. He wasted no time, sucking and licking her
creamy juices off her fingers, one by one.

"Now . . . that's the shit I'm talking about." He sucked them
clean. She pulled them out of his mouth and delicately glossed
them over his lips. Sitting on the edge of the bed, she stroked
him with both hands before wrapping her soft, pouty lips over
the head. Both hands still stroking, she licked, sucked on the
head and stroked him until the dick seemed to swell to another
size. Smiling at her handiwork she looked up at Kaylin. His eyes
were closed and his arms were bent, just like D'Angelo's were
when he was getting his dick sucked in his video.

How Does It Feel? Angel began to lightly massage his balls
while trying to suck the skin off his dick.

"Ooooohhh . . . shit!" Kaylin's voice went up a notch. He placed
both hands on top of her head and began fucking her throat. "Red,
baby . . . oh, fuck!" he grunted, his voice dropping down an oc-
tave, as her bobbing head deep-throated almost all of him.
When she felt his balls tense up, she released him slowly until
his dick was free and it was spitting all over her lips, face, neck,
and breast.

"Got damn . . . fuck!" he groaned as his knees gave out and he
almost tumbled on top of her. "Shit," he panted as he fell over
onto his back. Angel immediately leaned over and sucked whatever was left off before crawling up and kissing his lips and allowing him to taste the fruits of her labor. He smeared his cream
all over her breasts and then smacked her ass.

She crawled up and got in position to sit on his face. With her
up on her knees, Kaylin looked up at her pussy. "Damn, it's beautiful," he whispered as she eased her pussy down to his tongue.
Her breathing got heavy and thick as he blew on her swelled
pearl. He slithered his tongue around and down before entering
every inch of it inside her tight, juicy walls, deeply giving her a

tongue-lashing. Throwing her head back, she begged, "Suck this shit, nigga." He grabbed her ass cheeks, squeezed them, and began eating her pussy as if he was trying to win a custard pie eating contest. Because she was pregnant her pussy was fat, warm, and tasty and Kaylin couldn't get enough of it.

"Get it, nigga! Right . . . there . . . fuck," she squealed in pleasure as he vigorously licked her clit. "Sw . . . ee . . . t Je . . . su . . . s, don't' stop . . . r-right there." Her orgasm started from her ass, shot up to her stomach, and then swarmed across her pussy, causing it to contract, jump, and twitch as she screamed and ground her pussy into Kaylin's mouth.

"F-fuck," she finally screamed out as Kaylin continued to lap up her creamy white liquid. "Oh my God," she whimpered. Now it was her turn to collapse onto her back. "I love you," she panted. "Damn, I fuckin' love you."

He leaned over and allowed her to taste her juices in his mouth, while he untied the strings holding her robe together.

"Mmmmm," she moaned as he squeezed her nipple between his thumb and forefinger. He then placed his lips over her other nipple, licking it and trying to suck on the entire tit, driving Angel crazy.

He stood up, pulled her up, and slipped her negligee off her shoulders. Her pussy was still jumping. As he stood there admiring her pregnant and naked body his pipe was now rising slowly to the occasion. "You know I gotta fuck you in those stilettos, right?"

She gave him that sultry look. "Why do you think I have them on?"

She reached over and began playing in the precum on the tip of his dick. "Make sure you fuck my back out. Daddy make this pussy talk in tongues."

Those words made Kaylin's dick jump as he walked her over to the dresser. He bent her over and she spread her legs, making that ass jiggle for him.

Kaylin nodded in satisfaction, then slapped her ass. "Mmmmm," she moaned seductively as she looked back at his dick and licked her lips, letting him know to bring it on.

He grabbed her ass and stood behind her, his dick in between her legs, pressing against her pussy lips. She instinctively began rocking her hips, sliding her pussy up and down the length of his nine and a half inches.

"Ssss . . . baby." She was rocking harder, harder, faster, and faster, her creamy liquid so plentiful it was turning his dick white. "Kaylin . . . please . . . give it . . . to . . . me."

Kaylin began moving faster, making sure the head of his dick kept rubbing her clit.

"Oh . . . oh . . . oh . . . shit," she whimpered as the orgasm turned her hip rocking into hip quaking. He kept his hardness pressed up against her pussy as he rained soft kisses all over her back.

"You want more?" he whispered in between kisses.

"Please, Papi," Angel begged. He gave her a little time to get herself together before he spread her legs wider and slid his dick over her dripping wet pussy, once more gliding the head to the opening, only giving her an inch at a time. Angel felt like she was going out of her mind. They both let out a groan as Kaylin put it all the way in, held it, and began grinding nice and slow, sending electric currents flying throughout her body, setting it on fire.

"Oh . . . God . . . it . . . feels . . . damn . . . please . . . Unnnnghh . . . oh . . . fuck this pussy," she yelled out, her fingers gripping the edges of the dresser so tight her knuckles were turning white. "Oh, yeah, baby, that's my spot," she squealed. "That's . . . it . . . oh G-God!" She squeezed her eyes shut as her body shuddered from her toes all the way up to her nipples. She shook and trembled and yelled out his name, a single tear rolling down her cheek as she gave in to the body-rocking orgasm. Her pussy was clamping around his dick.

Trying not to bust, Kaylin pulled out, stood behind her as he massaged both of her nipples. Her head was down on the dresser, as her sweat-covered body heaved up and down. As soon as her breathing returned to almost normal, he stood her up, turned her around, and set her on top of the dresser.

"Gimme that tongue," he ordered as their tongue kisses sounded off into the quiet room. Running her soft small hands all over his chest, she wrapped her legs around his waist. He pulled her to the edge of the dresser and eased back into her. This time it was all about him. She leaned back and let out a moan as he fucked her deep and slow.

"Damn, you got this snap-back pussy!" He closed his eyes as he let the feel of her soft, gushy walls ride him to oblivion. She clamped down on his dick with her pussy muscles, causing him to shudder and mumble shit she couldn't understand.

"Fuck this pussy, get yours. Do that shit. Take it . . . Daddy, long-stroke this pussy. Sssss . . . yeah," she teased him. She reached down and pressed on her clit, as he hammered in deeper. When her clit began to skeet, her walls contracted . . . clenching on to his dick. His face twisted up, body stiffened, he let out a long grunt and Angel thought she felt his cum hit her throat.

The following day by noon they were still in the bed. Malik had been blowing up all the phone lines. When Angel's cell phone rang, Kaylin groaned as he reached over her to answer it.

"Yeah."

"Hey, Dad."

"What's up?"

"When you coming to pick me up?"

"As soon as I wake up and get in the shower."

"You woke now. So you gonna get in the shower?"

"Malik! Gimme that phone," Kaylin heard Bianca yell. "Kaylin, I'm on my way out, I'll bring him over there."

"Aiight, then." Kaylin hung up and looked down at Angel, who was fast asleep. He kissed her on her forehead and closed his eyes in an attempt to get another hour in.

Ding, dong. Ding, dong.

Kaylin groaned as he lay there willing whoever it was to go away.

Ding, dong. Ding, dong.

He tore himself away from his warm spot in the bed. His tall, naked frame stretched as he clutched the thick carpet with his toes. Throwing on a pair of sweatpants, he headed for the front door.

Ding, dong. Ding, dong.

"All right, damn," Kaylin bellowed out as he unlocked the door and opened it.

Mr. Harry, his neighbor, was just turning away. "Young man, I was just about to leave." Mr. Harry reminded Kaylin of Ossie Davis. He had a Macy's bag filled up with neatly stacked mail that he had collected for them while they were away.

"Morning, Mr. Harry."

"I heard you and the missus pull up last night. It was too late to bring your mail over." He held out the bag for Kaylin.

"'Preciate this, Mr. Harry. The wife is still asleep but she brought you and Miss Emma sumthin nice back."

Mr. Harry grinned. "Very nice of you. I'll tell the missus." He tipped his hat and wobbled away.

"Damn," Kaylin mumbled as he stuck his hand in the bag and thumbed through the mail. He pulled out two large envelopes that didn't have postmarks on them. Locking the door, he then set the bag on the couch before sitting down and inspecting the envelopes.

Shaking them, feeling them, and smelling them, he finally decided to open them. Dumping out the contents onto the coffee table, he began to get pissed. "What the fuck!" he spat as he sprawled out pictures of Angel, Malik, Bianca, New Day, Papi Chulo, and him. There were also pictures of the rest of Game Over staff and artists going into the building. He sat back onto the couch, rubbing his hands over his face.

Chapter 13

Phillip Johnson was swerving his Rolls-Royce along the Forty-ninth Street Bridge into Queens Bridge, one hand on the steering wheel, the other waving animatedly as he cursed the past events. His brother, Dougie, pulled out a Black N' Mild and lit it. He was half listening, as his oldest brother continued to vent.

"I can't believe that a couple of bitches are trying to chump me! Do they know who the fuck I am?" Phillip spat as he recklessly handled the Rolls.

Dougie let out a grunt. Phillip went on to answer himself.

"Shit, I'm muthafuckin' Phillip Johnson, ain't nobody gonna chump me. You should have seen that pussy-ass Kaylin, he wouldn't even check his bitch, yo! Then on top of that, the bitch Lily talking about she carrying my baby! She smokin' somethin', because I know my sperm ain't get that bitch pregnant. Tryna ruin my reputation and upbringing. She got me fucked up."

Dougie grunted again, fighting to remain cool as his brother ranted some more. *I wish this nigga would shut the fuck up, complaining like a little bitch. You fucked her, so why can't she be pregnant? With his punk ass.*

Phillip had been pissing a hissy fit ever since Angel punked him. But when he saw on MTV news that Game Over Records stole the show over there in Spain and Greece he went ape shit.

In his twisted mind, he came to the conclusion that they did it all by using his artist Lil'E. He still considered her his property and couldn't wait to show her just that: she belonged to him.

To add insult to his already bruised ego, when the artists in his camp began questioning him about doing a hot tour like the one 'Game Over' pulled off, he felt even more threatened.

"I got sumthin for them bitches!" He was vexed but also excited because they had one stop to make; then they were on their way to the strip club, Runway 69, to meet up with Perry G.

Tired of his brother's repetitious rantings, Dougie turned on the radio.

Phillip shot him a nasty look, turned it back off, and started yelling. "Don't touch my shit, man, like you don't want to hear what the fuck I got to say . . . punk muthafucka!"

Dougie had heard enough. "Look, bruh, all I'm saying is, how you know that you can trust this kid?"

"Trust? What the fuck do trust got to do with anything? I just want some fuckin' info! What—"

"Yo," Dougie cut him off, "dude got fired, so obviously he's pissed and got motive. What the fuck can this little punk-ass bitch tell you that you can't find out for yo' got damn self? Shit, you bigger than that. Plus, you been in this game longer than both of them cats. And Kaylin, he just tryna come up. He's not even close to your status. You got niggas and hoes pullin' in major stacks. So, bruh, I can't understand why you nuckin' off this little white bitch, and gettin' your blood pressure all up. Nah mean?"

Phillip balled his face up and spat, "Who the fuck side you on, nigga? Shit, let me find out. What type of shit you on? And hold up, who the fuck you talking to like you crazy or sumthin?"

See? I can't talk no sense to this bullheaded nigga. Dougie smirked to himself as he looked out the window.

"That's right, I've been in the game longer. I'm Phillip muthafuckin' Johnson, so I'm not about to let no new cat come up and just fuck me, nah mean? You right, bruh, I don't know what this cat can tell me, but as sure as hell is hot, I'm gonna listen to what the nigga got to say."

Phillip hit Twenty-first Street and his eyes caught somebody he had been looking for since last month. "Oh yeah," he mumbled as he skidded onto the sidewalk, threw the stick shift in park, and jumped out. Dougie sprang out of the other side. "Yo, Wes, thought I wouldn't roll up on yo' punk ass, huh?"

"*Fuck.*" Wes glanced at Phillip, then at Dougie. With his deformed hand he threw the bag of groceries at them and jumped on top of the Rolls. He grabbed on to the storefront's awning, trying to pull himself up, but instead of getting away he came tumbling down, flat on his back, landing on the hood of the car. "Unnnnghh," he grunted.

Phillip had caught one leg and Dougie grabbed the other and both men started raining blows at his face and on his body. Most passersby scurried around the action, but the rest were enjoying the show.

"Bitch, where . . . my . . . muthafuckin' . . . rims . . . at?" Phillip kept punching the now screaming man. "You . . . fuckin' . . . thief."

"Yo, pop the trunk. Let's get this nigga outta here before the po-po roll up," Dougie warned.

"Yo, I'ma get you your rims," Wes, the thief, screamed.

"Nigga, I paid you over a month ago. Who the fuck you take me for? Some sucka-ass busta?"

"Naw, man. Ohhh . . . shit," Wes screamed out as Dougie pulled him off the car and his head hit the ground. Dougie was dragging him across the cement. "C'mon, man," he pleaded.

"What the fuck y'all looking at?" Phillip yelled at the bold spectators. They were right up on the action. This was his hood and he felt as if he was king. He moved a few items out of the way in the trunk as Dougie lifted their victim and stuffed him inside. Dougie's six-two, 245-pound solid frame came in handy.

"Yo, man, c'mon now. Don't close me in here. I'ma get your rims." Panic was evident in his voice.

Phillip punched him in the jaw, grabbed his head, and mashed him down. He stood back as Dougie slammed the trunk.

"Yo, why you gotta slam my shit? I keep asking you nicely not to do that. All you got to do is press it closed. The latch will catch."

"Man, go 'head with that fuckin' bullshit. Let's get the fuck outta here. We got a nigga in the trunk and you bitchin' about a fuckin' latch."

When they got back into the ride, Dougie clicked on the radio and turned it up real loud. Phillip reached over and turned it down. When he heard the dude in the back yelling and screaming he turned it back up and mumbled some threats to Dougie.

They pulled into the strip joint Runway 69. Phillip maneuvered the car all the way into the back of the lot and parked.

"What the fuck we gonna do with him?" Dougie nodded to the back.

"I haven't decided yet." Phillip turned the engine off and got out.

Dougie shrugged and got out too. They were searched and allowed through the velvet rope.

"Oh my Gawd!" Phillip yelled as he walked through the club looking at all of the many beautiful asses, tits, and faces. "I'm in my element fo' real!" He slapped a bronze beauty on the ass as she walked by, swinging her weave.

Several people said what's up, and there were several "there go Phillip Johnsons", but he kept it moving.

Perry G stood up and waved Phillip and Dougie over. Perry was hard to miss, especially since he looked like he was wearing Bishop Don Juan's hand-me-downs, hat included.

"Look at this nigga." Dougie smirked.

Perry G came up and gave them both some dap. "I got you the best table in the house, Mr. Johnson." He immediately began to kiss ass. "What y'all want to drink? I appreciate y'all coming out."

"I'm in the mood for some Patrón!" Phillip yelled as he placed a five-dollar bill in the white broad's thong.

"Get me a scotch on the rocks, Mr. Kiss Ass," Dougie cracked.

The DJ was spinning "Déjà Vu" by Beyonce, and two dancers were on the stage, throwing their money makers around.

"Mr. Johnson." He shot Dougie a fucked-up look. "I've been in A-and-R, as you probably heard, for the last ten years. I'm the b—"

"Hold up, money," Phillip interrupted. "This ain't no job interview. I came here to get me a lil' pussy and to hear about a pussy. What's the deal with this Kaylin nigga?"

"I can tell you whatever you need to know."

"Then talk." Phillip leaned back into his chair.

"Yo, my man is just trying to come up. He go hard on finding that talent. He's focused on building a big team and building it fast. He's goin' hard at it."

"Where the nigga getting all this money from? Fuckin' office in the Time Warner Building!"

"Yo, he used to be big in the game. Him and his boy, Trae. Their names used to ring loud. Them niggas caught a case, beat it, and hauled ass out of the game. Turned everything legit. Both of them got married, got families, and is just trying to enjoy the fruits of their labor."

The more Perry G was talking, the madder Phillip was getting. "So, that's really his wife? That fine, yellow lawyer broad?"

"Yeah. I know you heard about that big wedding they had. That shit was off the chain. His nigga, Trae, got shot up, yo. Angel's ex, this nigga named Snake, came rolling up in there with his boys and halted that whole shit. Everybody had to leave. Kaylin walked out on his bride to be."

"So they ain't married!"

"That nigga came to his senses. They just got married recently."

"Damn. I know he did. That's a bad bitch."

"That's a crazy bitch. After her wedding got crashed and Kaylin walked out on her she came to the office acting like nothing happened. She's about her business."

"So who's really running the label?"

"They both are. They are a team. Like Bonnie and Clyde."

Phillip reached over, grabbed Dougie's drink, and threw it back! Too lazy to open the bottle of Patrón the first waitress brought over, he signaled for another waitress.

"So who was this nigga that crashed the wedding?"

"Her ex. All I know is his name, Snake. They say he used to be a pimp."

"Aiight, my man. Where can I reach you if I need you?"

Perry G, not wanting the meeting to end, took his time at retrieving a business card.

"I might have some work for you," Phillip told him, then stood up. He took the business card and slipped it in his suit jacket. "Aiight, money, I gotta go get me a lap dance right quick." And he left Perry G and Dougie sitting there at the table.

A little after midnight, several lap dances, some head, and a VIP fuck, Phillip and Dougie were coming out the club. As soon as they made it to the parking lot, Phillip smacked Dougie on the back of his head.

Dougie stopped dead in his tracks. "Man, what the fuck is your problem, yo?" Dougie swung at him and Phillip ducked.

"You said I was wasting my time, nigga. You gonna learn from me one day, boy!"

"What the fuck is yo' crazy ass talking about?"

"I knew I saw that bitch before!"

"What bitch?"

"Remember when we was on the ticket with Carl Thomas? We had to give Snake some tickets because he was killin' us in some Cee-Lo. Snake, man, think about it."

They were getting in the car and Dougie was still trying to jog his memory bank.

Phillip, losing patience as always, yelled, "Keenan, man! Dino, Steve, Mark. The Hightower's fool!"

"Oh, shit." Dougie grinned as the memories crept back. "Me

and Keenan used to get mad pussy together. Get the fuck outta here! That's my nigga."

"Hell yeah. And you know I don't believe in that muthafuckin' coincidence shit. We caught bodies with them fuckin' wild-ass Hightower niggas. They went from gangstas to pimps. I ain't never saw no shit like that before. And only a nigga like him would crash a damn wedding. That ho must have been tearin' that track up, for him to go do some shit like that. But hell, she is fine. You gotta see her."

Dougie had to laugh at that one. But he stopped when Phillip pulled into an alleyway and turned the car off.

"Let's handle this nigga." Phillip turned stone-faced.

They both got out and Dougie pulled out his burner. Phillip stuck the key in the trunk lock and turned it. They both held the trunk closed and moved on opposite sides. Phillip nodded at Dougie and he stepped back with the burner aimed. Phillip let his hand go and the trunk eased open. Their victim was just lying there, balled up in a knot. Phillip chuckled when Dougie smacked him across the head with the gun.

Wes, the thief, let out a gut-wrenching moan. Phillip grabbed him by the collar and yanked him out the trunk. "Get yo' little ass up!" He threw him onto the ground, after he told him to get up and kicked him in his ribs.

"Oowww," he groaned and went into a coughing fit.

"Your life is only worth a set of five thousand dollar rims, nigga?" shouted Phillip as he grabbed the lug wrench out of the trunk. He kicked Wes again, causing him to roll over on his back. "I'ma teach you to keep your word, nigga. 'Cause you obviously forget who you was fuckin' with."

Phillip held the lug wrench up as if it were a stake and brought it down forcefully, driving it into his throat. His blood gushed out as if he had just struck a tiny oil well. Phillip ducked to his left, barely missing a splash of blood on his face. But it did get on his shoulder. "Fuck!" he spat as he grinned wickedly at his handiwork. "I thought I could pull this off with precision." He pulled the iron out and stood up.

Dougie threw him a towel and he ran it across the bloodstains on his suit. He then wiped off the lug wrench, wrapped the towel around it, and set it in the trunk.

"Yo, I don' know what the fuck to think." Kaylin was sitting on his mother's back porch, showing Kajuan the mystery envelope that had the pictures in it.

"My gut is telling me that it's not Snake," Kajuan told him.

"Well, my gut is telling me who it is, but hold up." Kaylin flipped open his celly.

"Where you at, yo?" It was Omar.

"I'm at my mom's. What's up?"

"We hit pay dirt. You wanna swing by the hospital and tell Tasha, or you want me to do it? That's why I was asking where were you."

"Can I get a name, nigga?"

"Jaden's little brother, Rome."

"Word?"

"Yeah. But that's neither here nor there, baby."

"Aiight, then. Real talk."

"I'm out."

Kaylin hung up with a smirk on his face. "That was O."

"Yeah?"

"That was Jaden's little brother who got at Trae."

"Who the fuck is Jaden?" Kajuan wanted to know.

"A nigga we fucked with who stepped to Tasha when we was gone. Trae had somebody get at him."

"Damn. Y'all niggas was wild, yo. Kill a nigga because he step to your woman. Whatever happened to the good ole days? The days when the focus was gettin' money and if you had beef you used your fists."

"Nigga, those are the gone ole days."

"I see."

"In any event, street justice has been served." Kaylin flipped open his phone again. "Yeah."

"Hey, baby." Angel cooed in his ear.

"Red, what's up?"

"Where are you?"

"At Mommy's."

"Marvin and Kyra are at the hospital with Tasha, they got in last night."

"That's love. I need to holla at Marv."

"You've got company over here," she said with excitement.

"Who?"

"You're fam from Puerto Rico."

"What family?"

"Who gave us the gold bars."

Shit. "Oh . . . that . . . family."

Carmen was looking at Snake all dreamy-eyed as he rose up to leave. "When are you coming back?" Her tongue was practically hanging out of her mouth.

"I'll call you later." He flashed that slick grin at her and pulled out a wad of cash. He peeled off a few bills and put them gently in her hand. "Keep it tight, aiight?"

Carmen giggled. "Fo sho!"

Snake and his crew left the condo that he set Carmen up in and they piled into his uncle Dino's Escalade. Dino had Bullet chauffeuring them around.

"Man, you hit that yet? She is open, dawg." Bullet was acting as if he would if Snake didn't want to.

"Nah. I don't want her. It's her sister I'm after. Not that little dumb bitch. She's just an end piece to this puzzle. Why you want her? I'll give you a deal on the ho."

"Where we going?" Bullet ignored Snake's last comment.

"Just drive, man. That hen dog got me feelin' nice."

"You decided if you was gonna put her on the track or not?" Dino asked.

"Nah, I'm still hashing out the details to everything."

"Man, pull over. Let me and this nigga out," Uncle Dino ordered.

Bullet pulled over. Everybody got quiet.

"What? Unc? What's up?"

"Get the fuck out, that's what's up."

"What I do?" sighed a confused Snake as he followed his uncle's orders.

They both got out of the Escalade and began walking down the strip. Snake was loving Miami and he was ready to call it his home.

"Boy, I'm sick of you scheming on that bitch, Angel. What the fuck done happened to your mind, boy? Here you done put a bitch up in a plush-ass condo, giving her money, and you don't know if you gonna put her ass on the track? I should fuck you up just on GP. You might as well hit the track yo' damn self."

"Unc, it ain't even like that."

"Fuck it ain't! I swear that beat-down you got fucked your head up real bad."

"Naw, Unc, she got me fucked up! No matter how long I was gone, she was supposed to wait. I don't care if I was gone for forty years, she wasn't supposed to get with the next nigga. And get pregnant and shit?"

"Well, she did, nigga, and that should tell you sumthin. And on top of that you didn't even have that ho out on the track!"

"Hold up, Unc . . . hold up. You married with a wife and Aunt Jill never hit the track. Why can't I marry and get a wife?"

"Fool!" His uncle pushed him. "You marry somebody that wants to marry you back. She obviously has moved on, Keenan. And I'm getting sick of you focusing on nothing but this bitch. Now you went as far as hooking up with her sister?" He gritted his teeth. "What the fuck is the matter with you?"

"Unc, you know how I left, man. We were engaged. I had to

dip. Now I'm back and I just wanted to see what's up. I haven't had the chance to talk to her in private. That's all I need. I know she still love me. She thought I was dead, remember? Why can't I just talk to her? What's the big fuckin' deal?"

Dino used his thumbs to massage his temples, thinking that this was a dumb muthafucka. And that he was right, that beat-down fucked his head up. The nigga was now insane, stuck on stupid. As they strolled down the strip, Snake was enjoying the warm Miami weather, the palm trees, the night sky, and the sounds of the city. Dino was quiet and thinking. Thinking about how could he help his nephew stop himself from self-destructing.

After a good ten minutes of silence, Dino said, "Look, nephew. I want you to listen to me. And I'm only gonna say it once. See if she'll talk to you one on one. Don't force her. If she gives you that, fine. Then ask her, what's up? If she wit it, cool. But if she ain't, I want you to back the fuck off. That's an order. This shit is crazy. I don't see any good coming out of this. Do you under-stand me? There's a whole sea of bitches out here. You embar-rassing the fuck outta your whole damn family. I don't know why I'm wasting my breath for real. I see now that I'm going to have to fuck you up my damn self."

The Escalade rolled up on them. "Yo, Dino, your phone, man."

"Do you hear what I'm saying?"

"I hear you, Unc."

Dino went over to his ride and grabbed his cell. "Yeah? He right here. Why the hell you calling him on my phone?" Dino barked. "Here. It's your uncle Steve."

"Steve?" Snake asked, surprised. Dino shoved the phone at him and headed back to his ride. "Unclc Stcve, what's up?"

"Boy, you got big people looking for you." Steve was the old-est of all his father's brothers.

"Big people like who? The only big people I know are the I, the R, and the S. And let's not forget the F-E-D-S. So what's up, Unc?"

"You ain't never had no job, so how would you know about the

I, the R, and the S? And the feds, you down there doing sumthin you ain't got no business doing?"

"Naw, Unc. I'm chilling. Just trying to get right again, that's all." He was hoping that his uncle Steve didn't know about him moving dope.

"How many hoes you got?"

"Three right now."

"Three? Aww, nigga, you are doing bad. You need to call this nigga back, right away, shit. He got money. Big money."

"Who, Uncle Steve?" Snake was getting agitated at both of his uncles for trying to tell him how to do shit.

"Phillip Johnson."

"Phillip Johnson?"

"Yeah, little P.J. and Dougie Johnson."

"Aww, hell no! What that nigga callin' me for? I know he need sumthin!" Snake laughed but was skeptical at the same time.

"I don't know, boy, but with three hoes, maybe you can get a job. Get one for you and your stable of three," his uncle cracked.

"I'ma make you eat those words, Unc."

"Well, I hope so. Here, boy, now write this number down so you can call little P.J., the big music man," he said proudly. "Even though I know it's just a front. That boy can't fool me."

"Unc, everybody ain't illegal."

"Yeah. Uh-huh. Come on, boy, get a pencil. You runnin' up my damn bill."

Chapter 14

Almost three months later, Tasha could drain the blood from the tube in Trae's chest with her eyes closed. After the task was done she cleaned up the mess and was back by his side.

It was just after eight and all visitors were gone, the twins, Marvin, Kyra, Jaz, and Faheem. It was a very busy day. Even her cousin Stephon flew in from Cali.

She leaned in and planted long and tender kisses on Trae's cheeks, the corner of his lip and forehead. She took his hand and held it against her stomach. Looking down at him, she said, "Trae, I am having a very, very hard time controlling my emotions today." She leaned over and kissed his cheek again and rested her head on his shoulder. She moved his hand all over her stomach. "We need you, baby. I need you. I miss you so much. I miss talking to you. I miss hearing your voice. I miss your touch. Baby, I need you to come back to me now." Her eyes were swelling up with tears.

"Seeing everybody today, especially Marvin and Kyra, tore me up. They remind me too much of our home, us living as a family, waking up in each other's arms, taking care of our children together, and sitting together at the dinner table as a family. Baby, I miss that. I'm ready to take you home. Then the twins today kept wanting to climb on top of you and was bringing you their toys, wanting you to play with them. They miss you so much. This is the first time they were this persistent about wanting your attention. They wore me out. I am so grateful for your parents, I swear, I wouldn't be able to do this without them. I know they are fine with them, but, baby . . . we need to go home." She was crying uncontrollably. "I'm . . . I'm sorry, baby." She sniveled.

"I'm just so tired. I want to go home. And I swear, if I have another emotional and busy day like today, I'm going to have a nervous breakdown. Lord knows what I'm doing to our baby. The reason why it hasn't happened yet is because of the baby, our son. That's right. It's another boy. You got your wish. I had the ultrasound yesterday. I already found a name. Caliph. It means leader, ruler. I wanted to wait and surprise you, but I'm hoping that this news will make you come back to us. I don't want nothing to happen to our son. And the twins? You gotta see them, they are getting so big and bad. Your mother said that they are going to be bossy just like you. She said that they are already trying to tell her what to do. She also slipped in that I'm going to want to have a girl because there is going to be entirely too much testosterone in the house. I swear, you got everybody working with you. I told her I'm done. After this no more. Right, baby?"

She kissed him on the corner of his mouth again. "Remember when I went into labor with the twins? You left home to make a run to the club even though you didn't want to. But I kept telling you to go handle your business, that I would be all right. It wasn't time yet. We already had, what, three or four alarms?" She giggled. "You could tell we were new at this. So when I called you, you was like, Tasha, stop playing. I said, 'Baby, my water broke.' And you stayed on the phone with me during your entire ride back from the club. You were sweating and everything when you came in. I think you were more nervous than I was. And, oh, when they both came out, you should have seen your face, you were beaming with pride. Remember that, baby?" She kissed his forehead. "Then you made that stupid comment about how your dick wasn't shootin' bullets but grenades. That's how you made two babies at once. The doctor and staff looked at you like you was crazy.

"And when we took them home from the hospital, you couldn't tell us nothing. The nurses acted like they didn't want us to leave. But when I got home that was the kicker. You had everyone there: your parents, Jaz, Faheem, Marvin, Kyra, and Angel. Kay got there later on that night. Stephon, you even sent for my sister and brother." She started crying again. "That was so beautiful, baby. You and our children are my everything. I love you so much." She hugged him tight, keeping her face nuzzled into his neck. "Hug me back, baby. I need you to hold me, baby. I miss you holding me." She sobbed quietly. "You know what else I miss? Your smile. How you smile at me with that look in your eyes that says I'm the only woman in the world for you." She continued for the next few minutes sobbing quietly and wanting him and anticipating him waking up right then, right now, her emotions and hormones going up, coming down. She felt as if she was losing her mind as she started grinning.

"I thought that after the nigga who shot you got what I wanted him to get, I'd be fine. But you know what? I don't feel any different." She ran her hands over his chest. "For real, if you were up and about, you would have been on the warpath. And who knows? Instead of lying here, you could be gone from me forever. So don't be mad at me for doing what I considered the best thing for our family."

She pressed her lips to his ear and whispered, "I need you, baby. I need you now. Don't keep making me go through this. I know you hear me, Trae. Your family needs you. Damn you, Trae!" She let out a gut-wrenching scream.

No more than a minute later, the head nurse came busting into the room. Tasha was standing in front of the window looking out and crying. She was hugging herself and mumbling something.

"Mrs. Macklin, are you okay?" The head nurse came over and hugged her.

"No . . . I'm not . . . okay," she heaved.

"Baby, you really need a break. Why don't you go home for the evening? I swear you're gonna have a nervous breakdown. You're pregnant, you've been here day and night for three months. That is not good for your physical or mental health, Mrs. Macklin."

"I know it's not good. And today I'm really feeling all the pressure. I can't leave him." She shook her head no. "I'll be okay. I just need a few minutes to pull myself together."

"We'll take good care of Mr. Macklin for you. Go home and get some rest, you need a break, chile," the nurse persisted.

"I can't. I can't leave him here. I won't leave him here. What if he wakes up and I'm not here? I'm not leaving my husband here. I'll be fine. I just miss him, that's all."

The nurse sighed as she went and grabbed some tissue off the table. She dabbed at Tasha's eyes and cheeks. She smiled at her. "He's lucky to have you, young lady. You are under a lot of stress, especially being pregnant. Since you're not going to leave, at least promise me you'll get a good night's sleep. I'll make a note for the duty nurse to change his drainage tube."

"I'll be okay. My body has grown accustomed to waking up every three hours. I'll be fine. But if I feel the need I'll tell them to come do it."

"You are a stubborn one, aren't you?"

"My husband says the same thing, so I guess I am." She let out a forced chuckle.

"Okay, then. I'll see you tomorrow, but I will check on you again before I leave tonight."

"Thank you, ma'am."

Tasha watched the nurse as she left the room. She let down the blinds and went over to his bed. She puffed up her pillow, adjusted the blanket in the chair before getting comfortable in it. She locked her fingers in between his, laid her head on his forearm, and cried herself to sleep.

* * *

Kaylin left his mother's house driving like a bat out of hell across town, ignoring speed limits, stop signs, and police vehicles.

When he pulled into his driveway, Don Carlos and his bodyguard were just leaving.

"Ah, here he is." Don Carlos came down the steps and greeted Kaylin with a hearty hug. Kaylin's glance met with Angel, who was standing in the doorway. "We were just leaving. We have another appointment. Come. Take a ride."

Kaylin looked up at Angel. "Baby, I'll be back. Do you need anything? Are you all right?"

"Of course she is all right! We wouldn't let nothing happen to her. Same old Kaylin." He laughed and looked back at Angel.

The smile she had faded from her face. "I'm okay." Then she looked at Juan. "Juan, have him back for dinner."

"Don't worry, Angel. I will. If I can make it back myself, I would be delighted to taste your cooking." They watched her close the front door and then they headed for the limo.

Kaylin got seated in the backseat of the limo with Don Carlos and his bodyguard, Jorge. He knew Angel was wondering what was really going on.

"Kaylin," Juan drawled in his Mexican accent. "You have a beautiful wife, beautiful home, growing business, you've done quite well for yourself. We are so proud of you. And Don Alexjandro sends his love. He always talks about you and Trae. How loyal you two are and of course, how rich you made us." He let out his signature deep, hearty laugh and Jorge joined in.

"Give Don Alexjandro my regards. And thank him for the very generous wedding gifts. And please, I mean no disrespect. Please get to the heart of the matter and answer the million-dollar question. What brings you to my home? Why do you take pictures of me and my family and send them to my home? What have I done to deserve such disrespect? If Don Alexjandro needed me, all he had to do was call." Kaylin wanted some answers and was obviously pissed off.

"The don knows that, Kaylin. That's why he sent me. You know the don. The pictures were just a . . . reminder. No big thing. You understand, Kaylin?"

"No, I don't understand. I received threats, and why? When all—"

Don Carlos held up his hand in protest, interrupting Kaylin. "It's nothing, Kaylin. No need to be alarmed. Just a friendly reminder. And you know we don't deliver threats, we deliver bodies." He burst into that signature laugh again.

Don Carlos quickly turned serious. "We have everyone praying to the saints for Trae's immediate recovery. He is a very good man. Loyal just like you. That is hard to find these days, even amongst family. Again, that is why I'm here. Don Alexjandro needs a huge favor."

"We're not in the game anymore, Don Carlos. We're trying to be good businessmen and even better family men. No disrespect, but do you understand?"

"Of course. Of course. But let me remind you that it was Don Alexjandro who made it possible for you to be legit businessmen and good family men. It was Don Alexjandro, not your attorneys, not your money, who got you out of Mexico with your lives and your freedom. You have no prison sentence, no parole, no nothing. You are both free to live life. You understand?" Don Carlos spat. "And you have gold, which you took from one of our people. You didn't get permission. We understand that things got crazy and you had to do what you had to do, no? But lucky the fat fuck was no good. He was bad for business, family or not. So with everything comes a price. You understand, Kaylin?"

Kaylin didn't respond. He allowed a huge sigh to escape his lungs.

"Good." Don Carlos pulled out a pipe filled with rich strawberry tobacco and lit it. He closed his eyes as he put his lips around the ivory pipe and pulled. "Now . . . this is good." He held it out for Kaylin, who declined. He allowed the rich smoke to ease through his lungs. "Smells heavenly, doesn't it?"

"Smells rich," Kaylin had to agree.

"I told my wife, Graciela, that when I die, bury me with my pipe and fill it up." He then locked eyes with Kaylin. "We need a matter handled. Don Alexjandro's unloyal nephew, Mickey Reyes. He's tarnishing the family's reputation. It's no good for business. He's bringing too much attention our way. The don would appreciate it if you would handle this matter for him. He also knows about your brother, who is doing twenty-seven years in state prison. You know the don always pays his debts."

"I know the don looks out for his own. But you do understand that we are out. We fulfilled our obligations. Our work is over, it's behind us. Tell the don if he wants the gold we jacked, he can have it, but we are out."

Don Carlos took another pull from his pipe, closed his eyes, savored it. "Don Alexjandro is very proud of both of you. He treated you like sons. We need this taken care of." He leaned up to the edge of the seat and lowered his voice. "Whose life is worth more to you? That of you and your family or a low-life disgrace like Mickey Reyes? I trust you will make the right decision."

The limo slowed down and then eased to a stop. No words were needed as Kaylin jumped out and flagged down a taxi.

That release of tension Tasha had earlier obviously did her some good. She had heard somewhere that crying heals the soul. Well, she was sleeping like a baby, that is until she felt something in the palm of her hand. When she looked up at Trae his eyes were open and he was writing letters in her hand. She had one hand over her chest, and her mouth was wide open. She was in shock. He was writing *Tasha, I luv u*. The tears fell down her cheeks as she began to shake uncontrollably. He started pointing to the tubes coming out of his nose and mouth. Tasha, still in shock, pressed the nurse station button.

"Is everything all right, Mrs. Macklin?" the voice over the intercom asked. When she didn't get a response, she said, "I'll be right there."

When the nurse came into the room Tasha was standing there looking down at Trae in tears. Trae was looking at her and wouldn't let her hand go. She ducked back out of the room and yelled, "Get Dr. Peters, stat!"

"Mr. Macklin, glad you decided to join us," she beamed. She turned on the light and proceeded to get his vitals. "Can you hear me? Blink your eyes twice if you can." He blinked twice. "Good, Dr. Peters is on his way." He raised his hand slowly and pointed to the tubes. "Dr. Peters will be here shortly. I know they are very uncomfortable, but bear with us for a short while, okay?"

She turned to Tasha. "Mrs. Macklin, are you okay?" Tasha nodded up and down and leaned over on Trae's shoulder. "I love you so much. Oh, God, thank you so much. Oh, baby." She hugged him.

"Mr. Macklin, you are a very lucky man. Your wife has shown incredible strength. Your vitals are stable. I'll be right back."

"Baby, do you have any idea how long you've been here?" He slowly shook his head no. "Were you aware of my being here and talking to you?" He slowly nodded yes.

"Mr. Macklin. Mrs. Macklin." Dr. Peters nodded towards Tasha. He was a small-framed black man who reminded her of the butler on the *Fresh Prince*.

He was accompanied by an Indian female, Dr. Gupta. "Mrs. Macklin, Mr. Macklin." She spoke in a thick accent.

"Can you hear me, Mr. Macklin?" Dr. Peters asked. Trae nodded yes. Dr. Peters picked up Trae's chart and began to read it.

Dr. Gupta came around to where Tasha was. She tried to break away from Trae's grip but he wouldn't let her go. Dr. Gupta smiled at the gesture.

Trae pointed once again at the tubes. Dr. Peters turned off the ventilator and respirator. "I can't remove the tubes, the anesthesiologist has to remove them. I'll have the nurse page him."

Trae had to release Tasha's hand in order for the doctor to complete his examination. Dr. Gupta was talking into her minirecorder, taking notes as Dr. Peters administered the exam. "Blink if you are in pain." He pointed to the tubes. Both doctors smiled. Dr. Peters took his vitals, checked his pupils and ears. Dr. Gupta helped turn him over on his side so that he could examine his spine. He stuck a special pin in it. "Blink twice at Dr. Gupta if you can feel it." He blinked twice. "Good." They placed him on his back. Dr. Peters stuck the pin in both legs. Trae couldn't feel the pin penetrate his legs. He shook his head no. "Don't worry about your legs. In a day or two, you'll get the sensation back. I was mainly concerned about your spine. But that's fine. If the sensation doesn't return in your legs, we'll do further testing."

Tasha was still shaken as she picked up the phone and called his parents. "Nana, it's me. He's up. Oh God, he's up." She swiped at the tears for the hundredth time. Apparently Nana was waking up Mr. Macklin since it was three thirty in the morning. She could hear Nana in the background crying and praising God.

"Tasha, are you still there?" Mr. Macklin grabbed the phone.

"I'm here. He's up. The doctors are examining him now."

"Thank you, Lord." Mr. Macklin sounded as if a huge burden had been lifted off his shoulders. "What is he doing? What is he saying? Tell him we love him and we knew he would come back to us."

"He wants the tubes out of him. He can't talk. He's been nodding up and down, blinking, and writing in my hands. He's been squeezing my hands." She was crying once again.

"Oh, glory be to God. We'll be up there first thing in the morning. Tell my son that, okay?"

"I will, Pop-Pop." She disconnected the call and stood watching as the doctors continued to probe, prod, press, and examine.

She closed her eyes and said a silent prayer; then she called Kaylin and told him the good news. He said he would spread the word and would be up first thing tomorrow.

"Okay, Mrs. Macklin. He appears to be in stable condition. In layman's terms, for someone who's been in a coma for the last three months, he's doing pretty darn good. Even though he has no energy, which is normal, make sure he stays put. Don't you dare try to get up." He glared at Trae. "I will page the anesthesiologist and get these tubes out and then I'll be back."

He patted Trae on his shoulder and they left.

Tasha rushed to his side, fluffed up his pillow, and straightened out his bedding. She grabbed his hand and began smiling through the tears. "I love you, baby. And thank you for coming back to us. I knew you would. Nana and Pop-Pop said they love you more than anything and that they'll be up in the morning." She kissed him on the cheek. "The boys are fine, getting bigger and talking up a storm. I can't wait for you to see them." He placed his hand on her stomach, which caused her to smile. "Do you remember what I told you we are having?" He nodded a slow yes. "What did I say we were gonna name him?" He drew the letters C-a-l-i-p-h in her palm. "Oh my God!" she gasped. "You really could hear me. Oh my God!"

A young blond Caucasian lady came in with a name tag that read DR. KIM WHITE, ANESTHESIOLOGIST. "Hello, I'm Dr. White," she said to Tasha. "I'm here to remove those irritating tubes."

"I'm Tasha Macklin and this is my husband, Trae. And, Dr. White, he's ready for them to come out."

Dr. White smiled at Trae. "They're horrible, aren't they?" She put on a pair of surgical gloves and picked up his chart, looked it over, and placed it back down. "This will be uncomfortable, Mr. Macklin. I'll take out the one in your nose first." She pointed to the tube in his nose. "No more uncomfortable than what you've been experiencing, right?" She talked him through it, as it slid out effortlessly. When she removed the tubes from his throat a blob of green pea-soup-looking bile came out with the tubes. It splashed Tasha's neck and cheek.

"Oh my!" Tasha squealed. "Gross."

"Sorry about that," Dr. White apologized. "I didn't think it would be that bad."

Tasha giggled as she headed for the bathroom to wipe it up.

"That's better, isn't it?"

Trae's gaze was fixed on the bathroom door where his wife disappeared. Dr. White was packing up her equipment when Tasha came out of the restroom.

"What was that?" Tasha wanted to know.

"Mainly drainage and it's backed up. It's also mucus. I'll page Dr. Peters and let him know that my work is done here. His throat will be sore, but after a couple of days it will heal. I would suggest that he doesn't try to speak. Take care, Mr. Macklin." She said it as if he were deaf. And then she was out the door.

Tasha had her husband back.

Chapter 15

Tasha was feeling totally rejuvenated. She was feeling as if her life was starting all over, that she could now go back to living. Life was great once again.

Even though her body was extremely tired, she was up at 6:00 a.m. giving Trae a sponge bath, shave, manicure, and pedicure. She was tired and happy at the same time. He still wasn't talking, but was now writing his words on paper.

By eight she had him fresh and clean, all propped up, ready to see the family.

She had arranged it so that when his parents came she was going to go home, take a nice hot bath, get her hair done, and then go pick up the twins from her sister's house.

By eight thirty his parents were bursting through the door, both of them so glad to see their only child, they were literally smothering him. Mrs. Macklin stopped crying long enough to say a prayer. Tasha stepped back to allow them time with their son, and it did her heart good to see it. She slipped out to the nurses' station to let them know she would be back by two and to call her if they needed her. She then went back into the room and debriefed his parents as to the doctor's comments upon examination. She also relayed what was to be expected of his recovery.

"Baby." She kissed him gently on the lips. "I'm going to go to the apartment, take a bath, and then go and get this knotty hair of mine done. After that I'll go pick up the boys and then I'll be back here. Okay?" She ran her fingers along his jaw. "I love you and I've missed you so much. I told the nurses to call me if they need me. But you should be fine with your parents," she teased.

He nodded yes as he ran his hands over her stomach. When the baby kicked he smiled.

"Tasha, you sure you don't want to take the whole day off? Maybe get some much-needed rest and relaxation?" Mr. Macklin asked but was really making a suggestion.

"No, Pop-Pop, I'll be fine. Spend some time with your son. I'll be back around two. That's enough rest for me. Pop-Pop, I feel . . . like this is the very first day of a wonderful life. My husband came back to me. My family is back. I feel like doing cartwheels." She giggled. "That wouldn't be good, though, would it?" Trae smiled and nodded.

"Girl, don't be doing nothing stupid," Nana scolded.

"I won't, Nana. I said I felt like doing cartwheels, not I'm going to do some." She went over to Nana and kissed her on the cheek and then kissed Mr. Macklin, and then she was gone.

Phillip Johnson and Dougie drove to Newark's Liberty International Airport to pick up Snake. They had gotten through all of the formalities during the course of several lengthy telephone conversations. Phillip circled around the airport until he saw Dougie and his old partner in crime flagging him down. The police were right behind him, giving out tickets, so Snake hurriedly threw his garment bag onto the backseat and jumped in behind it while Dougie jumped in the front. Phillip pulled off.

"Man, what's up with the eye patch?"

"Damn, Phillip, no hello, how was your flight, how's the family?" Snake joked.

"Nigga, I talked to yo' fake, wannabe, pimp ass this morning, two times yesterday, and once before that. How many times you want me to ask the same ole shit? This is a business trip, not a high school reunion," Phillip snapped.

Snake tapped Dougie on his shoulder. "What the fuck does my eye patch have to do with business? How do you put up with this control freak? It's always business with him. I guess that's why yo' paper so long, right?" Snake teased.

"And you know this, mannnn!" Phillip joked back.

"I'm feelin' this ride, man. A got damn Bentley Continental! This bitch goes up to 195 miles a hour. Damn, nigga! You really have come up. So what was so urgent that you had to see me today? I had other shit to do."

"Nigga, don't try to skip the subject. What happened to your eye? I doubt if it's a fashion statement."

"I got hit in it, man. It's completely damaged. I only have about ten percent vision in it and it's very sensitive to light, even sunlight. So that's why I keep it covered. But it's cool, the bitches still like it."

"I'm sure they do."

"So what's up?"

"Several things. You and I have the same people and issues in common. A nigga and a bitch that's in our way."

"Oh, really?" Snake's interest was piqued. "Who?"

"Kaylin."

"Kaylin?" To say that Snake was surprised was an understatement.

"Yeah, you heard me right. Small fuckin' world, ain't it?"

"Well, I'll be damned. What? He fuckin' your woman too?"

"No but he's fuckin' with my paper and that's not as bad but worse. He pulled this bitch I signed, and I got major attitude."

"So what does this have to do with me?"

"You owe me a favor, if my memory serves me right. And I'm a very public figure now. I can't be getting my hands dirty."

"I can't get mine dirty either, shit. I'm a pimp, nigga!"

"Yeah, and a broke pimp at that who needs major stacks. 'Cause according to Uncle Steve you only got three hoes and them bitches lookin' for a job."

"Ha, ha, ha. You scary punk muthafucka, you gots to remind me to fuck you up like a broke pimp would do! So watch yo' mouth. Uncle Steve don't know what the fuck I got," Snake snapped.

"Anyway, so what about the favor you owe?" Phillip glared back at him through the rearview mirror.

Snake didn't reply at first. He mumbled under his breath and shot glances at Phillip and Dougie. "What the fuck you need done? I know you got niggas to handle your dirty work. What the fuck, P?"

"Man, this is a special job. I don't feel right or see myself giving it to any ole joe blow or else I would have been done it. This is too important. And I can't be linked to this shit in no kinda way. Shit, nigga, you do owe me. What, I gotta throw in sumthin extra? Damn, nigga, what you need? Cash, a coupla birds, what?"

"What you need done, man?" Snake asked reluctantly.

"Can you believe this nigga?" Phillip asked Dougie.

"I told you he was going to want sumthin," Dougie stated matter-of-factly.

"Well, I'll be damned. You sure called it," Phillip told him.

"Oh, so now y'all niggas gonna just sit there and talk about me like I ain't even here?"

Phillip pulled into JE's, a diner on Halsey Street in Newark. "Let's talk this shit over some grub." He pulled into a parking spot and the three men poured out of the '07 Bentley convertible. He gave Snake a brotherly hug. "Even though you trippin' it's good to see you, man. And it was real good talking to Uncle Steve. That nigga takin' pimpin' and hustlin' to the grave. I bet you, him and Dino still treat yo' ass like a snot-nose punk, don't they?"

"Hell yeah. They still getting on my nerves thirty years later."

Dougie and Phillip laughed as they made it inside the crowded diner, bypassed the customers in line, placed their orders, and found them a booth.

"You look good, man. So, tell me, where the fuck you been? And how you gonna leave the fabulous East Coast for the dirty South?" Phillip wanted to know.

Dougie opened up his case that held his black-'n-milds and lit one before offering Snake a stick.

"No, thanks." Snake waved him off.

The waitress came by to take their orders. As soon as she left, Phillip nodded for him to tell his story.

"After some bitch tried to poison and kill me, I stayed in a hospital in Philly for almost a month. After that my uncle Dino put me on to his hookup in Canada and I was over there for those few years. My physical therapy took damn near a year by itself. I had broken bones in over four spots. By that third year everybody started acting like they missed a nigga. The only time I eased back over here was when they told me where my ho, Nell, was. I had to do to her what the bitch did to me. An eye for an eye."

"Damn, man, one of your own hoes tried to kill you? That's fucked up. So why Miami? How long you gonna leave the money-makin' East?"

"Nigga, please, there are plenty of hoes in Miami. Plus, I needed a change, a new start for a new me."

"New you? Nigga, you still pimpin' bitches! Ain't shit new about that!" Phillip cracked.

"Nigga, I don't know why you tryna sleep on the M-I-A. I'm just getting my foot on solid ground. There's a lot of money to be made down there."

"Man, you need to find you a legit hustle and stop the bull-shittin'. Ya ass gettin' too old to be doing time. That's where I come in at. You handle this for me and you won't have to get your hands dirty again. Invest in sumthin legit. That is unless you want to, which would be stupid."

"I'm listening."

"First, tell me why the fuck you going around crashing weddings and shit. That's some crazy shit, man. What, she was making millions on the track?"

"Man, go 'head with that bullshit. That's "wifey," right there. All I wanna know is: How in the fuck she gonna try to marry some other nigga? She know better than that shit!"

Dougie and Phillip burst out laughing but stopped when the waitress put the food in front of them.

"Okay, look nigga." Phillip wasted no time digging into his mile-high whiting platter. "I got this little white bitch who done switched sides and went with that nigga Kaylin. She over there feedin' them all types of bullshit. Talking about she pregnant and shit."

"Well, is she?" Snake asked while trying to swallow a mouthful of corn bread.

"Yeah, so what? Since she says it's mine and she ain't my wife I want that baby stomped the fuck out of her and then I want the bitch to disappear."

Snake let out a chuckle. "You want me to kill a baby? Why didn't you just make the bitch get an abortion?"

"Nigga, are you listening to me? I want her and the baby put to sleep," Phillip coldly stated. "If I can't pimp her the next nigga sure enough ain't. I know you can dig that. Plus, it's fifty thou in it for you."

Snake looked at him. Then looked over at Dougie. They both could see the wheels churning in his head, considering what all he could do with fifty g's.

"Make it one hundred and you got yourself a deal."

"Nigga, fifty. You still owe me, remember?"

"One hundred. I need to go legit, man. Plus, you talking about two bodies."

"Fifty, son, take it or I'll make it three bodies," Phillip gritted.

"Y'all ready to go see Daddy?" Tasha asked the twins as she had them seated in the gift shop tying "Get Well" balloons on each of their wrists. "Daddy misses both of you." She helped them off their chair and they headed for the elevator. She spoke to several people as she passed them by. She was indeed a regular. The guard monitoring the desk and elevators loved her. For the last three months he had made extra money allowing visitors up to see them, all day, every day.

The twins' eyes grew large as the elevator rose higher. This was the only time of day that they remained still. But as soon as the doors opened, they ran.

"Shaheem, Kareem. Hold it right there." They stopped but bounced up and down in place. She grabbed them both by their hands and led them to the room.

The door was open and Tasha's heart felt as if it skipped a beat. Trae was sitting up eating a meal consisting of soft foods.

"Baby," she squealed. "You're sitting up eating." She and the twins bum-rushed the bed.

"Daddy, Daddy", they yelled.

Trae pushed his tray of food over to the side and smiled as he admired his family.

"Where's Nana and Pop-Pop?"

"Here we are," Nana said, as Pop-Pop followed behind her. "We went down to the cafeteria and snuck Trae up a few things."

Mr. Macklin held his hands up in surrender. "I ain't have nothing to do with this."

"Nana, what did you get him? He should only eat what the doctor ordered."

"It's only some broccoli cheddar soup, some real applesauce." She turned up her nose at the tray they brought him. "And some fresh-squeezed carrot juice. That's the best of what they had down there, but it will hold him until I can get home and cook him sumthin better."

"Nana, don't go cooking him fried chicken, corn bread, and all of that stuff. He'll have time to eat that. He needs to stick to what the doctor ordered. Right, Pop-Pop?" She looked to Mr. Macklin for a little help.

"She's right, sweetheart. He got all the time in the world to feast on your good cooking."

Mrs. Macklin waved them both off. "I'm not crazy. Whatever I fix will be in soft form, thank you."

Trae shook his head no, telling Tasha to let it go.

"Look who's here to see Daddy." Tasha picked up Kareem and sat him next to Trae, who immediately stole a kiss and hugged his son. "Aren't they getting tall?"

He whispered in a raspy voice, "They sure are."

"You're talking, baby! You're talking! You're not supposed to be talking. Oh my God!" Tasha couldn't conceal her excitement.

He grabbed her hand as he smiled at Kareem and palmed his head. The boy was already trying to squirm down off the bed. Tasha helped him down, and picked up Shaheem.

"Daddy, here." Shaheem held out his arm, wanting Trae to take the balloon off his wrist. Trae stole a kiss and hug from Shaheem and then untied the balloon. It floated to the ceiling, causing both boys to giggle.

Kareem, seeing that, ran back over to the bed. "Daddy, do mines."

Tasha helped Shaheem down and helped Kareem up once again. He untied the balloons and they rose to the ceiling. He jumped off the bed by himself. The twins occupied themselves with trying to reach the strings.

Trae pulled Tasha toward him. She placed her hand on his cheek, leaned over, and pressed her forehead to his. "I love you."

"Love you more," he whispered.

"How are you feeling?"

"Tired."

Tears welled up in Tasha's eyes. "I'm so glad you came back to me. You scared me, Trae."

He wiped her tears away. "I was scared too. I could hear but I couldn't find you. You were . . . far away. But I always knew you were around."

"Baby," she cried softly as she hugged him. "I did sumthin bad, Trae. At the time I thought it was the best thing . . . but now I . . ."

"Don't worry about it. It's over. We move forward from this moment on. All right?"

She nodded yes and then brushed her lips against his. She kissed him gently, as if she would break. Then she kissed him harder. He kissed her back. She eased her tongue in his mouth, and he played with it.

"Hey, hey, cut that out!" Omar tried to startle them.

"Yeah, break that shit up!" Kaylin yelled. Kajuan and Bo were behind him, laughing.

"This ain't no motel, nigga," Omar announced.

"You boys need to watch your mouths. This *is* a hospital," Mrs. Macklin scolded, in a teasing way.

"Nana, what's up?" Bo gave her a big hug.

"Hey, Auntie. What's up, Unc?" Omar greeted his relatives.

Kaylin and Kajuan went over and hugged them both.

"Trae, we'll be back later on." Mr. Macklin scooped up both of the twins, who were trying to snatch the balloons down. "Tell your father you'll see him tomorrow." He took them over to the bed and Trae kissed his sons, his dad, and his mom.

"We're taking your wife with us while you spend time with these knuckleheads. Keep a close eye on my boy," Nana said to no one in particular.

"We got him, Nana," Bo assured her.

Tasha leaned over and kissed him once again on the lips. And she left with the twins, Nana, and Pop-Pop. Omar closed the door behind them and they all gathered around the bed.

"Man, you scared the fuck outta us, son," Bo snapped as he gave Trae a warm hug.

"Dude, what the fuck happened?" Kajuan chimed in, using his surfer boy interpretation.

"Nigga, I missed the hell out of you. I feel like a bitch." Kaylin caused everyone to burst into laughter. He hugged Trae as well.

"Yo, fam, glad to see you up. What's good?" Omar wanted to know.

"Can *you* talk or what?" Kaylin asked him.

"A little" he whispered. "My throat is raw."

"Damn, maybe this will help." Bo had a twinkle in his eye as he pulled out the bottle of Patrón. Kajuan opened up a case that held some champagne glasses.

Trae smiled and shook his head. "Crazy niggas." He rubbed his neck where his throat was.

"Aiight, nigga, we get the point. We won't make you talk tonight. We'll do all the talking. We gotta shitload of stuff to bring you up on. But first let's make a toast." Bo was filling up the glasses. Kaylin was trying his damnedest not to choke up. He was grateful beyond words that his boy was all right. "Can you hold your glass, yo?" he asked Trae.

"Yeah. I'm not a cripple"

"All right, then, nigga." Kaylin raised his glass to Trae's, and everyone followed suit. "To our nigga, first and foremost, and to our fam. We thank you, OAllah, for keeping this nigga here with us. We thank you for all the peace and prosperity you have bestowed upon us, even though we still have to get down and dirty every now and then. We thank you. This toast is for my nigga, my brother from another mother, the one and only nigga who can live through bullets and die and come back to us." Everyone chuckled. "The one and only Trae Macklin."

"You still got jokes," Trae whispered.

Everyone clinked glasses and drank up.

"Can we light up or what?" Bo asked.

"Nah, man," Kajuan snapped.

"Why not?"

"Because, nigga, look where the fuck we at!"

Kaylin gave Trae another big hug. "Man, don't do this shit no more," he whispered in his ear. Everyone gave him more brotherly hugs and spread love.

"Ain't no music up in this piece?" Omar teased.

"Yo, listen up." Kaylin got serious. "Trae, we know you need your rest and everything, but when you get stronger, we want to hear what happened. And I got a lot of shit, deep shit to share with you. But what I have right now is pressing. Very pressing. Everybody listen up, because you all were there except for Kajuan. The don came to see me."

"Who?" Omar asked, trying to make sure he heard him right.

"Don Carlos. He had a message from Don Alexjandro."

"What?" Trae's real voice broke through.

"Aw, this can't be good." Bo poured himself another drink and threw it back.

"What the fuck they want? I agree, this can't be good," Omar added.

"So when did all this go down?" Bo asked.

"Right after O hung up from telling me he handled that other situation."

"Damn, who are these people? I ain't never seen y'all hard-ass niggas shook like this. Y'all acting like real bitches. Damn, bro, why the fuck y'all so shook? Y'all out, right?" Kajuan was trying to get some understanding.

"We thought we was out. They told us we were out," Trae whispered as he shook his head no.

"Yo, they showed up at my fuckin' house," Kaylin spat, drawing a bunch of "oh, shits" and "goddamns."

"He knows about the gold and what we did to El Gordo. Bottom line, he needs some work put in. So if anyone in this room doesn't want to get dirty, I'ma ask you to leave now. Me and Trae, we don't have a choice in the matter. So trust, I won't be mad." He looked everyone dead in the eye. Nobody moved. He poured himself another glass of Patrón and threw it back. "Aiight, then. He wants someone, a family member taken out."

"And what if you don't do it?" Kajuan wanted to know.

"Nigga, did you just hear what I said? This cat sent me pictures of me, my wife, my son, my baby's mama, and my business. He told me they are praying to the saints for Trae's speedy recovery. So they know every fuckin' thing about us. He said he knows that Kyron is doing a twenty-seven-year state bid." He looked at Kajuan. "So what the fuck does that tell you?" Kajuan let out a whistle. "Yeah, nigga, that's what I thought."

"Yo, so who says that after we handle this, he won't come back?" Omar wanted to know.

"I can't say, man," Kaylin said sincerely. "I can't say."

"Fuck! After this, I got a feeling he's gonna try to pull us back in," Trae warned.

Chapter 16

"Yo, Unc, I'll be up this way for a minute. Send Bullet and White Boy up here."

"So, what's up?" Dino wanted to know.

"I'ma kick it with Phillip for a few. Check out a few things."

"Ummm, hmmm. So you need Bullet and Whitey to chill with you?" Dino was already suspicious. "Don't let that nigga get you caught up in no bullshit. I don't give a fuck how much money he got."

"I got you, Unc. That's why I'm sending for Bullet and White Boy." Snake tried to be reassuring.

"Aiight, I'll tell them. But I'm tellin' you and you know I ain't muthafuckin' playing. Don't bring no bullshit and no heat to our fucking family or our reputation. One!" Dino hung up the phone.

That evening, Snake was at the airport circling the arrival terminals, in an attempt to avoid getting a ticket, when he finally caught a glimpse of Bullet and Whitey. Bullet turned around and was signaling, obviously to get someone's attention. When he saw Carmen rushing toward him with a big suitcase he was ready to flip. He jumped out of the car and yelled, "Bullet! Whitey!"

They both looked up at the same time. Bullet grabbed Carmen by the arm and led her to the car.

"Keenan, what's good?" Whitey grinned.

"I sent for y'all muthafuckas, not this bitch. So what the fuck is up? Y'all should know what the business is, y'all about some stupid muthafuckas acting like y'all new to this and not true to this. And, bitch, I told your stankin' ass to sit tight until I got back. Now why the fuck are you here?"

"I miss you, baby. Plus, I was bored. And I do have a few dollars for you. I had a good night dancing at the club last night."

He threw Bullet the keys while Whitey put the bags in the trunk. He pushed Carmen into the backseat and got in behind her. He then hauled off and slapped her so hard, her nose squirted a stream of blood. Her eyes grew big with surprise and fear.

"Bitch, when I tell you to stay put, that's what the fuck I mean," he gritted and then backhanded her. She yelped as she crouched back into the corner. This was the first time Snake had ever exhibited this kind of behavior toward her.

"I—I'm s-sorry. I di-didn't think—"

He grabbed her by the neck and punched her in the face. Bullet and Whitey had jumped into the front and Bullet had pulled off. "I do all the muthafuckin' thinking around here. You got that?" Carmen nodded her head up and down. "Speak, bitch!"

"Yes," she sobbed.

"What the fuck y'all bring her for? Y'all fuckin' her or somethin'? If so, run me my fuckin' money. Y'all know what time it is," he spat.

"Naw, man," Bullet lied.

"C'mon, dude," White Boy said. Snake looked at all three of them. "Drop this dumb ho off at the first hotel you see." He snatched her by her hair and looked into her eyes. "You gettin' high? And without my fuckin' permission?"

"No," she wailed.

"She did a couple of lines before we left the club." Whitey ratted her out.

Snake punched her repeatedly in her face. "Oh, now you lying too?" He was raging mad.

Bullet turned off the radio. Between the music and her screams, he was feeling as if he were sitting in a surround-sound movie theater, watching a blaxploitation flick.

The car was silent except for Carmen's sniveling. Bullet finally pulled into a Holiday Inn on Route 1 and 9. She grabbed her purse, pulled out a wad of bills, and held them out to Snake. He slapped her again. "I don't need your funky-ass money, bitch! Plus, you need a lot more than a couple of lousy dollars to be on my team." That made Carmen cry even harder. "I'm going to Canada, first thing in the morning. I want yo' ass to stay put until I send for yo' funky ass. You understand me, bitch? And if I ever find out you told somebody where I am . . . well, you know what we talked about. You got that?"

"Y-yes," she stammered.

He leaned over and pushed the door open and shoved her out.

"I'm sorry. I just wanted to see my mom and sister. But if you want me to go back, I'll go get the first flight out," she pleaded as she looked up at him.

"Nah, you was bored, remember? So sit yo' ass at this hotel."

Bullet mashed the gas pedal and they were out of the parking lot. "She gonna take a lot of work," Whitey said as he looked back and saw that she was still on the ground crying.

"Niggas, I can't believe y'all brought that bitch to tag along on a fuckin' mission! What the fuck y'all niggas smokin'? I thought y'all was smarter than that," Snake spat.

Bullet and Whitey both knew it would be foolish to say a word. Just let Snake vent and hopefully he would let it go. But as usual, Whitey couldn't resist. "Yo, Unc just said you wanted us to come and chill. So how was we supposed to know? Cut us some slack."

"What?" Snake looked at him in disbelief. "You challenging me, you white muthafucka! Yo, Bullet, pull over, man. Get the fuck out!"

Whitey cocked his head at Snake. "Get the fuck out? Nigga, you put me out and I don't know where the fuck I am. I'm from tha South. Got me all the way up here in New York. Shit, I just got a call saying Snake need you. I ain't ask no questions. I ain't even know where the fuck I was going until I got to the airport. I'm at your beck and call, nigga. The only thing Unc told us was that you wanted us to chill with you. You the one sent for me. Now you wanna put a muthafucka out? And over a bitch? I wish the fuck I would get out. Put me out. You trippin', man."

"Get this fool out of my ride," Snake said nonchalantly.

They were on Route 1 and 9. Bullet pulled into a BP gas station. Whitey got out and before he slammed the door he warned, "You need me, nigga."

Bullet pulled off. "Where to?"

"Just drive, nigga. I gotta get geared up for this work we gotta put in." He leaned back into the seat and thought about it. At the first exit he said, "Turn around and go back and get that white nigga."

"You know you was wrong."

"Man, shut the fuck up!"

"Aiight, Snake. You can't keep disrespecting us like that. Get us down here and acting all grimey. You shut the fuck up!"

Three days later, low on funds and her suitcase still in the trunk of Snake's car, Carmen found her way to her mother's house. Embarrassment swept over her face as she rang the bell.

"Carrrrmen," her friend Shae called out. Carmen rang the bell again, waved at her but kept her back turned.

"C'mon, Mommy," she mumbled as she willed her mother to come to the door.

"Who is it?" Mrs. Smith called out.

"It's me, Mom." Carmen held her breath as she felt her mother pause. She exhaled as her mother slowly took the locks off the door.

Mrs. Smith cracked it, looked at her daughter's bruised face, and almost fainted. "Oh my heavenly father."

"Mom, please. Save the drama, the prayers, and the speeches, because I don't want to hear them. I just need a place to stay for a couple of nights and I need to pack a few things. So just open the fuckin' door." She pushed the door open so hard it damn near knocked Mrs. Smith on her ass.

Lil'E and Papi Chulo were seated in Kaylin's office, discussing Papi Chulo's album release party and Lil'E's remix single just turning gold, when Angel walked in. Even though she was eight months pregnant, when she felt the urge, like today, she would still wear a pair of stilettos, despite Kaylin's never-ending protests.

Papi Chulo jumped up and gave Angel a hug.

"Hey! Hey! Stop trying to feel on my wife, man," Kaylin teased.

"Mrs. Santos, will you marry me?" He got down on one knee.

She slapped him in the head with the folder she was carrying and everyone burst into laughter.

"See, you kiss-ass. That's what you get," Lil'E scolded.

"Mami, I have to kiss ass. I'm not prego like you. You two are road dawgs." Everyone laughed again.

"I need to talk to my husband. Are you guys done here?" Papi and Lily stood up. She was now six months pregnant and was doing well. "Both of you guys are doing extremely well. I'm proud of the both of you."

"Does that mean you'll marry me?" Papi tried again.

"Sorry, Mr. Chulo, I'm already married."

"Even if she wasn't she wouldn't marry you," Lil'E snapped.

"Well, will you marry me? You can become Lil'E Chulo. You like that, huh?"

Lil'E rolled eyes at him. "I'm not sure if you know your ABCs."

"Is that sumthin new?" Angel asked.

"Ms. Angel, nowadays you gotta make sure that, a, your man don't have an attitude, b, no baby mama drama, c, not a convict and, d, don't like dick."

"Oh my God! Baby, did you hear that?" Angel asked her husband.

"Yes, I did. What up, Papi? I know you know the a, b, and c. What's up with d?" he teased.

"Man, Mr. Kay, that is my cue to leave. I'm Audi 5000." Everyone laughed as he whizzed out the door.

"Lily, don't forget our doctor's appointment tomorrow," Angel reminded her.

"I'm not. We're gonna take separate cars, right? Because I gotta hit those two Philly stations for interviews."

"That sounds like a plan as long as you have someone with you." Angel was being overprotective as usual. "And make sure you go straight home and chill out."

"Don't worry, Ms. Angel, I will. Later, Mr. Santos."

"Be easy, Ma."

Lil'E left, closing the door behind her. Angel walked over to Kaylin, stood in front of his chair, leaned over seductively, and kissed him.

"Mmmmm," Kaylin moaned. "What was that for? And why am I seeing you for the first time today?"

She kissed him again, this time longer and harder, making her pussy wet. "Which question do you want me to answer first?"

"The latter."

"I went to visit Trae, I had that meeting with Puma, then I spent the rest of the day working at home. And this kiss was to let you know that I've been fantasizing about sucking your dick all . . . day . . . long." She kissed him hungrily, leaving no doubt in his mind that she was definitely ready to fuck. When she wasn't getting the response that she would usually get, she slowly stood up, placed her hands on her hips. "What's up? What's the matter?"

"I want you to save all this pussy for me until tonight."

"Noooo," she whined. "I wanna suck your dick." She pecked him on his lips. "And fuck now."

"What's the rush?"

"When you ready to fuck, I don't offer you any resistance, so why am I getting some? Plus, we're having company tonight."

"Who?"

"Your son. I told him I would pick him up tonight."

"What! Malik! Awww, that lil' nigga . . . sumthin gotta give," he joked. "That lil' nigga always blockin'. Why does he have to spend the night? What's his excuse this time?"

"I promised to let him go to the Lamaze class with us in the morning."

"Aww, hell nah. I might as well stay my ass home and let him take you."

"Kaylin, I'ma ask you to stop acting like a big baby. What are you going to do when the baby comes?"

"It's a girl, that's different."

"Boy, stop it."

"Yo, for real, though, me and Malik gonna have to talk."

"Let me find out you're jealous of a six-year-old." When he didn't say anything, she tried not to laugh. "Awww, baby." She hugged him and patted him on the back like you would a baby. "You'll always be my baby, okay?" She kissed him on the lips. "Be good and after you tuck Malik in, Mommy's gonna give you sumthin really nice."

"Oh yeah?"

"Oh yeah."

His mood changed to somber. "Come here." He held his hand out and she took it. He pulled her gently onto his lap. "There's sumthin I've been wanting and needing to talk to you about, but I had to wait until I looked further into the situation before I told you. So, before I begin, please keep an open mind, hear me out, and draw on the faith that you have in me, your husband, who needs you to understand what I'm up against."

She got comfortable in his lap, while looking at him with skepticism. "All right, talk already before you scare the shit out of me even more. Baby, you know that no matter how crazy I get about things, or what the situation is, I'll always have your back. Now what's up?"

"The people that came to the crib, yo, they are made men. We worked for them. When we thought it was our attorneys who got us back over here and scott-free, it wasn't. It was them. We got snagged up in Mexico when we were over there, overstepped our boundaries, and they let it go until now. I need you to trust me. I gotta do sumthin that comes with some . . . risks." He cleared his throat.

She glared in his eyes. "All I'm hearing is risk, Kaylin. That's all I'm hearing. What do you mean risk?"

"Risk, baby. You know what that means. I can't sugarcoat or change the meaning." He watched Angel as she got up, walked around the desk, and plopped down in the chair in front of him.

"Fuck," she spat. "I think I would have been better off if you had kept this little bit of information to yourself."

He shrugged his shoulders. "You damned if you do, and damned if you don't. You just said you had my back no matter what."

"Don't get smart, Kaylin. Look at this shit from my point of view. I take 'risk' to mean that one day I'll get a phone call say-ing, 'Mrs. Santos, you can come and identify your husband's body.' Baby, I take 'risk' to mean, Mrs. Santos, you have been served an indictment for three hundred kilos of . . . whatever. Jump in here anytime, Kaylin. I take 'risk'—"

"Angel, I asked you to trust me on this. I didn't want you to hear this from anyone else."

They were staring each other down. Kaylin hoping for some understanding, Angel wishing that they weren't having this conversation.

"Come here, baby." She remained seated. "Come here, please." She wouldn't move. Couldn't move. He stood up and made his way to her. He pulled her up and hugged her.

"Why did you tell me this, baby? I'm trying . . . I'm honestly trying to digest it to be positive. Tell myself everything's gonna be all right. But damn, you gave me a little too much to swallow. What's our options, or do we have any?"

"Yeah, move out of the country, go into hiding. But, baby, come on. I'm asking you to, I need you to trust me on this one and to be positive."

"Well, answer me this, if all goes well, is it over? There won't be anything left that can be held over your head? And are you going to be here when the baby is born? Is that sumthin I have to worry about, Kaylin? Because if you're not going to be here when the baby is born, then I don't wanna hear nothing else you got to say."

"Ma, I can promise you I'll be here when our daughter is born. I can't believe you'd even ask me that. You don't have to worry about anything. I really need you to trust me on this. Don't I always come back to you?"

"So far, baby, but—"

"No buts. Trust me on this one. You know Daddy will never and can't leave his Angel. Come on now."

As she thought about it a little more, a small smile crept up on her lips. "And you know I'll always have your back, baby. But that doesn't stop me from worrying." Her voiced cracked even though she tried to stop the tears from falling.

"Miss Angel, your mother's on line three and she says it's urgent," Bobbi's voice surged over the speakers.

Angel immediately reached over the desk and pressed line three and then hit the speaker button. "Ma, is everything okay?"

"Your sister is here, and if you don't come here now, I'm going to call the police. I honestly don't know who this child is. She had the nerve to tell me to ask you for a thousand dollars, that it was important. And, Angel, her face is all bruised up. Looks like she got run over by a Mack truck. And she hasn't been here a good three hours and two of my credit cards are missing. I don't know whether to cancel them or let her keep them, because she looks like she's been living in the streets . . . and she's so skinny." She choked up.

"Oh my God, Mommy. Tell me you're joking."

"I wish I was."

"Hold her there until I get there."

"She said she'll pay you back and for you to wire it to her because she can't stay. She only came by to get some clothes and money. The clothes she's wearing look as if she'd been sleeping in them."

"Tell her I'll give it to her but I'm not wiring it. I'll bring it down. I'm on my way, Mommy."

"Please hurry," Mrs. Smith pleaded.

Angel looked at Kaylin, disgust and hurt all over her face. "Let me lock up my office. Call Malik and tell him sumthin urgent came up and if I don't get back too late I'll swing by and pick him up." She stormed out of Kaylin's office, forgetting to disconnect the speakerphone.

By the time they made it to Trenton, it was almost eight. Kaylin pulled up into the driveway and turned the engine off. "Hey." He turned Angel's face toward his. "You gonna be all right in there?" He gazed into her eyes, looking to see something.

"I hope so."

"Red, you are eight months pregnant. I don't want any arguing or fighting. Your sister is going to do what she wants to regardless. Do you understand?" She nooded yes. He leaned in and gently kissed her lips. Angel sat back into the seat, closed her eyes, and took a deep breath, not knowing what to expect. Kaylin opened the door and helped her out.

Mrs. Smith was standing in the doorway with the door cracked.

"Hi, Mom."

"What are y'all doing sitting out there? Come on in."

"I was trying to tell your daughter not to get all worked up. You know how she can get." He leaned over and kissed Mrs. Smith on the cheek. Her eyes were puffy and he could tell she was crying.

"How are you, Kaylin?"

"When my wife stresses, I stress. How are you? You need anything?"

"A strait jacket. That girl in there is trying her damnedest to drive me crazy. I want to commit murder."

"You can't let her do that. I know it's easier said than done. Especially since I only have a six-year-old and one on the way. What do I know?"

They watched Angel head straight for Carmen's bedroom. She knocked and eased the door open. Carmen had just got out of the shower and was getting dressed. Angel came in, shut the door behind her, and locked it.

"Why did you lock my door? Don't think I'ma let you hit me again. Pregnant or not I'm hitting your ass back." She smirked.

It took every ounce of strength she had to remain calm. Carmen's left jaw was swollen and discolored. Her eye was healing. It was bloodshot and all around it was black. Her lips were still swollen. To make matters worse, the way she was fidgeting and the glaze in her eyes let Angel know that she was high.

"Who did that to you, Carmen?"

"Look, I'm not in the mood to have you playing twenty questions. I don't get into your business so stay the fuck out of mine," she spat.

"What business do you have, Carmen? You are only seventeen."

"Why do you give a fuck?"

"I don't believe you. You are my sister, Carmen, that's why I give a fuck. Why can't I care about you?"

"Why start now? Are you gonna loan me the money or not?" she asked impatiently.

"Not until you tell me where you been and who did that to you. Do you even care or think about how much we, especially Mommy, have been worrying about you?"

"Angel, please. Mommy only worries about you. She doesn't give a damn about me or Mark. That's why he never comes around. So that's why I won't be around either."

Angel was shocked beyond words by that statement and was beginning to look at Carmen as if she were sprouting two heads.

"Close your fuckin' mouth, Angel. You know this is true."

"I can't believe you said that."

"Well, I said it and please believe it."

"And please believe that you and I both know that that is not true. You're just using that as an excuse to run the streets and get high."

"Oh, it's true. It was always, Angel is doing so good in school, she's going to law school, she pays all of the bills, if it wasn't for her this family would be naked and out of doors. Angel, Angel, Angel!" she spat. "She was acting like you were her only child, and God's glory. And you, you didn't care about anyone but yourself. You couldn't wait to up and leave. Then when you left it was still Angel this, Angel that, she sends me money, she bought me a house, she gotta a good man, she's getting married, she lives in a nice house. Ugghhh . . . I hate hearing your name," she screeched through clenched teeth.

Angel was trying to hold back the tears. She was beginning to see just how sick her sister really was. "All of my struggling was for you and Mark as well. You benefited just as much as anyone else, if not more. Not just Mommy, Carmen. So you can save all the theatrics and just keep it real. If you was feeling like this, why didn't you ever say this before?"

"What for? You and Mommy were so in love with each other. Y'all couldn't've cared less about what I said or did. Plus, it's too late now. I can't front anymore. I hate your uppity ass. You may be the apple to Mommy's eye but you wasn't shit to me then and ain't shit to me now."

Angel shook her head in disgust. "That is such bullshit. You need to stay off the fuckin' drugs, Carmen. The drugs are eating up your brain cells. You are really sounding stupid."

"Say what you want. Are you gonna give me the money or what?"

"Not until you tell me who did that to you and where you have been."

"I got into it with my man. Okay? Now are you gonna give me the money or what?"

"What kind of man would beat a seventeen-year-old's ass?"

"You should know. He used to beat your ass." Carmen regretted the words as soon as they left her mouth. She didn't even see Angel get up off the bed, but she was now standing in front of her face.

"What the fuck are you trying to prove, Carmen? Don't you see Keenan ain't shit? He's using you to get at me, Carmen."

"He doesn't want your stuck-up ass. I'm younger, prettier, and my pussy is much tighter, you bitch!" Carmen shrieked as she shoved Angel, and on instinct, Angel smacked her.

"Angel, open the fuckin' door," Kaylin demanded as he banged on it.

"Yeah, younger and dumber, Carmen. Perfect to turn your dumb ass out."

"Fuck you, bitch. He wants me for me. He put me in my own condo. I don't even have to do anything, unless I want to!" They were both screaming.

"That's how it starts, Carmen. That is what he wants you to

think. Then you'll be offering him money, offering to trick for him."

"Angel, open the fuckin' door!" Kaylin yelled again.

"Give me a minute, Kaylin," she screamed at him.

"That's your problem," Carmen continued. "You think you know everything."

"I know more than you. I'm not the one calling you for money, all beat the fuck up and been wearing the same outfit for days. Call him, since he loves you so much. Ask him for a thousand dollars." Angel headed for the door.

Carmen ran after her and grabbed her arm. "I will, bitch, because he's my man now."

Angel turned around and grabbed her by her hair and slammed her head into the wall. "I'ma beat some sense into your dumb ass." She pinned her there. "I see what your problem is. You want to be me. You're fuckin' jealous of me, Carmen. And why? I'm the fuckin' sister who loves you, unconditionally!" She was ramming her head into the wall.

Kaylin kicked the door in, with Mrs. Smith on his heels.

"Back up, Kaylin, Mommy. Or else I will pop this whore's neck." Next thing you know Kaylin had lifted them both off the floor. Carmen started throwing blows. Kaylin put Angel down.

"Bitch, I'm better than you. Keenan told me that. My pussy is tighter than yours."

"You dumb bitch," Angel growled as she charged at Carmen, but Kaylin managed to keep them separated.

"Get your hands off me, nigga," Carmen yelled at Kaylin.

"Where is this nigga at?" Kaylin asked.

"Wouldn't you like to know!" Carmen spat. "You would have to kill me, 'cause I ain't no snitch!"

Mrs. Smith held on to Angel, who was raging mad.

"Tell your nigga to get his hands off me." She snatched away from Kaylin. "I'm leaving." She grabbed her suitcase and bag.

"Don't let her leave. I'm not finished with her yet," Angel yelled.

Carmen reached into her bag and pulled out a gun and aimed it.

Mrs. Smith gasped, "That's my gun," and went toward her. It went off and the bullet surged through the door. "Now get the fuck outta my way. Because the next bullet won't miss." Carmen stormed out.

Chapter 17

Jaz, Angel, and Kyra were in Tasha's living room. They were helping Tasha get ready for Trae's homecoming. For the last two weeks he had been walking with a walker and going through intense physical therapy. The doctors said he could go home when he could use a cane.

The girls were enjoying a break, and were chillin' in the living room. Angel had just arrived, but Jaz and Kyra had spent the night. Jaz was sitting on the floor, Kyra was reclined back in the La-Z-Boy, Angel was seated on the couch next to Tasha, who was stuffing her face with fried chicken, potato salad, and rolls.

Angel let out a deep sigh. "Look, I'm getting ready to tell y'all some deep shit, and on the real, this cannot leave this room. Y'all know the drill." Her gaze met with each of theirs, to let them know that this was indeed serious.

"Come on with it," Jaz told her. "I knew sumthin was up because you've been looking tired, worn out, stressed, worried, the whole nine."

"I should and I am. I had the last twenty hours from hell. First, my husband tells me that he was just informed about an unfulfilled obligation to his supplier, and that they are now ready to collect on it. He said he shared that info with me, just in case he disappeared, I wouldn't have to hear it from someone else. Ain't that some shit!"

"What?" Jaz and Kyra said in unison.

"Hold up." Tasha almost dropped her plate. "Kay and Trae worked for the same people. And Trae hasn't mentioned this to me."

"Then don't mention it to him. Trust me, they know where he is and why," Angel stated with conviction. "Chill out."

"Chill out?" Tasha was now up and pacing the floor. "My husband has been away from me for months, Angel. Now you're talking about going back out there to fulfill an old obligation? I wouldn't be able to take it if he didn't come back." Her voice choked up. "What do they have to do?"

Angel regretted that she even mentioned the possibility to Ms. Drama Queen herself. "Tasha, I don't know. He didn't go into detail. But from what I understand, Trae won't be needed, he can barely walk. I'm sorry I even brought it up, but you can imagine how I feel, can't you?"

"I'm sorry, Angel. I mean, just how much can a bitch take? I will be talking to Mr. Macklin tonight. You best believe that." She sat back down on the couch.

Angel jumped up out of her chair. "No, the fuck you're not, Tasha. We will fall the fuck out about this shit. Because I'm telling y'all this in confidence. So keep your damn mouth shut. Hell, I told your drama queen ass that Trae most likely won't and will not have any hands in the shit, so chill out. For real, I don't even know if he knows or not," Angel fussed.

"Angel, please. You know better than I that if nobody else knows, Trae knows. So you can let that go. And you're the drama queen."

Angel gritted her teeth. "Tasha, my dawg, I'm asking you to don't say a word. Because we both know no matter what we say, we're gonna go with the flow. These are the old suppliers and we know how powerful those folks are and what they are capable of.

Now, don't we? If they don't get what they want . . . well, you can fill in the blanks."

"Yeah, Tasha," Jaz interrupted. "Chill out for a minute. Don't go stressing Trae out. The man just got out of a coma. And I need to inform both you drama queens, you are now married. It's no longer about us and a relationship. It's about the future, the whole family, kids, dogs, and goldfish included."

"Well, damn, Angel, and you too, Jaz, you still can't blame the sister for being worried. When Kaylin told you what the deal was, I'm sure you allowed some slick shit to fly out of your mouth because you were worried as well," Kyra snapped.

"Yes, I did. But I still don't want her saying anything to Trae, and can I finish? I didn't come over here to argue and fight with my girl, I came here to share the troubling events of last night."

"Drama queens," Jaz mumbled.

"But listen, it gets better. While he's dropping this bomb on me, my mother calls and says that my sister is at the house. She hadn't been there for more than two hours and Mommy's credit cards were missing. We get down there and this bitch is fucked up on coke or meth, I couldn't even tell."

"Oh my God!" Kyra gasped, knowing from firsthand experience how detrimental a drug habit was.

"Let me finish. Her face was all bruised up and she was asking me for a thousand dollars."

"Who beat her up? Where has she been?" Tasha wanted to know.

"Hold up, Ma, the plot thickens. I gotta save the best for last. Then she starts talking about how me and Mommy only cared about each other, how we didn't give a damn about her and Mark. She said she always hated me, I wasn't shit, Mommy was always talking about Angel this, Angel that, and how it made her so sick just to hear my name."

"Oh my God! What has gotten into Carmen?" Jaz shrieked.

"She needs some counseling," Kyra added. "When can you bring her to Cali?"

"Please, that girl is not thinking about any counseling, she is too busy chasing Snake's ass."

"What?" Jaz was too rough.

"You gotta be kidding me." Kyra was very disappointed.

"That is so sad," Tasha remarked.

"Hold up. It gets even thicker. Anyways, she's fucking him and didn't want to hear any of my warnings and accused me of being jealous. We got into a fight and Kaylin had to kick in the bedroom door. He broke us up and asked her where Keenan was. She said we would have to kill her, because she wasn't telling us shit. Kaylin wanted to do just that. I could see the look on his face. Then the bitch had the nerve to pull out a burner on us and fired it off. Then just like that"—Angel snapped her fingers— "she was gone."

"That is unbelievable," Jaz said.

"Well, believe it because it happened. And now Kaylin is so mad I can't even hold a conversation with him. We were supposed to go to Lamaze class this morning, but he left and didn't even say anything." Angel sighed. "He's going to kill him," she whispered. "And you know what? I wish he would hurry up. He could get someone else to do it, but he's hell-bent on doing it himself. I don't know what I would do if sumthin happened to him. I am so worried about him."

"Girl, worried about him? What about yourself?" Tasha asked. "Look at you. You don't look good at all. You're working nonstop, worrying about Carmen, worrying about Snake, worrying about Kaylin, the business, girl, it is eventually going to catch up with you. I am very worried about you."

"Well, don't be. I go to the doctor's when I leave here and I plan on staying home until it's time for me to have the baby. I plan to take it easy from here on out."

"This has been a little too much for me." Kyra sighed.

"My sisters, you exemplify tremendous strength." Jaz beamed. "I am so proud of you ladies. The strength of the black woman never ceases to amaze me. And trust me. Whatever is troubling us at the moment will soon pass. I honestly don't see how y'all do it. So much drama up here in the East. I'm taking my ass back down to the dirty dirty."

They all stood up and engaged in a group hug, wiping the tears off one another's faces. Then they all giggled. "We have too much fun being such strong crybabies," Kyra teased.

"We do, don't we? And I would love to stay and cry some more but I have to get going to my doctor's appointment. I miss you guys a lot and can't wait to spend a couple of days of quality time with all of us together, minus the drama." Angel hugged everyone at least one more time. She whispered, "I love you" in Tasha's ear.

"Yeah, as soon as you chicks drop them loads, we must plan a getaway," Jaz told them, and everyone was in agreement.

"Angel . . . keep your head up, my sista." Kyra pumped her fist, Angela Davis style. Angel smiled as she left.

Lil'E had left the doctor's office ten minutes before Angel. Angel cursed under her breath as she looked at the flat tire on her ride. She dialed Kaylin's cell phone and it transferred to the office line.

"Game Over Records, this is Bobbi. How may I direct your call?"

"Hi, Bobbi, it's me. Where is he?"

"Right this moment he's in the main conference room, conducting about three meetings at once. Do you want me to interrupt him?"

"Yes, thank you."

"Okay, hold on." Bobbi hit the intercom button. "Mr. Santos, wifey is on line two." Line two blinked for a few seconds, then stopped.

"Baby, what's good?"

"Don't baby, what's good me! Remind me to check Bobbi about that wifey bullshit. I'm the wife. Now, did you forget how you left the house pissed off this morning, skipped our Lamaze class, and acted as if I did sumthin to you? I know you're in meetings right now, but I will deal with you tonight."

"Yo, Ma, cut me some slack. I—"

"Yo, Ma nothing! I'm just leaving Dr. McCombs's office and Lil'E already headed to Philly. Unfortunately I have a flat tire. I'm going to leave the car here and catch a taxi."

"No, stay right there. I'll come pick you up."

"Baby, I'm tired and you are way across town. Get back to your meetings but get your cell and turn it on. I called it first and it went to the front desk. Handle that please."

"Oh, my bad. Call me as soon as you flag a taxi."

"I will." She hung up.

Angel trudged around the corner and stood in front of the office building. When a taxi finally pulled up, she waved, and it zoomed over to the curb. She jumped in the back and shut the door. The other passenger door flew open and a man jumped in.

"Where to?" the cabbie asked as Angel was dialing Kaylin.

"Central Park," Snake answered.

"Central Park it is," the cabbie obliged as he started the meter and pulled into traffic.

Snake gently took the phone out of Angel's hand and turned it off. Her heart felt as if it was skipping every other beat. Her hands were turning sweaty and clammy. When his cell rang she jumped. *Breathe, Angel. Breathe.* She made a feeble attempt to control herself.

"Yeah," he answered.

"We got a tag on this pregnant white bitch," the voice on the other end said.

"Just stay on it. Move when you can. And keep me posted." Snake hung up.

This was Angel's second time being this close to the man she used to love. "I can't believe I used to be in love with such a creep," she blurted. "How could you do that to my sister, Keenan? How could you fuck my baby sister?" She hawked and spat in his face.

He remained calm, pulled out a handkerchief, and wiped his face. "She's lying, Angel. I never fucked her. The only reason I'm putting up with her crazy ass is that I can't get rid of her if I wanted to. Plus, I needed to get your attention."

"You're such a fuckin' liar, Keenan."

"She wants to be you so bad, it's scary. I mean I've heard of sibling rivalry, but damn. You know she was talking about going to law school? The girl seriously needs some help."

"Make her come back home, Keenan. Don't do this to my baby sister." Angel was so mad that she wished she had a gun on her.

"What's it worth to you?"

"Nigga, what do you mean, what's it worth to me?"

"Her coming home, or rather her wanting to come home?"

She looked at him, unable to hide her disgust. "You are the one who is sick, Keenan."

He let out a sigh. "Why do I have to talk to you in the back of a fuckin' taxi? Why the fuck are you taking me through all of this trouble? Dealing with your sister, flattening your tires, showing up at a damn wedding, Angel? What we had was worth more than how you're treating me."

"Keenan, you left me, remember? For years, if I'm not mistaken. Hello! It's over. I've moved on, Keenan, there will never be anything between us. I love someone else. I have a new family. How else can I put it? It is O-V-E-R."

"It's not over until I say it's over, Angel. Don't forget who the fuck I am."

"Keenan, why are you doing this? Do you realize that your behavior is considered stalking?"

"Call it what the fuck you want to call it. Do you realize, technically, that you're still my muthafuckin' fiancée? So when can we muthafuckin' talk? Over dinner, the easy way, or all out the hard way. Which way would you like it? That's all I'm asking. You owe me some answers."

"Owe you? I don't owe you shit! Owe you? You think I want to have dinner with you and you're fucking my baby sister? And you beat her ass?" She slapped him. Slapped him again. Then she started raining punches all over him.

"Hey! Hey!" the cabbie yelled when he saw Snake's hand around her throat. Angel pressed her finger into his Adam's apple, forcing him to turn her loose.

"Let me out, now! Stop this fuckin' cab or I'll call the police on this psycho nut."

"No. Keep driving," Snake spat.

"Stop the fuckin' car." She picked up her phone and dialed 911. He snatched it from her and turned it off.

She snatched it from him and slapped him across the face with it. She opened the door while the cab was still moving, ready to jump.

"Hey! Hey!" the cabbie yelled as he came to an abrupt stop, causing the car behind him to rear-end them. Angel felt the impact but didn't care as she jumped out and ran across the street, jumping into another cab.

"Go! Please go! That man is following me," she cried. The taxi slowly merged into traffic.

"Where to, ma'am?" the female cabbie asked as she shook her head. Anything is likely to happen in the Big Apple.

"The new Time Warner Building." She sniveled as she dialed Kaylin. Before he could answer, Snake was running beside the cab, oblivious of the horns blowing around him. "Hurry up!" Angel screamed. He tried to pull the door open, but Angel locked it. "Can't you go any faster?" she yelled.

"Traffic is not moving fast, ma'am," she answered as she glanced at Snake from her side-view mirror.

"Cut around somebody. Lose him, damn it! He probably has a gun."

The cabbie made a sharp left and zoomed down a side street. Snake was running behind them but soon gave up.

"Are you okay back there? I lost him." She looked at her through the rearview mirror. Angel had her head back and was crying. Her hands were shaking so bad she could hardly pick up the phone. Kaylin was screaming her name. He had answered the phone as soon as it rang and could hear her voice and knew that sumthin wrong was going on.

"Talk to me, Angel. C'mon, baby. I can't do anything if you don't tell me where you're at. Please, baby. Give the phone to somebody. Angel!" he screamed. "Damn it, say sumthin, let me know you're all right!" He was pacing the conference room like an angry tiger. Everyone had cleared out as soon as they saw him jump up and start to cuss.

"Baby . . . " her voice finally strained through the line.

He was trying to remain calm. "Just tell me where you are and what the fuck just happened. Are you all right?"

"I'm . . . in . . . a taxi. I'm coming to the office." She glanced back, hoping not to see Snake.

Kaylin let out a huge sigh of relief. He was definitely thinking the worst. "Just tell me you're not hurt, baby. Tell me that," he pleaded.

"My w-water broke." She couldn't stop crying. "He was in the cab with me. Why won't he leave me alone? Make him leave me alone," she sobbed.

Those words ate at Kaylin's heart. "I'ma take care of him. I promise." Kaylin was now at the elevators pressing frantically on the DOWN button.

"Oh, shit!" She screamed as she began to pant the way the Lamaze coach instructed. This was her first contraction and the cabbie thought that her eyes were gonna bulge out of her head.

When the contraction subsided she said, "It's happening baby. It's time . . . I'm scared."

"Oh shit!" It had just dawned on Kaylin what it meant when the water broke. Now he had to really focus on being calm. "I'm at the elevator now. As soon as you pull up, we will go to the hospital. Don't I need to call your doctor?"

"No!" she screamed. "Don't hang up, baby, please."

"Okay. Okay. I won't hang up. I'm here, baby. How far are you?" He looked around. "Call an ambulance!" Kaylin yelled at the guard stationed at the front desk. "My wife went into labor. She'll be pulling up here in a cab. Are you there, baby?"

"I'm still here. I'm scared. Are you out front?"

"I'm right here waiting on you. I need you to try and relax for me."

"Okay." She closed her eyes and laid her head back. She heard Kaylin instruct someone to call Dr. McCombs and let her know that Angel's contractions were eight minutes apart and that they were on their way.

When he stopped talking she said, "Eight minutes? That's all? Oh . . . here comes another one! Oh, shit!"

"Breathe, baby."

She was holding her breath. "I can't, it hurts."

"C'mon, baby, breathe." He heard her make feeble attempts at the breathing exercises. "I hear the ambulance getting closer," he told her as he listened to her breathe, even though the contraction had stopped.

"I'm about two blocks away. Oh God. That was a hard one."

"The ambulance is here. Where are you, baby?"

"Almost there."

"Hold on." She listened as he spoke to the paramedics.

The female cabbie beeped the horn as she pulled in front of the building. Kaylin turned his phone off and jogged over to the taxi. He opened the door and helped Angel out. When the spectators and passersby saw her belly and the paramedics wheeling the gurney they all started clapping and whistling.

As they helped her onto the gurney another contraction hit. She grabbed Kaylin's hand and they did the breathing exercises together. She was then lifted up onto the back of the ambulance. Kaylin jumped in behind her, they closed the back doors, and they were off to the hospital.

Chapter 18

"Don't hurt her," Whitey snapped at Bullet.

"Shut the fuck up, you groupie muthafucka!" Bullet was tying Lil'E's hands behind her back. Her feet were already bound and he had taped her mouth shut.

Lil'E was kicking herself because the boss lady told her not to travel to Philly by herself. Since she had the twins with her, Smith & Wesson, she had told the boss lady that she wasn't alone. Now she was hemmed up in some seedy motel room with smelly orange carpet and two crazed lunatics.

On the way back from her interviews, she was traveling the turnpike and stopped at one of the rest stops to gas up, freshen up, and grab a sandwich. A white guy came up to her asking for directions to New Brunswick and before she finished explaining the way, he had the burner pressed at her stomach telling her to get inside the Chevy.

She could tell that the white dude was from the South. His accent and the gold grill were dead giveaways. The big black dude didn't say too much but his accent wasn't screaming, dirty South. In any event she got caught slippin' and here she was.

"Shawty, I was feelin' you flow. You got mad skills on the mic," Whitey was cheesin' at her.

Is this what the superstars go through? Is this why they hire body-

guards? To protect themselves from crazed, kidnapping fans and groupies? she asked herself.

The more Whitey looked at her, the more in awe he became. "Damn! Lil'E!" He lustfully looked her over. "I can't believe I kidnapped muthafuckin' Lil'E! Shit, my muthafuckin' niggas ain't gonna believe this shit." He licked his lips. "Damn, you finer than a muthafucka. Lookin' like Alicia Keys. Boy, and that new remix . . . you put it down hard. Them strippers be at the club, wigglin' real nice like to that shit." He was trying to imitate the strippers' moves and began singing the hook "In ya face, in ya face." He dropped it like it was hot and was laughing. "Ya know what I'm sayin'? I'ma have to take ya panties for some proof. My homies ain't gonna believe me, though." He stared at her before it hit him. "You think you can autograph them for me?"

"Man, why don't you shut the fuck up!" Bullet had heard enough. "Shut the fuck up and leave her alone."

"Fuck yeah," Lil'E tried to mumble under the tape, which tasted horrible and was burning her lips. "And tell him to stop staring at me. Go watch TV or sumthin. Let me be a hostage and die in peace. Lord, why I gotta be tortured by dumb and dumber?"

"I can't believe what the hell I'm hearing." Bullet continued with his tirade. "I don't see why I've been hanging with yo' stupid ass for this long. What the fuck you mean proof? You tryna get us a case? And over some bitch? A white bitch at that! They'll fry us and then hang our asses. Your stupid white ass got me fucked up. I'm not tryna catch a case with a stupid, talkative, potential snitch ass."

"Snitch? You got it fucked up! Man, stop trippin'. This Lil'E. And what the fuck you mean white bitch? I'm white!"

"Well, act like it, then," Bullet snapped. "And find you some common sense. Oh, I forgot, y'all go looking and go running to find the noise and run right into all the trouble."

"Ha, ha, ha. Punk muthafucka, you got jokes. It's whatever, 'cause that white bitch can spit."

Oh God, Lil'E screamed to herself. *I'm kidnapped by Beavis and Butthead. How the fuck I'ma leave my twins in the ride? I got to hit Hot '97, BLS, 105 tomorrow and I'm tied up in some fuckin', stinkin'-ass motel room. Boss lady is going to kill me if these clowns don't go ahead and do it first.*

"I think she like me, man."

Now, what the fuck I do to make him think that?

Whitey grinned as he sat facing Lil'E. "She really look like Alicia Keys. He reached out and touched her cheek. E squirmed away. "You think the boss man will let me hit this? I need some of that! And she pregnant too! Shit, I ain't washing my dick for a month after I hit that! I'ma fuck the shit out of her. She gonna wanna be with me. Don't worry about it, boo, you gonna love me in the end. We a match made in heaven."

"Aww, man. You's a dumb-ass bitch. Ask him yourself, dummy. He's pulling up right now." Bullet tossed the remote onto the bed and went to open the door. He looked at his watch and blurted, "Eleven forty. Damn. We been waiting on this nigga for almost three hours." He snatched the door open and watched Snake get out the car. They were in the boondocks in Jersey somewhere holed up at a joint that reminded you of the Bates Motel.

"Damn, how the fuck y'all found this place?" Snake snapped.

"I know you ain't complaining. You gonna let us do what we do, right?"

"Hell yeah, but damn." His gaze went over to the bed where Lil'E was. She was a tiny little thing. "Put that bitch on the floor." He was being careful not to show his face. "And blindfold the bitch!"

"Why? Dead men can't talk," Whitey snapped. "I know y'all gonna let me enjoy my job. I like looking at her."

Dead men? Lil'E froze in panic. *Oh, shit. My baby. My unborn baby, my grandma. Who's going to take care of her? I didn't even get a chance to take her to Italy. Lord, I'm only eighteen. Don't let me die now. Damn. Why did I travel by myself? Who are these clowns? And what the fuck do they want with me?*

"So what's up?" Bullet wanted to know. Because he was ready to get this over with. They watched Whitey pick her up and place her on the floor. She had tears streaming down her cheeks. Bullet said in disgust, "You'se a sick son of a bitch," when he saw Whitey kiss a tear off Lil'E's cheek.

"Gotta wait on this nigga to collect the dough. He claims he knows where the spot is. I wish he would hurry up." Snake ignored the both of them.

"Yo, can I hit this real quick?" Whitey wanted to know. "Do you know who this is? She got that hot joint, the "In Yo Face" remix. This Lil'E, nigga," Whitey gloated, as he talked to Snake.

"Man, I don't give a fuck who she is. Just want to pay off this debt and collect what's owed to me. I might need this nigga again."

"So, I can get up in this or what?"

"Man, where you gonna take her? I damn sure ain't gonna leave the room to give yo ass privacy. And I definitely don't want to sit here while you rape a bitch," Snake said matter-of-factly.

"Shit, I'll get me a muthafuckin' room, you know how we do. Shit, I know the pussy good. Fuck it, there ain't no sense in lettin' good, pregnant pussy go to waste. We killin' the bitch so it really ain't no shit. We can all hit that!"

"White boy, if you don't shut the fuck up! You ain't stop runnin' yo trap about this bitch since we got here. I'm starting to think you wired!" Bullet fired off.

Snake got wild with a gritty look on his face and said, "You bitch, muthafucka, you wired?" At the same time he began to pat him down.

"What you think, nigga? Hell naw, I ain't wired! I been with y'all paranoid asses for at least seventy-two hours and frankly I'm sick of both of you niggas. Matter of fact, let's get this shit over with so I can take my ass back home away from you sorry-ass muthafuckas. Y'all got me fucked up, talking about wired. Don't call me no muthafuckin' mo!" he spat. "Let me pat yo' ass down."

"Here come that nigga now." Snake left Whitey alone to go

peek out the window. He looked around to make sure it was just Phillip and Dougie. "Let them in," Snake ordered, as he sat down at the small round table.

Dougie stepped through the door first. His gaze scanned the room, then Whitey and over to Bullet. He nodded at Snake and stepped inside. Dougie followed him, his glare scanning the room for Lil'E.

The two men remained standing. Bullet stepped over to the TV and turned it off. Dougie pulled out a black n'mild and lit it. Lil'E was on the floor shivering. She was trying to control her bladder.

"Where is she?"

When she heard Phillip's voice she froze and pissed on herself.

"Over there on the other side of the bed," Snake told him as he watched Phillip head over to where she lay. He stooped down and yanked the tape off her mouth and eyes.

"Yo, what the fuck is he doing? I thought he didn't want her to see him?" Snake asked Dougie.

"What difference do it make? He paying y'all to merk the bitch, right?" He pulled hard on the black-'n-mild.

"I know you didn't think you would get away with fucking up my money, threatening me, and having this baby? Um, um, um." He waved his index finger back and forth. "Lily, you've been a bad girl, and Daddy's very disappointed in you. I was planning on taking you places you've never been." He wanted her to say something. "You don't have anything slick to say?"

"Fuck you. Whatever you gonna do, do it and get it over with." Her throat was so dry she could barely get that out.

Phillip let out that signature laugh. Dougie and Snake joined him. "All righty, then. That's what I'm talking about. So, tell me, you thought that bitch was gonna protect you, huh?"

"Let's do this, Phillip. Oh, I forgot. You had to hire some flunkies to do a man's job. Hurting little ole me." And she grinned, causing him to stand up and kick her in the face.

"Now, bitch." He watched her writhe around in pain. "Oh,

you can't talk now, can you?" He kicked her in the stomach. She began to cry out. "Uh-huh." He kicked her again. "Y'all niggas, I want this bitch to take three bullets to the stomach. I don't need no fuckin' babies. I got a family." His cell rang. He hawked and spat on her. He turned the cell off. As he walked over to Snake, he reached inside his suit jacket and threw a stack of bills at him.

Snake snatched the stack out of the air and thumbed through it. "Yo—"

"Nigga, that's half. Hit me up after the job is done for the rest. Let's dip, bro."

"Hold up! What the fuck you mean half? That ain't the muthafuckin' agreement we made. Don't be walking off. We ain't talked about this shit. I'm not the only muthafucka gettin' paid. We need to fuckin' discuss this shit. I'm not yo' bitch, so you definitely ain't gonna be treating me like one. So what the fuck is up? Talk, nigga."

"Man, this is business. What the fuck you wanna talk about? The job is half done, so you get half the dough. When it's finished, hit me up and I got you. I ain't tryna skip on a funky-ass twenty-five g's. Shit, nigga, my suit cost more than that." Dougie opened the door for his brother and they walked out, slamming the door behind them.

"Man, who in the fuck that nigga think he is?" Bullet snapped. "I got beef with him and don't even know the pussy."

"Damn." Whitey looked down at Lil'E and frowned. "He fucked you up. I guess I won't be gettin' none of this pussy."

"I guess you won't be. Let's get this over," Snake ordered. Then he turned to Bullet. "If that nigga don't pay up, then you can have all the beef you want with him. Now get this bitch so we can take care of her, get the rest of our money, and take our asses back home."

They left the motel room carrying Lil'E. Snake and Bullet got in the front of the pimped-out Chevy while Whitey jumped in the back with Lil'E, who didn't appear conscious.

They drove to New York and advanced through the Verrazano Bridge.

"Damn, look at all these homeless muthafuckas." Bullet scanned the long dark alley.

"Fuck them. They'll steal her clothes and shit, but will keep it moving. Go down there." Snake pointed to what looked like a deserted area. "Handle that, Whitey."

Bullet brought the car to a stop. Whitey opened the door and shoved Lil'E out. He pulled out his burner, shot her three times in the stomach, slammed the door back, and Bullet sped off. The vehicle came to a screeching halt, then backed up and out flew her purse.

Ten hours later, Angel was finally fully dilated. Kaylin had to call his sister to bring a video camera. He was there when Malik was born and was grateful to be here for his daughter. Half of the Santos clan was at the hospital anticipating the arrival of a new member.

"Okay, Mrs. Santos, it is almost over," Dr. McCombs assured her.

"Almost? Almost?" Angel damn near screamed. "I want this agony to be over with now!" she breathed as the contraction threatened to knock her out.

"Okay. Here we go. I see the head. I want you to give me a nice big push," Dr. McCombs instructed. Angel pushed, as the doctor tugged at the baby.

"All of that hair for you to comb, baby," Kaylin teased.

"Shut up, Kaylin!" Angel snapped.

He laughed. "I got this all on video," he joked. "I'ma sell it as baby mama gone wild on delivery table, 19.95."

"Make him leave, somebody!" Angel said between breaths.

"I love you too, baby," he teased.

"Okay, Mommy. I need another push, but this one needs to be a little harder. Go ahead and push."

"Oh God." She gritted her teeth as she bore down.

"That's good. Go ahead and push again, but a little harder for me," Dr. McCombs coaxed. "Good," she said as she pulled the baby all the way out. "And it's a baby girl!"

"Oh God," Angel panted as she lay back, exhausted, and looked at the slimy little being.

"Come on, Daddy. Give the nurse the camera, while you get the honors of cutting the cord."

Kaylin's eyes were glued to his baby girl. "She's pretty like me," he stated as he took the cutting instrument from Dr. McCombs. He clipped the cord and smiled.

"Congratulations, you guys did very well." She handed the baby to the nurses who immediately started cleaning her up, and Dr. McCombs began cleaning Angel in preparation to apply the stitches. The baby was yelling at the top of her lungs.

Kaylin came over to Angel's side and kissed her. "You did real good, Ma. Real good." She rolled her eyes at him and he smiled and kissed her again.

"Okay, Mommy, you only needed a couple of stitches. And again, you did very well. Congratulations to the both of you."

"Here's your baby." The nurse handed the bundled-up baby to Angel.

She stared at the baby for several minutes, taking her all in. "I'm a mommy." She beamed as the tears welled up in her eyes.

Kaylin was glad to catch that moment on camera before putting it down. "Let Daddy hold her." Angel kissed the baby on the cheek and passed her to Kaylin.

"Jahara Kayliah Santos," he said proudly. "Daddy's precious little angel." He explained the meaning of Jahara.

"Daddy, we forgot to weigh your little one," Dr. McCombs told him. "Here. We'll let you once again have the honors." She led him to the scale by tugging at his elbow. He gently laid her down but wouldn't let her go. "She'll be okay." She smiled at Kaylin, as he reluctantly let a screaming Jahara go.

"Man, just like her brother she has a strong set of lungs."

"That's a good thing. Well, she comes in at seven pounds, one ounce, and . . . she . . . is twenty-one inches long." She skillfully swooped up Jahara, wrapped the receiving blanket back around her, and handed her back to Kaylin. "Wow, Mommy. I can't imagine how much she would have weighed if you went full term."

Angel smiled at her. She was happy that it was all over and only wanted to fall into a deep comalike sleep.

As soon as Jamaica heard gunshots, she grabbed her grandfather's hand and they stepped back but peeked around the Dumpster. When the car pulled out of sight they ran over to Lil'E. Now they were standing there going through her purse.

"Grandpop, call the ambulance," Jamaica pleaded. "She's bleeding and she's pregnant."

Her grandfather's hand shook uncontrollably. He was excited that they had a few dollars and excited about the pregnant white woman lying on the ground. He pressed 911 on E's cell phone. "Hello. There's a white pregnant woman lying here on the ground. She was shot, what sounded like three times. She needs an ambulance in a mighty big hurry."

"Where are you, sir?"

"Down here under the Verrazano Bridge."

"Is she breathing, sir?"

"I don't know and I ain't touching her to find out. She's lying down here next to two beat-up vans. A white one and a red one. You can't miss her."

"Sir, can you stay there with her until the paramedics arrive?"

"Jamaica, turn this thing off. Let's get outta here." He handed Jamaica the phone, as he thought about where they could go spend the night. Eight hundred dollars should keep them out of the alley for a week.

* * *

"Yo, P. It's me. That's done," Snake said into Phillip's voice mail for the tenth time. He was getting angrier and angrier.

"Man, if this nigga is trying to gank us, I'm going back to get the body and dump her right in front of his place of business," Whitey vowed.

Chapter 19

This was Trae's first night home and Tasha was ecstatic. He was walking slow, and with a cane, but it was okay. Omar and Bo had helped them from the hospital, and the kids were at their grandparents'.

The apartment was silent and Tasha stepped back to allow Trae his moment. She knew what he was feeling and knew that the moment for him was ten times as intense for him as it was for her. This was his home long before he met her, and he had a lot of history here and it held a lot of memories. This same apartment went from being his bachelor's pad, to his one-wifey-only pad, to a family dwelling. They only used it once in a blue moon.

Trae stepped into the kitchen and looked around. He recalled Tasha blending the hell out of strawberries and bananas while pregnant with their first baby, the one that she lost. He turned around and stopped once again in the living room and looked around. This was where Tasha first gave him some head. His dick jumped at that memory. He made his way down the hallway and opened the door to what used to be his weight room. Now it held two twin beds, a crib, stuffed animals, and toys. *Damn*, he said to himself. Leaving the door open he made it to the bathroom, peeked in. A woman's touch. Tasha's touch. She had the same mauve and light gray color scheme as their guest bedroom at their home in Cali. He went to the master bedroom and sat down on the bed, taking it all in. So many memories . . . of his hustling days. He didn't even notice Tasha standing in the doorway.

"Baby, you need anything? Are you all right?"

He skimmed his face over his hands. "I shouldn't be here. I shouldn't be alive," he mumbled.

"Come again?"

"Nothing, baby. Come here." He patted the spot next to him.

She sat down and ran her hand over his bald head. "It's weird, isn't it?" He nodded his head yes. "I know. It got me too. My stomach does somersaults as soon as I pull up in front of the building. It doesn't seem real. I remember the first time I stepped foot in this apartment. It feels just like it was yesterday. You were so sure that I would be a permanent part of your life. I was so unsure, scared, and confused," she confessed. "You seemed . . . so for real about us and I didn't want to throw myself out there and then learn that it was all a game to you."

"See what you would have missed out on?" he teased. "Disappearing on you, three babies, a coma, you would have missed all of that good stuff."

She giggled. "Whatever, nigga. I can laugh now, but at the time I didn't know if I could hang. A damn roller-coaster ride."

"Yeah, I can say it's been that. But over all, have I made you happy? Have I kept my promises to you?" He leaned over and brushed a strand of hair away from her eye.

She pretended that she had to think about it, before finally answering, "Yeah, so far."

"Aww, you got jokes, don't you?" He stared at her for a while. "Thank you for being there. Thank you for being there when I woke up. You ever had those dreams where you were falling, and when you woke up you were trying to catch yourself?" He closed his eyes for a minute. "Well, that's how I was feeling. I was falling, and you were holding your hand out to me smiling, but I kept falling further, further away. I was scared to look down so I kept looking up at your hand. When I couldn't see it anymore I panicked and couldn't breathe and when I woke up your hand was in mine and you were snoring."

"No, I wasn't." She slapped the back of his head.

He smiled at her. "It didn't matter. You were there and that allowed my heart rate to return to normal, as well as my breathing. For real, if I would have woken up and you weren't there, I don't know if my heart and breathing would have returned back to normal, yo. I think I was going to actually cash out at that point. I try not to think about it, but the thoughts keep coming back."

She could actually see the panic in his eyes. "Baby, it did get scary at times. In my mind and my heart at times I could feel you slipping away from me. But over all my spirit was telling me that everything would be all right, that you was not going to leave me. Some nights, some days, I couldn't breathe, eat, or sleep! Then one morning, and it wasn't the first time or the last, I felt as if I could go no further. I was forced to get down on my knees and start praying. I felt like I was having an anxiety attack. I prayed and prayed. I don't even know how long I was on my knees but I didn't stop until a peaceful surge came over me. That surge confirmed that you were coming back to us.

"I will always be there for you. You are my soul mate. They would try to get me to go home and get some rest, but I couldn't leave you. I knew you needed me and I wouldn't, I couldn't take that chance. You are my everything, Trae. You are a part of me."

"It's over. You don't have to worry about losing me anymore. It's all behind us now."

"Is it?" Her thoughts went to Angel's conversation.

"Believe me, baby. It's over."

She believed him. Desperately wanted to.

Later that evening, Trae was propped up in the middle of the bed watching Tasha as she lit candles and then poured him a glass of wine and fired up his blunt. He was butt naked with only a towel spread across his lap. She had on a see-through negligee and was seven and a half months pregnant. He made a mental note to try and fatten her up a little more. She handed him the ashtray with the lit blunt.

"Are you okay? Why are you looking at me like that?" she wanted to know.

He gave her that lazy grin. "Just checking out how good you look and mad that I missed so much of this pregnancy. I was also thinking how I need to fatten you up."

"Don't be mad, baby. And look at it from the point that you could have missed all of this pregnancy, and the rest of the children's lives. And fatten me up? Between Mama Santos and Angel, I've been eating. So don't even try it. The doctor said I'm doing very well."

"I'm your doctor. And I said you need to gain some more weight."

She lifted the lid off a platter and placed several chocolate-covered strawberries on a glass saucer and sat on the bed next to Trae. She placed one to his lips and he took a nibble. "I brought them for you to enjoy." He took a pull of his blunt. He knew they were her favorite. He watched as she closed her eyes and bit into the delicacy and moaned.

"All right now. Let me find out. I'll toss them all into the trash," he said.

"You'll have to catch me first."

"Aww . . . that was low. That was way below the belt."

"You know you can't fuck with my strawberries or my milk shakes. Have you forgot?"

"I guess I did."

"Well, now your memory is refreshed," she teased and closed her eyes, biting seductively into another one. "I've been waiting for you to come back to me before I indulged. I knew you was coming back, you just took longer than I expected." She bit into another one and let out a soft moan.

"I'm getting jealous and a hard-on at the same time."

She giggled. "You are so silly. Don't be jealous, I got you."

"Do you?" His eyebrow arched.

"Umm-hmm. Are you nervous?"

"A little."

"Me too." They both shared a laugh. "So I guess we'll both be getting our cherries popped tonight."

"Well, have mercy on a nigga. And keep in mind that I just got out of a coma," he teased as he put his blunt out and set the ashtray on the nightstand.

"Oh, I'ma have mercy all right. If that guy quits early on me, I'm pulling out the Viagra. I ain't trying to hear no shit. I've waited too long for this moment."

"Baby, you really got some Viagra?"

"I sure do."

"Oh, shit." He lifted up the towel and looked down at his dick. "Yo, nigga, you hear that, don't you? I'ma need you to stand strong or she's gonna pump you up with some dope."

Tasha chuckled. "I sure am." The room got silent as they gazed at each other. "I missed you so much," Tasha whispered. Trae took the empty saucer from her and placed it on the nightstand. "God, I missed you." She choked up.

"I'm here now." He gently squeezed her thigh and began rubbing on it. His gaze traveled over her belly, up to her breasts, lips, back down to his hand rubbing her thighs. "You are my world. You know that, right?" He patted her, coaxing her to move a little closer.

She was already breathing hard and he wasn't doing anything but rubbing her gently. "And you are my soul," she whispered as his hand went farther until he was rubbing her pussy.

"Your soul needs Daddy, doesn't it?" Her head fell back as she opened her legs wider. "Doesn't it?"

"Y-yessss," she moaned as he dug two fingers inside her. "Fuck y-yess, we need Daddy."

"I can tell," he whispered as the electricity flowed from her pussy to his dick. She was juicy and hot. "You thought Daddy forgot how to make this pussy scream, didn't you?" He was now playing with her pearl tongue.

"Shit, baby, yes, that . . . feels good. Oh God." She was grinding against his fingers.

"Daddy didn't forget, Tasha. Did he?"

"Nooo," she squealed as he pressed down on her clit and her legs went to bucking . . . jerking . . . trembling. He released her clit and eased two fingers inside her pussy. He smiled as her muscles squeezed and clamped around his fingers. If he had been well, he would have leaned down and eaten her pussy until she screamed and begged him to stop.

"Oh God," she said as she caught her breath. "I know what you're thinking." She was on her back, legs spread open, looking at him.

"What?" He was slowly working his fingers in and out.

"I know . . . oh, babe . . . know how you think," she moaned. He had slid up to her clit once again. "Oh yesss." She tried to squirm away, but he grabbed on to her tight with his other hand.

"I'm not that hurt."

"Nigga . . . oh . . . yess . . ." She began to skeet, tremble, shake, and he allowed her to scoot away from him. He watched her pussy jump and unconsciously began stroking himself. He had a handful of dick.

"Tasha." He was about to explode. "Tasha, look what Daddy got for you." She heard the urgency in his voice as she sat up and saw that big, black, hard, long dick that she missed so much.

He saw that naughty gleam in her eye as she crawled over to him. His head rolled back as she tossed her hair back over her shoulders, leaned down, and wrapped those soft luscious lips around the head of his dick and began teasing him with her tongue.

"Unnngh," he groaned, sensations shooting all the way down to his toes. He grabbed on to her head, watching his dick disappear down her throat. "Fuck," he grunted as she eased up.

They both looked down at his throbbing pipe. "Are you comfortable?"

"Do I look comfortable?" He looked back down at his outrageous hard-on.

"Not that, silly. Your back?" she purred.

"Yeah, I'm okay. It's your show. Daddy's all yours."

She slowly began to straddle him, while they both pulled the negligee up, over her head. She leaned into him and kissed him hungrily.

"Aiight. Stop playin', Tasha."

"Nigga, I'm trying to let you get it together. Because if you cum as soon as I get him up in me, we're going to fight."

"I got him. Come on now." He squeezed her ass.

She got in position, grabbed on to the bedposts and shuddered as she slid down on that fat, long pole. The both of them released long-awaited, satisfactory groans.

"Big Daddy." She slowly glided up and down. "Damn, I've been long . . . ing for this." She shuddered as she felt his hands massage her ass and glide over to her hips to control her moves.

"That's it, baby," he whispered as his firm grip glided her up, down, up, down in a jack-off motion. "Damn, this shit feel so good." Up, down, up, down. "I missed this. You miss this, baby? You miss stroking this long, hard, fat dick?" He slapped her ass and she began to bounce faster. "Unh, unh, baby . . . we gone . . . nice . . . and slow . . . sss . . . yeah, baby . . . that's right . . . just . . . like . . . that." He took a nipple into his mouth and then as much of her tit as he could swallow and made her slow down.

She shrieked, "Right there, fuck just like that." He released her hips and she went all the way down, gripping and swallowing all of his dick, trying to make it drive so deep that she could feel it in her throat. Trae was enjoying the ride and she could feel from his breathing and grunts that he was getting ready to nut. Sliding all the way down, keeping his dick hitting her spot and grinding from side to side, she burst out of control, forcing them both to ride an uncontrollable body-rocking orgasm.

*   *   *

This was Angel's second day home from the hospital. And Kaylin hadn't left the house.

"Baby, you know this is important, especially to Papi. Me and Jahara will be fine until you come back." She leaned over and shared a passionate kiss with Kaylin while Jahara was enjoying her breast milk.

Kaylin looked down at his precious little Angel. "She's so beautiful." He beamed.

"She is, isn't she?" Angel agreed. "Look at all of this thick hair." She sighed.

What should have been a very happy and celebratory atmosphere was anything but that. Kaylin was stressing more than Angel over Lil'E. To compound matters even more, their public relations maven, Courtney Moran, was having a hard time doing damage control since she didn't show up at any of the New York radio stations to do her interviews. Rumors were flying, and negative speculations were at an all-time high. And tonight was Papi Chulo's album-listening party and she needed Kaylin focused on that. Tonight was Papi's time to shine.

"You sure you're going to be all right?"

"I'm fine, Kaylin. What about you? Are you going to be all right? Tonight is Papi's night. He's gonna need you. Give him all of your attention. Work your magic and work that crowd. Then when it's over, come back home to worry about Lil'E."

He stared at her, admiring that after-baby glow.

"It's going on seventy-two hours, so the missing persons report is in, the investigator is combing the hospitals, sumthin will eventually turn up. Okay, baby? You can do this." She ran her hands through his hair. "I love this side of you. Your wimpy side," she teased.

"And I love this side of you." He kissed her. "The think-you're-running-the-world side of you," he teased back.

"Nigga, you must have forgot. The world is mine. You promised me the world, remember?"

"Am I giving it to you, baby?" He kissed her again.

"Yes. Yes, you are." She gently eased the nipple out of Jahara's mouth, and placed her on her shoulder to burp her.

"When is her birthday?"

"She's only four days old, silly." She giggled. "And your son is going crazy. He has no understanding as to why he hasn't been over here to see his baby sister. You gotta pick him up tomorrow."

"I will."

She watched him get dressed. *That is my nigga.* Her thoughts then immediately shifted to Lil'E. Her gut was telling her that the worst had happened, but she was praying for the best.

The phone woke Angel up. She looked at the clock, 12:57. "Hello."

"Hey, you asleep?" Kaylin asked.

"I was, baby."

"My bad. Are y'all okay? I love you."

"We're fine. I love you too." There was silence. Angel giggled. "You want me to ask you how it's going?"

"That would be nice."

"I got you so spoiled. How's it going, baby?"

"They are loving the new King of Reggaeton, Red. They went bananas over nine of the eleven tracks. And the three they didn't go bananas over, we're gonna remix them and make it a done deal. This boy is going to be big." Kaylin was amped.

"That's what's up. Congratulations. Where is the man of the hour? I need to congratulate him."

"That nigga is getting lifted, he so amped."

"Well, don't let him get too drunk. He is an assest. Keep an eye on him."

"Baby girl, let him have his fun. He's been grindin' on this album for the last six months."

"I feel you, but still keep an eye on him."

"I hear you, Ma. But Courtney did a good job. We got everybody out for this. Magazine editors, DJs, artists, even club owners."

"Is Papi pleased?"

"That nigga was on pins and needles acting like a bitch. But now he has thanked me at least a hundred times. I had to ditch him."

"Baby, that wasn't nice." Angel giggled. "You are so silly."

"All right, I just wanted to share that with you. Go back to sleep."

"It's too late now, your precious little baby Angel is squirming around. It's feeding time."

"My bad. You want me to wake you up when I get in?"

"Of course, I miss my big ole baby." She could feel him blushing.

"Love you."

"Love you more."

Angel lay perfectly still, listening to see if Jahara was going to go back to sleep. Suddenly the phone rang again, startling her. She immediately snatched it up.

"Hello."

"Hello. Mrs. Santos, this is Derek, the PI you hired. I called your husband first but it jumped to his voice mail."

"It's okay, Derek. He was talking to me. What's up? You found out anything?"

"We found someone who fits the description of Miss Penzera. However, she's in critical—"

"Oh God, no." She dropped the phone not hearing the rest of what he had to say and began trembling. "Oh God, Lily. Oh God," she cried before picking the phone back up. "Derek, call my husband, okay?" She hung up on him. "Oh, dear God. She's . . . Lily's just a baby. The baby! Oh my God." She picked up the phone and dialed Kaylin. "How could I forget about the baby?"

"Red, I'm on the line with the investigator now. I'm on my way home."

"Oh God. Hurry."

* * *

Before Kaylin could get in the house good, his cell went off again.

"Yo, nigga." It was Kajuan.

"What's up?" Kaylin asked him.

"You listening?"

"Yeah." Kaylin stopped dead in his tracks.

"Got sumthin real juicy for you. It's your lucky night, nigga. Papi is drunk as fuck, flapping his gums as if he's trying to win a prize. Well, check it, he says his man is *Mickey Reyes.*"

"What?"

"You heard right, nigga!"

Kaylin's heartbeat damn near tripled. His mind was racing and adrenaline was rising. "Yo, tell Kendra, I need her for this. Tell her to suck that nigga's dick if she has to. I need her to stick to him like glue. Put somebody on him around the clock. You got that?"

"I'm already on it, nigga."

"One."

Chapter 20

The Santos clan was out representin' and in full effect. They all were half black and half Puerto Rican. Coming up they always lived close to each other, in Spanish Harlem, went to school together, fought together, hustled together. As they grew up, they all went their separate ways but still remained tight. With the exception of Kendra and Kendrick, the twins, they still ran as thick as thieves.

Game Over Records went all out for Papi Chulo's album-listening party. They redecorated Club Envy and everyone was seated around the huge specially designed round table drinking and smoking, and Papi was on top of the table singing and dancing.

"Yo, Kendra, I got a message for you from Kay." Kajuan, Kendrick, and Kendra had stepped out to take in the cool night air.

"What's up?" Kendra wanted to know. She knew that Kay never came with no bullshit.

"Yo, big cuz need you to work Papi. He needs you to squeeze out everything he got on his dude Mickey Reyes. You know who Mick is, right?"

"Mr. Big Time himself, of course. I've heard of him, but never met him."

"Well, he got control over all five boroughs. Why this nigga throwing his name around is baffling the fuck out of everybody. So we need you to find out. You got that? Kay said to suck his dick if you have to, yo. We need an address, like, yesterday."

Kendra rolled her eyes and looked from her twin back to Kajuan.

"You straight?" Kajuan needed to confirm.

"Don't press me, nigga. I ain't no ho. Shit, I gotta get my mind right."

"Well, get it together, the clock is ticking," Kajuan warned and Kendrick snickered.

"What's so fuckin' funny, fool?" she snapped at her brother. He blew her a kiss and held the door open for her. "Tell Kay he owes me big time for this one."

"You ain't do nothing," Kendrick teased, causing her to mush him in the face.

"Well, watch a bitch work. Y'all better be lucky y'all family."

"Yeah, yeah, yeah. Just handle the family business," Kendrick told her. They all knew and expected nothing less from her as they all headed back inside the club to join the party.

Kelis's joint "Bossy" was blaring through the speakers. A waitress walked by carrying some drinks. Kendra snatched one off the tray, not caring what was in it. She stood there nursing the drink as she scanned the room for Papi. She smiled at Daddy Yankee and tried to see what Kelis had on.

"Everybody, let's do another toast." Tito, Papi's manager, was doing his best to gather everybody around, especially Papi, who was dancing all around the club. Tito had snatched him by his shirt.

Kajuan nodded to Kendra. She rolled her eyes at him and then sashayed her way over to the round table. She purposely stood directly in front of Papi and began looking bored, sticking out like a sore thumb. She caught Papi's attention immediately. Especially since she only had on a Biggie T-Shirt dress that barely covered her ass and a pair of Christian Cacroix crystal wedges.

Two waitresses carried out a huge sheet cake and set it on the table. It had a picture of Papi and the words *Papi Chulo, King of Reggaeton, the album.* Everyone clapped, hooted, and hollered.

"Who's gonna cut the cake?" Tito looked around. "Papi, can you handle it?"

Papi looked around. "Yo, Mami, come do this for me." He pointed the knife at Kendra. "She don't look like she's enjoying herself." Everybody laughed. "Come on, Mami, Papi won't bite you."

Oh brother, Kendra said to herself. But smiled as she headed toward Papi. She was eyeing him seductively and he was looking at her as if he wanted to sop her up.

"Yo, Ma, you lookin' good."

"Congratulations, Papi, you've come a long way." She eased the knife from between his fingers.

"Damn, you mo' sexy than a muthafucka." He eased up behind her and placed his hands over hers. "Let me help you cut this."

She giggled. "Oh, so you think I'm not capable?"

"Nah, I'm not saying that. It just gives me a reason to be close to you. Plus, I wouldn't want you to hurt yourself."

"Oh, so the King of Reaggaeton got jokes!" She took the first piece of cake and held it to his lips. He took a bite and everyone clapped and snapped pictures. This was indeed Papi's night.

"Now you take a bite," he told her. As he put the cake to her lips, she licked the icing from his fingers. "Woooooooo," everyone snickered.

"Now, yo, everybody take a seat! Let's get this toast off." Tito was still trying to control the crowd and was waving for everyone to sit down. Papi held out a chair for Kendra. The waitresses came over and began cutting the cake and placing the slices on saucers.

Tito continued. "On behalf of the new King of Reaggaeton, we thank all of you for coming out. Daddy Yankee, Kelis, Nas, Rhiana, Scott Storch, XXL, Hot 97, Scratch Mag, BLS, Don Diva, Feds, Felon. Damn Papi, you got the world at your fingertips! This is just about everybody!"

Papi stood up. "Thank you. Thank you, Tito my manager, who does his best to keep me in line. I appreciate you, man. You know that. To Kaylin and his wife, Angel Santos." He held his glass high up in the air. "They are the Bonnie and Clyde of the record industry. Watch what I tell y'all. They took me in, believed in me, when no one else did. I owe them, big time. I'm gonna show them that Papi Chulo appreciates them. Thank you for all your support and your love." He bowed his head.

"This toast is to you, Papi." Tito hugged him as everyone held up their glasses in the air. "Drink up and let's really get this party started!" Tito screamed. Balloons and confetti rained from the ceiling as Papi's first single, "I'm Not Trippin'", blasted from the speakers. The crowd went wild.

Papi threw back another shot of Hennessey, grabbed Kendra by the hand, and pulled her onto the dance floor. Kendra fell into her dangerous slow wind. "Oh yeah," Papi said in her ear. He was all up on her ass. She was trying to hold her breath. He smelled like a distillery. "Damn, girl, you got a body like Jessica Rabbit, but you look like Janet. That's a deadly combination."

"You got a body like Fifty, but you look like Sean Paul and got an ass like Tyrese. That's a deadly combination."

"Oh, shit, you got jokes."

Kendra rolled her eyes. *This drunk-ass lame*, she said to herself as she backed that ass up. "Damn, this my jam, you did dat."

He looked around and cheesed, as if the entire club heard what she said. "You're Kendra, right? I know you belong to the Santos clan. Boss man ain't gonna cut off a leg or my contract, is he?"

"Boy, stop playin', you family now," she assured him.

"Shit, I don't know. There's a lot of y'all. I know growing up, y'all were some hell-raisers." He turned her around and grabbed her ass.

"How did you know my name?" Kendra smirked as she continued to mesmerize him with her slow wind.

"Don't worry about that."

"Oh, I see nothing gets past you, huh?" She stroked his ego.

"Sho' you right."

"So you know that you're platinum material, right? Well, then you already know you're going to go platinum real fast."

"That I am."

"The world is yours, playboy."

"Yup, the world is mine! The . . . world . . . is . . . mine!" he yelled. "Damn, I wish my homeboys could see me now. Especially Micky."

"Where are they? Shit, they should have been here. This is a big night for you."

"Baby girl, my fam runs shit. They're big time."

"Well, you're big time too."

"I know, but I'm talking big, big mafioso-type niggas."

"Uh-oh. I hear you. You mean some Michael Corleone–type niggas?" She chuckled.

"Hell yeah. Maybe I'll hook you up. We'll see how you do tonight."

"Tonight, huh?"

"Tonight." He wanted to get into them panties right then and there, and was telling her whatever she wanted to hear.

"Well, what do you have planned?"

"Leave those details to me."

"Aiight, then. Just remember I'm the boss's family so you gotta treat me real special."

"I got you, Ma."

Kaylin hung up the phone. Sitting there he buried his face into his hands. Angel was standing in front of him, holding the baby and crying softly.

"Is it that bad? No, baby. Please say it's not that bad."

"It's bad."

"Dear, God."

He sighed. "She was beaten and shot three times in the stomach. The baby didn't survive and she is in critical condition and at this point she's not stable."

"Oh God!" Angel sobbed. "Her grandmother! Who's going to tell her grandmother?" She placed the baby in the crib.

"I guess that I'm going to have to be the bearer of the bad news. Fuck!" He hurled the phone across the room.

"I'm going with you."

"No, you're not."

"Kaylin, I need to see her."

"Why? You're staying right here."

"Baby, please. I'm coming with you. Let me go with you."

"Red, you are staying your ass in this house with our newborn baby. You are not even healed yet. What are you thinking? The baby ain't even a week old yet, and you're talking about going somewhere. Plus, it's four in the morning." He grabbed her and hugged her tight, trying to calm her down. "I know you care about E but you are going to have to sit tight."

"She's a baby, Kaylin. I told her to take somebody with her. Why would they do that to her? She's pregnant. I should have made sure somebody was with her." She sobbed.

"Baby, calm down. At least she's alive. And look at it this way. She's young, she can always have another baby. She's living, at least we got that." He gently caressed her back, trying to get her to calm down and stop crying.

By the time the baby and Angel fell asleep it was almost six in the morning. Kaylin slipped out of the house and headed to Lil'E's grandmother's.

Kendra was in Papi's bathroom running bathwater. Papi was knocked out cold. She looked at her face in the mirror and sighed. "I need some sleep." Glancing at the iced-up Chopard still on her wrist, she saw that it was 6:24 a.m. She had been up all night long and her skin showed it and her pounding headache confirmed it. The night wouldn't have been all that bad if Papi was a better fuck. She dialed Kaylin's cell and made a mental note to try Papi again when he was sober.

"Yeah."

"Why do you sound like your mama just died, nigga?" She joked. "I'm the one who should be sounding all down. I can't believe what the fuck you had me do. You owe me big time, nigga. I've been up all night pumping a drunk-ass, can't-stay-hard-dick nigga, for information. I got bags under my eyes and my skin looks a hot mess! We popped a few E tabs, and that caused the nigga to flap his gums all night long. If his dick would have been going all night I wouldn't be mad. He ate my pussy until—"

"Whoa, whoa!" Kaylin yelled into the phone, cutting short Kendra's tirade. "Chill out, Ma! You giving out a little too much info! You family, girl." He had to grin and was grateful that she did get him to smile. "I got you, cuz. What you did was very important to this family. That's why I love yo' gangsta ass!"

"Well, act like it, nigga! You know for the fam, I will step up to the plate. But you know I ain't fucking any Tom, Dick, and Harry, so at least act like you glad to hear from me and not like you on your way to a funeral."

"Kendra, check it out, yo. Lil'E was shot three times in the stomach. The baby is dead and we don't know if Lil'E is going to make it or not. I'm on my way to tell her grandmother now. I'm trying to beat the police over there."

"Oh . . . no. Kay, I am so sorry. I didn't know. I'm sorry, cuz."

"You know other than that, I would be jumping up and down, clapping and shit. And showering you with all the praise, props, and attention that yo' ass thrives off of. So tell me, what you got?"

"Your man lives all the way down in Maine. He flies in on a private jet up to the city twice a week, Sundays and Thursdays. Papi sees him on both days. I don't know if Papi is coppin' from him, working for him, or what, but he keeps saying that's his fam. I'm stuck like chuck on that one. But you keep an eye on Papi and you'll get your man. I gotta go."

Kendra saw the daylight sun creep into the bathroom when the door opened. She hung up the phone and sauntered over to the Jacuzzi and turned off the water.

"Good morning, you were snoring a few minutes ago," she said to Papi.

"I snore, but I'm a very light sleeper. But yo, why you all in my bathroom on the phone like you tryna hide somethin'?"

"Whatever." She snapped her neck back. "That was my cousin. Lil'E . . . they killed her baby. She's in the hospital. He's on his way to tell her grandmother."

"What? Oh, nah, mami. Lil'E? Not Lil'E, that's my little nigga. What the fuck happened? Who the fuck would do some shit like that?"

"I don't know. I don't think Kay knows either, not yet anyway."

"That's fucked up, yo. She family, man! What hospital?"

"I don't know. I only talked to my cousin for a few minutes. Give him time to talk to her grandmother and then try and call him back."

"Somebody gotta pay for this!" He stormed out of the bathroom.

Kendra recited a prayer as she stepped into the Jacuzzi.

Angel sat in the waiting room of the pediatrician's office. Jahara's navel cord wasn't healing as fast as she thought it should be so she brought her in to get it checked out. Everyone was telling her that she was overreacting but she didn't think so.

When she went to grab her phone to call Kaylin it started ringing. "I was just getting ready to call you." She smiled.

"Well, that's good to hear," Snake answered. "We've obviously been thinking about each other."

"What do you want?" She gritted her teeth. "How did you get this number?"

"That's not important."

"Why are you calling me, Keenan? Do I need to report you to the police?"

"Look, Angel. I'm done playing these silly-ass games with you. I want you to come down here and see me. We need to talk. And I'm not taking no for an answer."

"Keenan, listen. I am not coming to talk to you, not now, next week, not ever. Let it go. Leave me the hell alone. It is over between us." She wished that she could break his neck.

"How important is she to you?"

"What?"

"You heard me. How important is your sister to you?"

"What's that supposed to mean?"

"What you want me to do? Put the bitch out on the track?" He paused for effect. "Or I'll just get the slut strung out? Fuck it! I can do both. Tell me right here, fuckin' right now. Or was your sister right? You only think about your damn self. So I'm leaving her fate in your hands."

"Fuck you, Keenan, let me talk to her."

"You can talk all you want when you bring your ass down here. I need to see you."

There was silence and Snake knew he had her right where he wanted her.

"Keenan, don't do this."

"I don't want to but since I can't get you to talk to me, you leave me no choice. It's either you or her. All I'm asking for is just one night."

"One night? What do you mean one night?"

"Mrs. Santos, the doctor will see Jahara now," the receptionist called out.

"Just a minute," she snapped nervously at the receptionist. "What do you mean one night, Keenan?" She felt as if she was going to have an anxiety attack.

"One night, that's all I'm askin'. You owe me that, you gonna give me that! Angel, look, you really don't have a choice in this matter. I know you don't want to see your sister all fucked up, so I'll get back with your ass in a couple of weeks. Let you get everything together. Keep this between me and you. When I call you again, just have your ass ready to move."

Chapter 21

Four days later

"Yeah," Snake answered.

"Yo, nigga, we got serious problems," Phillip screamed into Snake's ear.

Snake held the phone away from his ears and looked at it. "You foul, P."

"Foul? Where you at? I need to come by and scoop you up."

"I'm back home, nigga. You got that off, and that twenty five grand ain't gonna make me or break me."

"Nigga, don't get it twisted. Twenty five stacks damn sho' ain't gonna break me neither. I wasn't tryna stiff yo' ass, I had some urgent shit that I had to handle. But yo, listen, sumthin way more serious than twenty five g's needs our attention. All over the news they talkin' about that."

"Talking about what?"

"Man, y'all failed. Homegirl is in the hospital in critical condition. Nigga, it's a very fucked-up situation. Very serious. It's not lookin' good." Phillip was trying to talk in circles but he was so mad, he was having a hard time. "It's not good. Too much at stake."

"So what this got to do with me?"

Snake heard a bang. Phillip was so mad he punched a hole in

the wall. Through gritted teeth, Phillip snarled, "You was supposed to handle that. You know how much I got on the line? A mutha-fuckin' empire! I could lose everything. She can finger me."

"Man, it was handled just the way you requested. You said three to the stomach. That's what you got. How the fuck was I supposed to know that the bitch was superwoman? And that was your decision to be all up in her face and shit."

Phillip let out a tired laugh. "Man, do you hear what you're saying? That bitch is a witness and can finger all of us. I suggest you come up with sumthin and sumthin fast, like within the next twenty-four hours." He slammed the phone down.

"Ain't this some shit!" Snake immediately dialed Bullet. "Nigga got me fucked up," he mumbled.

"'Sup?" Bullet answered.

"Man, get Whitey. I need to see y'all." He hung up and looked down at Carmen, who was kneeling in between his legs. She had snorted some coke off his dick and now she was sucking his hard-on as if her life depended on it. He grabbed her by her hair and motioned for her to stop. She looked up at him, eyes wide as saucers, and started giggling. "Go take a shower and get dressed. I got some people coming over."

Twenty minutes later, Bullet knocked on Snake's front door. "'Sup?" Bullet sauntered in wearing a big straw hat, a wife beater, and a pair of Docker's shorts and sandals. He noticed how Snake was looking at him. "Why you lookin' at me like that? I was chillin' sittin' by the pool, man. It's hot out." He smiled, sporting his white and yellow gold teeth.

"Whatever, nigga. Sit down. I just got a call from P.J. That lit-tle white bitch survived."

"She what?"

"She survived, she's in critical condition."

"Damn." Bullet sighed.

"Tell me about it. My concern is, she saw y'all faces. I don't have a problem with you. But Whitey, he be on some other shit sometimes. I might have to do sumthin with him. Can't have no witnesses, yo."

"Hold up. Hold the fuck up, Snake. We straight. We fam and everything but that's family. That white nigga is like my little brother. He act dumb as shit sometimes but we been running thick as thieves since elementary school. And I ain't never saw no signs of weakness."

"So, what are you saying? You vouching for the cat?"

"Snake, we got so many bodies together it's sickening. Don't forget we not new to this, we true to this. If he wanted to get funky on you he had several chances to do it. The last time being when you put him out of the car, he could've tripped then. But what he do? Went on with the job."

Snake was mulling it over, knowing deep down that Bullet was right. However, he needed to be sure.

"He cool, so don't trip. He least of your worries. So what? We gonna go back for her or what? And you know I want that nigga, Phillip. A deal is a deal. Let me *do* that nigga!"

"I don't know. I'ma have to talk to Dino, sumthin I'm not looking forward to. This nigga gonna preach a whole sermon and jump all in my ass."

They both turned to Whitey, who let himself in. He never knocked like everyone else.

"What it do?" He flashed his gold grill.

"Bullet will fill you in. I gotta make a run. Show yourselves out," Snake told them. "I want y'all to lie low. Real low until y'all hear from me."

"What's up?" Whitey asked as they stepped onto the front porch.

"Aw, shit. Let's get the fuck outta here," Bullet mumbled as the Escalade pulled up in front of them. "He looks pissed the fuck off."

"Who that with Dino, Big Steve?" Whitey tried to shield his gaze from the sunlight.

"Yup. That who that be." *They must have found out*, Bullet said to himself as he watched them get out of the car. "Dino. Big Steve. What's up?" Bullet gave Steve a hug. "You mean you left big pimpin' Jersey to come down to slow-ass Miami?" Bullet joked.

"Only for a minute. What y'all boys up to? White Boy, what's up? You still tryna be black?" Steve gave Whitey a hug.

"Steve, you still tryna be a pimp?" Whitey cracked back. "And the last time I looked I was black. The last time you looked was you still a pimp?"

"Only a white boy would say some dumb shit like that." Steve smirked.

Dino looked at both of them. "I'll get with y'all later. My nephew inside?"

"Yeah, he in there." Bullet jumped into his Denali and cranked it up.

Whitey walked around to the driver's side. "What the fuck is going on?"

"Meet me at the crib," Bullet told him and he started his ride and pulled off. Whitey jogged over to his Ferrari, got in, and pulled off behind him.

Dino and Steve let themselves in. Steve fixed him a shot of vodka and cranberry juice and sat at the bar. Dino made himself confortable on the huge butter-soft leather sectional.

"Look at those pimp of the year trophies." Steve beamed as he eyed the spacious glass china cabinet that held about twelve trophies.

Snake and Carmen emerged into the living room, looking as if they were on their way to a pool party.

"Whoa," Snake said as he stopped dead in his tracks. "My two favorite uncles." He looked at the no-nonsense expression on Dino's face and handed Carmen the car keys. "Go wait in the car for me." She smiled at the two men and followed his instructions. "What's up?"

They waited for Carmen to leave. "P.J. called and said you fucked up. What you done did, boy?" Steve wanted to know.

"Yeah, you care to fill us in?" Dino added.

"I was gonna get with you tonight, Unc." He looked at Dino. "To make a long story short, I owed P a favor from way back when and he asked me to pop this broad for fifty stacks. We did it how he wanted it done but she survived. Now he wants me to come back up that way and fix it."

"Bullshit, nigga. You know how hot that shit is by now? What's the matter with you, boy? First you going koo-koo over some bitch that don't want you and now you pulling penny-ass murders for some other nigga. I think I'ma have to send your ass away again. You too hot and you are starting to draw too much heat. Miami is mine. And I'll be damned if I'ma let some little snot-nosed punk, family or not, fuck up what I done built." Dino was outraged.

"I hear you ," Steve uttered as he chomped down on some ice cubes.

"But, Unc—"

Dino cut him off. "You gave me the impression that you was gonna see him to talk some legit shit. Not no bullshit. Hell, if I had known you was going up there to do some petty shit like this, I would have cracked yo' muthafuckin' skull my damned self and saved us all some drama."

"Unc—"

"Don't Unc me. All y'all niggas lie low. I'll let you know what I'm gonna do with y'all. I mean that shit."

"Damn. That bitch lived? What? She was P.J.'s jump-off who got outta line?" Steve cracked.

"Unc, it ain't funny. She was some white broad he got pregnant."

"Aww, Lawd!" Steve yelled, sounding like Steve Harvey. "Boy, you done killed a white broad? And a pregnant one at that? You's a big dummy! And I mean a big dummy. Shit sounds like twenty five to life to me and ain't nothing me and your big uncle Dino can do about that. You's goin' down. Boy, that's double murder! What the fuck was you thinking? And only fifty stacks? Oh, you're a cheap murderer, and stupid. Yup, brother Dino, I think you're right, that ass whupping that his ho put on him fucked him up. He's a goner. But check it, at least your commissary gonna stay stacked. And you might as well give me them three hoes for that."

"Steve. Shut up, man," Dino warned, then turned to Snake. "Just lie low and make sure your two sidekicks do the same." He shook his head in disgust. "You just keep disappointing me, nephew. Let's go Steve. I done worked me up an appetite. I'll get with you later, nephew, and stay the fuck put! And I mean stay the fuck put."

"Checkmate," Steve said as he closed the door.

Kaylin was sitting up in the dark, thinking. Angel was sound asleep and he had just rocked Jahara backed to sleep and she was still on his shoulder.

He had a tail on Papi and they followed him to a hotel where he picked up Mickey and then they went to Papi's house. But they were still baffled as to Papi's connection to Mickey.

"Nooooo." Kaylin's attention went over to Angel, who was squirming and moaning in her sleep.

"Keenan . . . nooo." Her breathing was sporadic.

Kaylin got up and laid Jahara in her crib, then went and sat on the side of the bed. He rubbed and squeezed her shoulder. "Angel, wake up, baby." He squeezed her shoulder again. "Baby . . . wake up. You sweatin' and shit."

"Noooo." Her eyes fluttered open and then she frantically looked around.

"It's me, baby. What the fuck you dreamin' about?" Kaylin didn't know if he should be jealous or pissed off.

She sat up slowly and the tears rolled down her cheeks. "Oh

God. He is in my dreams. My dreams." She clutched on to the sheets.

"He hasn't tried to contact you again, has he? You saw him recently?" She looked over toward the crib, and then closed her eyes. "Angel, you talked to him? You saw him again?"

"No, baby, I haven't." She forced herself to lie.

"This nigga got you shivering, sweating, and crying in your sleep. After I do this other thing, I gots to handle this nigga." *This shit has gone too far. This nigga has to be dealt with.*

Kaylin and Kajuan were standing at the nurses' station. The nurse had paged the resident physician so that he could come and fill Kaylin in on the status of Lil'E. The nurse wasn't telling Kaylin what he wanted to hear and he had become impatient. Lil'E's grandmother was in the room with her. Kaylin couldn't stay in there for too long; it hurt his heart to see her fragile body with tubes traveling all through her. To him, she looked worse than Trae did. She was still unconscious and in critical condition, but at least she wasn't comatose. Kaylin was more anxious for her to wake up than the police, who stopped by at least once a day.

"Ahhhhhhhh!" The scream caused everyone to freeze in their tracks. A figure with a hat pulled down over his eyes and hair all over his face came walking briskly out of Lil'E's room. "It's him again!" Lil'E's grandmother slammed Lil'E's door and you could hear her moving stuff around trying to barricade herself in.

Kaylin and Kajuan took off running behind the guy. They saw him head toward the stairwell. Kajuan jumped over the railing and landed right on top of the dude. They tumbled down a flight of stairs and the dude was trying to grab his gat.

Kaylin caught up and stomped on the hand that was trying to reach for the heater. "Nigga, you should have pulled that out before you started running." He pressed down with all his weight onto his hand, causing Dude to yell out in pain. Kajuan was punching him in the face and mouth, trying to get him to stop yelling.

"Get up, nigga." Kaylin yanked him up and Kajuan was already feeling him for the burner. Hospital security came rushing down the stairwell.

"We got him, go check on my grandma in CCU. There's two more up there," Kajuan lied.

The guard hesitated and then yelled into the walkie-talkie, "Moss and Bingham, report to CCU, two suspects on the loose." He looked back at Kaylin and Kajuan and took off running.

Kajuan cocked the nine and pressed the barrel against dude's temple. "Don't shoot, man. I don't got beef with y'all," Dude yelled out.

Kaylin was going through the dude's pockets. "Who sent you?" He pulled out a wallet and opened it, scanning through its contents.

"C'mon, man. Let me get out of here. I don't even know y'all . I don't got beef wit y'all fuckin' good Samaritans."

"Good Samaritans? Fuck you, that's my peeps in that room!" Kaylin rammed his head into the wall.

"Unnghhh." He slid to the floor and was breathing as if he were in labor.

Kaylin stood him back up. "Who sent you? This is my last time asking."

"Fuck you, man. This ain't got nothing to do with you."

"Aiight, cool." Kaylin pulled out his license. "I'll see you later." He looked down at the license. "Wallace Taylor, 124 West 119th Street, aptartment S10." Then he pulled out photos of children. "Oh, look, Wallace Junior and Krissy. Oh, who is this?" Kaylin taunted.

"Man, hold up."

"Nah. You hold the fuck up. Who sent you? Is his name more important than your family?"

"He'll kill me, man."

"What the fuck you think I'ma do? Along with your whole damn family."

"Awww, man." He started bawling.

"Let's go." Kaylin motioned to Kajuan, who hauled off and punched Dude in the face.

"See you later." Kajuan smirked.

"Hold up. Phillip, Phillip Johnson."

Kaylin turned around in his tracks.

"That's who sent me, man. Please give me back my wallet."

Kajuan emptied the shells out of the nine, wiped his prints off on his shirt, and dropped the gun onto the floor.

"Please, give me back my shit," Wallace pleaded.

"Dawg, you better get the fuck outta here, unless you ready to go to jail," Kajuan warned him as the footsteps coming up the stairs became louder. Kajuan left him there and jetted up the stairwell and caught up with Kaylin.

"All right, here is the deal," Kaylin announced when he stepped onto the Critical Care Unit. "This is a celebrity. She's in critical condition. There have already been two attempts on her life, you have no security in here so I want her moved to an undisclosed location. Right now! I'm calling my attorney and if you don't honor my request, he will make sure that I own this fuckin' hospital!"

Kaylin, Kajuan, Bo, and Omar were all seated in Trae's living room. He was getting stronger and healthier. And he looked to have put on ten or fifteen pounds.

"Man, this joint holds a lot of history." Omar snickered.

"Don't it, though?" Bo agreed. "Kay, tell Trae how Kajuan jumped over the rail at the hospital and nabbed Dude. He turned into supercop!" Bo and Omar started laughing.

"Don't tell him, bro." Kajuan was embarrassed. "I don't know what the fuck got into me."

Trae smiled and looked over at his boy, Kay. "Nigga, you need to talk. You been in your own little world over there. You lookin' stressed the fuck out. Talk, nigga. Say sumthin."

"Where do you want me to start?"

"Anywhere. Spit, nigga."

"Everything is happening at once. It's shit in the pressure cooker and it's getting ready to explode. And everything needs my attention. Red, she fuckin' having nightmares about this nigga. It's a must that I take care of his ass soon as I handle this Mickey shit. And then there's Lil'E. Phillip Johnson sent the same nigga up to the hospital twice to finish her off. I had to get her moved to a hospital up in Jersey. That took the mayor's office and everyone else to pull that off. Then Papi. I was planning to make mad loot off this cat, but it looks like the only time I'll catch Mickey is when he is with Papi." He sighed as he rubbed his temples.

"So, what's the status with the Don's work? Where are we on that again?" Trae quizzed.

"The dude, Mickey, comes in twice a week. We've had a tail on him for a couple of weeks. He either goes to a hotel or spends time with Papi."

"Who is this Papi cat? What does he have to do with Mickey?" Trae asked. "Are they lovers or some shit like that?"

"We haven't figured that out yet." Kaylin sighed. "But I got an investigator working on that as we speak."

"So, what's the plan?" Trae wanted to know.

"The next time he goes to Papi's we gonna make our move. We have a better chance getting into Papi's crib and getting right out. A hotel, that shit is too damn risky. We would have to find the room and get past security. Again, it's too damn risky."

"Well, what about your star? You're going to merk him too?" Trae prodded.

Kaylin sighed. "If I have to . . . yes."

"You're going to have to. No ifs, nigga. You can't leave a witness. Star or no star. Y'all understand that?" Trae looked everyone in the eye. Everyone nodded. "Aiight, cool. So the only thing left is to get it done and over with."

Everyone stood up to leave. Kaylin went over to Trae and said, "Yo, if sumthin happens to me, just make sure my family is straight."

"Nigga, we already discussed this, ain't nothing changed. I got you," Trae assured him. "I'm just mad that I can't go along."

Chapter 22

"I'm takin' over the world/one city at a time with every nickel and dime . . ."

"Yeah, yeah, yeah, dis is DJ Kay Slay, showing mad love to Lil'E. That was her joint, 'Hustler's Anthem.'"

"Whooooweeee! That joint is pumpin'!" Whitey was still jamming to the beat of "Hustler's Anthem."

"Man, shut up," Bullet snapped as the DJ continued.

"The industry scoop is, for those of you who have been living under a rock, Lil'E was beaten, shot three times, and her unborn child is dead. The latest news is that Phillip Johnson, CEO of Tyrant Music, is a suspect and that the baby was his. Deep, ain't it? Anyways, get well soon, Lil'E, we all pullin' for ya. And shout out to Game Over Records. And to you, Phillip Johnson, run, negro, run. But . . . I don't think you can hide! As a matter of fact, you might as well come on back. Prove your innocence, bruh, you lookin' guilty. Come on in."

"I wish I could have hit that. Man, that bitch must have nine lives. I may still have a chance to get up in that. You think she'll go out with me?"

"Fool, didn't you just hear what he said? She hotter than fuck. Plus, she can ID yo' dumb ass."

"I'm only playin', man."

"No, you wasn't."

Lil'E was now conscious and in stable condition in intensive care. She told Kaylin and the police that Phillip Johnson was the responsible party. She said nothing about the white dude, the big black guy, and the third man whose voice she heard but whom she didn't see.

The Santos household had been on pins and needles, Angel being unusually withdrawn and secretive. Kaylin was thinking it was because he had been focused on making sure Lil'E was safe, Phillip was being hunted, and he finally had a definite lead on Snake. He could reach out and touch him whenever he wanted. But tonight was Mickey Reye's night. All of this was in Kaylin's mind as they were tailing behind his car.

"Mama Santos, how is she?" Angel had just landed in Miami on a private jet.

"Stop worrying. She's my grandbaby and she's fine."

"I can't help it. This is my first time leaving her. I had planned on nursing for at least three months, but things are beginning to get crazy." She tried to tell herself that, more than Mrs. Santos.

"You could have squeezed some milk into a bottle," she scolded. "I nursed her father for ten months. I wish you would have nursed longer. She is only five weeks old."

"I know, let me go because you're making me feel guilty. Kiss her for me. I'll call you later. Bye-bye."

Angel flagged down a taxi and handed the driver a slip of paper with the address on it. He got out of the front seat, took her bags, and threw them in the trunk. She slipped into the backseat, popped on her shades, and focused on the task at hand.

*   *   *

"Good," Kaylin said. He was glad that Mickey went to Papi's house tonight instead of a hotel. He didn't want to prolong this mission any longer. They were hoping to get into Papi's house, handle Mickey, and get out quickly. They parked in the cut and let the engine run. Kaylin's cell vibrated and he started to ignore it but changed his mind when he saw the Miami area code. "Pras, I'm tied up, what's good?"

"Man, I don't even know how to tell you this."

"What, nigga? Spit it out. I'm in the middle of sumthin." He kept his eye glued to Papi's house.

"Wifey just pulled up in front of your boy's spot."

Kaylin got a nasty taste in his mouth and his head began to spin. "Come again?"

"Wifey just pulled up in front of this pimp nigga's house."

"Man . . . what is you talking about? My wife is home."

"I know what I see. And this is wifey. But hey, I just figured I'd let you know. What you want me to do?"

"You know what I want you to do but it's sumthin that I need to handle. Damn! Just stay posted. I'll get back at you." He ended that call and frantically dialed his house phone.

Omar, Kajuan, and Bo all looked at one another and shrugged.

After Kaylin accepted that he wasn't going to get an answer, his heart rate sped up. He dialed her cell phone.

"Hello."

Kaylin breathed a sigh of relief. "Hey."

"Hey back. I love you."

"I love you more, what's up? I called the house, no answer. Where you at? The baby with you? Why you ain't call and tell me you had to run out?"

"Sumthin came up. The baby is at your mother's."

"What? What is so important that you felt the need to leave our child?"

"I got sumthin to take care of, Kaylin. Just like you always got sumthin to take care of."

"Oh, it's like that now?"

"Oh, believe me, it's been like this for a while."

"It has? Well, when were you planning on filling me in?"

"I shouldn't have to if you'd pay more attention to me and our newborn baby. But c'mon, Kaylin, it's not what you're thinking."

"Then what's the real deal, Red? 'Cause you and I both know you spittin' bullshit right now."

"Please, trust me like I trust you, and this is not a good time."

Kaylin started laughing his pissed-off laugh. "Yo, I'll see you lat—"

She cut him off. "I gotta go." And she ended the call by turning her phone off. He was still laughing, crazy, as he dialed her back. When it went to voice mail he hung up and called Bobbi.

"Hello."

"Bobbi, it's me. Have a private flight ready for me within the hour."

"Oookay . . . uh . . . where to?"

"Miami."

"Okay."

"Thanks." He hung up and had this crazy look in his eyes. "The Grim Reaper is definitely earning his stripes tonight. Y'all ready to do this?"

Everyone nodded, put on gloves, and gripped their heat.

"You gonna fill us in or what?" Kajuan asked what was on everyone else's mind.

"Let's do this first." He opened his car door and everyone followed. Kajuan remained focused on the house with the car running.

Angel still could hear the hurt in Kaylin's voice but she tossed him out of her mind and plastered on her game face.

Earlier the taxi had eased into the driveway of a stucco-covered condo, surrounded by palm trees. The driver beeped the horn. After several minutes, Snake came out of the house and looked at Angel with a smirk on his face. The cabbie popped the trunk and grabbed Angel's garment bag.

Now, two hours later, they were finishing up their dinner. He had cooked a meal of steamed lobster, baked potatoes, spinach salad, and grilled vegetable shish kebabs.

"You hardly touched your dinner. I'm a little hurt."

"Don't be. I told you I wasn't hungry."

"You used to love my cooking. I taught you a few tricks around the kitchen, remember?"

"Of course I do. That was when I *used* to love you." She sipped a little of the wine that he served.

"Used to, huh?" He smirked. "You like that wine? I had that shit imported."

"It's all right, a little too sour for my taste."

"Damn, I just can't get it right with you, can I?"

"That should tell you sumthin, don't you think?"

He let go of a huge sigh. "Why, Angel? How could you so easily walk away from what we had? How the fuck am I supposed to understand that?"

"What we had! What I had was a lot of muthafuckin' ass whippings and a whole bunch of excuses for why you did it. Sorry this and sorry that. And understand? Understand what? Understand why I loved you for who you were and unconditionally. But you never respected me, loved me, or cared about me. Is that what you don't understand? But what I do and what you need to understand is that you never knew what love was. I had to eventually come to terms with that. And you know what? You did me a favor by leaving me and I thank you.

"After I accepted that you were dead, I began to move on. Then I met Kaylin and I fell in love with him, Keenan. I love him. And you can't change that. He took your place in my heart. Do you understand?"

Snake poured himself another glass of wine and gulped it down. Despite how sure of himself he sounded, he still had a hard time letting go and it pissed him off for being so gone over her. She leaned back into her chair and they indulged in a stare-down.

"You are so fine. And if, in the morning, you can look me in the eye and tell me that bullshit you just spoke, I'ma let you go."

"Whatever, negro. So, what? Is this the part of the evening where we are supposed to fuck?"

He smirked. "Yeah, we'll see if that nasty attitude will be with you in the morning."

"We will, won't we?" She got up from the table. "I'm going to take a nice, long, hot, bath."

"Can I—"

"Alone, Keenan," she said as she sauntered off to the master bedroom.

He pumped his fist and mouthed, "Yesss!" as he excitedly began to clear the dinner table.

"Who is it?" Mickey Reyes answered as he unlocked the door. "Mijo, you expecting company? Or did you order another one of those doughy Greek pizzas?" He cracked the door, and Kaylin pushed it open and rushed him, pressing his .357 to his head. The other two men with ski masks on came in quickly and quietly behind him and closed the door.

"Shh!" Kaylin put his fingers to his lips. The other two men began to search the house, with guns drawn.

"What is it? You want money? Do you know who I am?" Mickey asked, showing no signs of fear.

"No one else is here, except for Dude," Omar whispered. "And he's in the bathroom."

"Good." Kaylin quickly screwed on the silencer. "This is from Don Alexjandro and Don Carlos."

"Wait, just don't kill my s—"

Plat, plat, plat.

The first bullet pierced his forehead, the second one entered his chest, and the last one tore through his stomach.

"Let's dip," Bo said.

As they turned to open the front door, Papi stuck his head out of the bathroom. "Hey, Papi, put on some music. I brought you a couple of CDs, a classic Chick Corea, Santana, and Celia Cruz. Plus, you gotta hear my first single. Dad! You hear me? What are you doing?"

The three of them exited quickly toward the awaiting vehicle.

Angel sat in the tub crying and trying to gas herself up to be so close to a nigga that she hated. He made her sick. She jumped when she heard a tap on the door.

"Yo, you still alive in there?"

"Of course. I know you're going to let me enjoy my bath."

"You on my time now. Come on out, I got sumthin nice for you."

"I'm coming."

"Yeah, you can bet on that." He smirked.

She rolled her eyes and hit the lever to let the water out. Snatching a towel off the rack, she stepped onto the marble floor and began to dry off. She slowly began to moisturize her skin with some Victoria Secret's Strawberry Delight. After she fixed her hair and applied some lip gloss she went into her purse and pulled out a glass vial. She slowly poured the oil onto her fingertips and carefully massaged it onto her neck, nipples, navel, and all over her toes. She carefully closed the vial and dropped it back into the secret compartment in her purse, then washed her hands thoroughly. She slipped on her stilettos and stepped into her matching bra, thong, and robe. Glad to be placing all of her belongings together, she looked at herself once more in the mirror, took a deep breath, and opened the door.

Kaylin, Kajuan, Omar, and Bo were on their way to Miami. The hour-and-a-half plane ride wasn't moving fast enough for

Kaylin. They all had to stash their heat, instead of taking a chance bringing it with them. Pras said he had all that they needed.

"I'm still in shock, yo," Kaylin confessed.

"I know. He called Mickey Reyes daddy." Kajuan laughed.

"Not that, man. My wife!" Kaylin was pacing back and forth like a caged animal, making everybody antsy.

Finally Kajuan couldn't take any more and yelled out, *"Chigado carnal, porque no te sientas tu puta, madre."*

"Don't tell me to sit my fuckin' ass down. Fuck this marriage shit! I had a baby with this bitch! Why? Why she gonna make me take her out? I hope I catch them lying on top of each other. I want one bullet to go through both of them and explode in both of their guts." He was looking crazy and no one said a word.

"Damn." Snake lusted. "My, my, my, you are still so . . . beautiful. Turn around, let me look at you some more." She turned around slowly. "Look at them long, sexy legs. I miss them sumthin terrible."

She sauntered over to the bar and poured herself a glass of white zinfandel. "You want a drink?"

"Nah, baby girl. The last bitch that fixed me sumthin tried to poison and kill my ass. You ain't gonna get me twice."

"Are you sure about that?" She winked at him.

"Oh, I'm sure."

Angel looked him over. His feet were bare . . . still nice. He had on a pair of silk pajama pants and his chest was bare. Rock-hard abs, muscular arms and shoulders. A little gray was beginning to dot his curly hair. That damn ugly-ass eye patch. It gave her the creeps. She drank that glass and turned to pour another one.

He stepped behind her, wrapped his arms around her waist, and clamped a diamond tennis bracelet around her wrist. "I got this for you." He held her tight.

"You shouldn't have," she said dryly.

"Strawberries. You remembered." He inhaled his favorite scent on her skin.

Oh, God, please help me get through this, she prayed. Her hands were trembling, causing the drink to splash over her fingers. She felt his dick harden and knew that, at this moment, there was no turning back.

"You don't miss me a little bit?" He was getting more aggressive, his hands sliding over her like an octopus.

"Don't make me answer that."

"Why? Go ahead and say it. That nigga ain't here." He took her hand and led her over to the couch. He leaned over to kiss her.

"No, Keenan, I'm not ready to kiss you yet. We're fucking on the couch?"

"Baby, we're gonna fuck all over this house. But yeah, this is where it's gonna start."

"Take off my shoes, then." He was still kissing her neck and squeezing her ass. "Keenan." She pushed him away, smiling. "Why are you in such a hurry?" She sat down on the couch. "Take them off."

He knelt down on the floor and slowly unstrapped her stilletos. "I wanted to fuck you in these," he told her.

"Only Kaylin gets to fuck me in these. You lost that privilege when you left me. I want you to suck my toes, Keenan. Suck them how you used to. Do you remember?"

He grinned. "Of course I do. And don't say that punk's name again in my house." He took off the other shoe, looked at her feet, and smiled. She leaned back onto the couch, placing one foot on his shoulder, and with the other one she ran her toes across his lips. He gently took her heel and began to slowly suck her toes. She closed her eyes and imagined that it was Kaylin. Her pussy was actually getting hot. "Mmm, that feels nice," she moaned. Snake was stroking his dick while sucking her toes. When she finally had enough, she said, "C'mon, Daddy, suck my nipples." He wasted no time in obeying her wish and began kissing his way up her legs, stopping at her panties. "No, Daddy, we got all night for that. Isn't that what you told me? I need you to suck my nipples." She slipped out of the robe and gently peeled off the see-through bra, giving him a little show. She grabbed his head and pulled him up toward her nipples. "This is my night, isn't it?"

He moaned, "Yes."

"Then suck them real good. This is what you've been waiting for, Daddy. Make my pussy dripping wet. Suck them. Mmmmm . . . yes, just like that," she purred. "Shit, yes!" She was imagining that he was Kaylin. "Suck them, Daddy, real good."

He sucked until her breathing told him that she was ready for more. He reached down and yanked off her panties.

"Awww, shit. You know how . . . long . . . I've . . . been . . . dreaming . . . about . . . this?" he said in between kisses trailing down her stomach and stopping to lick her navel. She giggled as she held his head there, forcing him to lick and suck some more. He ran his nose all around her pussy and then began to lay his head game down. Once he got with Angel, her pussy was the only pussy he would eat. He felt her grab on to his head and arch her back.

"Ohhhhhh," she squealed, exciting him more as he lapped at her clit. "Oh, shit . . . this . . . oh, baby . . . oh, eat this . . . pussy . . . Kaylin—"

His head bobbed up. "What the fuck did you call me?" *Plop*. Not giving her a chance to respond he punched her in the face and then raised his fist to punch her again. She kneed him in the nuts, but couldn't get them good enough.

"You bitch!"

That brought her enough time to roll onto the floor. He grabbed her foot as she tried to crawl away. "Keenan, stop!" she screamed. Her jaw was starting to feel numb from his punch. He pulled her to him and punched her again . . . and again. "Keenan, stop it, please! I hate . . . you!"

"Fuck, you gonna call me some other nigga's name! I'll kill yo' ass, bitch!"

"What is the matter with you, Keenan? Why . . . are you shocked? I told you . . . I don't want you," she screamed as she tried to protect herself from his blows. She broke loose and could feel her eye swelling shut. She crawled as fast as she could but ran smack into a cabinet. "Owww!" Her head felt as if someone hit her with a pipe.

Snake reached her and they began trading blows. He was running out of fuel and she was fucking him up. He sensed that he was getting weaker and he was beginning to see doubles.

"What did you do to me, bitch?"

"I poisoned your stupid ass." She smiled a bloody smile.

He lunged at her and she backed up against the cabinet and it came tumbling down. Glass went everywhere and trophies slid across the floor.

"I'ma kill you, bitch." He was still coming after her.

"Not if I kill you first, punk faggot. Oh, shit," she groaned as a piece of glass pricked her hand. "God, that shit is supposed to have him going into convulsions by now," she mumbled. She crawled over shards of glass, cutting her knees and hands even more. She grabbed a trophy and swung it backward, slapping him across the head with it.

"Fuckin' bitch!" He fell backward. "I . . . can't . . . breathe."

She crawled over to him and banged him over the head, much harder this time around. Then again, again, and again. She zoned out as she kept hammering the trophy against his skull, oblivious of her surroundings. She didn't even feel Kaylin lift her up.

"Red."

"Get away from me! Don't touch me. Stay away!" She held the blood-and-flesh covered trophy out as if it were a gun. Her chest heaved up and down.

"Stay away from me . . . leave me alone. I hate you." She swung the trophy at Kaylin. "I dream about you. I hear your voice in my head. Stay away from me."

"It's me, Angel," Kaylin said softly but with force.

"Stay away from me. Leave me alone." She stared at him with a crazed look in her eyes.

He couldn't believe what looked to have just taken place. "Give me a minute, yo," he yelled to everyone without turning around and taking his eyes off his wife.

Omar, Bo, Pras, and Kajuan backed out of the front door, which never was locked. They had walked right in on the action ready to go to battle. Now sympathy covered their faces.

"Baby, it's me. Kaylin. Put the trophy down. It's over. He won't be bothering you anymore."

"No?" she said, in a childlike voice. She kept shaking her head no.

"Yes, baby, it's over." He wanted to grab her and take her into his arms. One of her eyes was swollen. The other eye was bruised. Her lips were bleeding, as well as her knees and hands, and she was naked.

"Angel, it's me, Kaylin."

"Angel!" Carmen came bursting into the house. She stopped dead in her tracks when she saw how her sister looked. Then she looked over at Snake on the floor in a bloodied mess and she started screaming. She ran over to him. "Keenan, baby, get up. Keenan, please get up. What did you do to him?" she screamed at Angel. "I know you did this! You bitch! What did you do to him?"

Angel dropped the trophy and ran over to Carmen. "It's over, baby sister. He's gone now. He won't hurt you anymore. You're free now. Mommy said for you to come home, you're in trouble."

"Nooooo!" she screamed. "You bitch! Why did you hurt him? Oh God, why?" Angel went to hug her and Carmen smacked her across the face and pushed her away, causing Angel to snap out of that daze that had her stuck on shock. Angel cocked her head to the side and that steely gaze caused Carmen and Kaylin both to take a few steps back. Angel lunged toward Carmen, who quickly reached in her bag and pulled out her heater. Angel grabbed it and they tusseled and before Kaylin could break them up the gun went off.

"Oh, shit," he groaned. Everyone had run back inside and was staring. "Oh, shit!" he groaned again. Both girls were frozen stiff. "Red, baby, don't do this to me," he panicked.

"Noooo," Angel cried out. "Oh God . . . no." Carmen fell back onto the floor, eyes wide open.

"Damn," Omar mumbled.

Angel was holding on to the gun real tight as she stared at Carmen. Kaylin, relieved, pried it loose from her fingers. He stood over Snake and shot him in the head one time . . . and again. Just to be sure that he was really dead.

All of the men immediately put on gloves and began going through the house. Kaylin grabbed the robe and put it around a shell-shocked Angel. She was shivering and was staring into space.

Pras immediately took charge. "Get her in the car, man. Me and my peeps got this." Two white dudes came in with duffel bags. "We'll handle the bodies and then we're gonna torch the place."

"Here's Angel's garment bag and I think this is her purse and suitcase." Bo held them up.

Kaylin threw Angel over his shoulder and took her out. Bo, Kajuan, and Omar were behind them.

"Later." Pras smirked.

"Later, nigga," Bo said.

Two weeks after all the drama

Angel, the baby, her mother, Kyra, and Jaz all flew to Mykonos. Angel hadn't expected to be back to her prehoneymoon spot so soon, but felt that this was the only place that would help her get her mind right. This getaway was more of a healing for Angel and her mother.

Two days before their trip they had a small, private burial service for Carmen's cremated remains. It was reported to the police that she was shot, possibly by a third party, and then the house was deliberately set ablaze with Snake's body included. The police had no suspects but the investigation was still open.

Kaylin stepped into his in-house studio at Game Over Records. Papi had been holed up in there for the last ten days. He looked and smelled horrible. He was in a zone, so Kaylin instructed everyone to leave him alone. He was writing and had sent for two producers. Another album was almost completed.

Kaylin set the Chinese food containers down next to him. "Papi, what up? You all right? I brought you some vittles. Why don't you take a break?" he suggested, glad that he finally caught him alone.

Papi looked up at him and said, "Boss man, what day is this?"

"It's Wednesday. Eat sumthin, man. What you living off of, the air?" he joked.

Papi grinned. "I'm on a roll, yo. This album . . . the people are really gonna feel it. Yo, you think the first one was off the chain! Well, on that one I was hungry, real hungry, no doubt. And that's what came across. This one . . . I'm in pain. I never felt like this before. Boss man, when I was a shorty I was thinking that my moms purposely kept me away from my pops." He reached for the Chinese food. "Until one day, a man walked up to me and said he was my father. Then at that moment I remembered how excited I felt. But that quickly turned to dissapointment, to anger, and then to me feeling overwhelmed. My dad kept it gully, even way back then. He let me know that he loved me and my moms and always will. But being the man he knew that he had to be, he couldn't be with us the way he wanted to. It was for our safety and for his loyalty to *la familia*. He explained to me that *la familia* didn't want him to be with a black Jamaican woman. Their ways were old-school ways. But he loved her, but again his loyalty was to la familia. It was la familia's business first. He snuck around to see us for a while. Then one day he stopped coming." Papi choked up.

"We just stared kicking it last year. I was enjoying that shit just like a little kid, yo. I was making up for lost time. Two nights a week, when he came into the city, I would get a couple of hours with him. Then one night, while I'm in the shower, bam!" He pointed his finger like a gun and shot into the air three times. "They shot him three times. They killed *mi padre* right in my living room. Ironic, huh? I know they did it. The *la familia* did it. They didn't even have the decency to invite me and *mi madre* to the funeral. . . ."

He rambled on, but Kaylin was no longer listening, lost in his own web of thoughts. He now felt fucked up. It all came together at that very moment. The urgency of why they wanted him to carry out the hit, why Papi was in the photos in front of the office building. *What else do they want from me? Why would they put me in the middle of this? Now I have to look at this man every day, knowing that I killed his father. Can I do that?*

"Boss man, boss man. Are you listening to me? What's wrong? I didn't mean to dump my sorrows in your lap, but I needed to unload that shit." He snapped Kaylin out of his reverie. Kaylin was staring Papi dead in the eyes. Eyes that were filled with guilt.

As Papi looked back into Kaylin's eyes he asked, "Why are you looking at me like that? Are you okay? You look as if your best friend just died, yo."

Damn.

Epilogue

Kaylin pulled up into his driveway. The clock on the dashboard read 2:47 a.m. He deaded the engine, opened the ashtray, and pulled out what was left of his blunt. He was already toasted. He just left his thugged-out bachelor's party the crew threw for him . . . once again. What was he doing sitting in his driveway, when there were a bunch of strippers, weed, drinks, music, his peeps, and his fam kickin' it big time? Simple. He needed to fuck his wife.

While she was away on her therapeutic vacation he was getting the ultimate hip-hop fairy-tale wedding together. Yeah, he went all out, but he owed her that much and refused to give her anything less. She had only been back for a week and they both had been ripping and running and it was time to slow things down. Hell, these last nine months, they never took time out to make slow passionate love. It'd been drama, chaos, ripping and running.

From what he could see, the trip had done her well. After all, she was pretty shaken. And once Mrs. Smith found out what had happened, she was even more shaken. She and her mother both willingly talked with a therapist. And with Jaz, and Kyra hanging out with them Angel sort of just bounced back to her normal self.

He had to give it to her. A true ride-or-die chick. She put her life and freedom on the line and went out like a gangsta. He could say that shit now . . . that the whole Snake ordeal was over. But at the time when everything was going down, he was pissed the fuck off and ready to rock the both of them to sleep.

He put some fire to the blunt and took a couple of pulls. Shit had been crazy since he quote, unquote got out of the game. Starting with niggas bum-rushing his wedding, Trae getting shot up, Lil' E still in the hospital, him taking out a made guy who was the father to his star artist, his wife killing a nigga . . . damn. The only thing missing was him moving weight. He shook that thought off, deaded the blunt, and got out of his ride thinking, *Is there really such a thing as out of the game?*

Stepping up onto the porch, he could hear the music. Her bachelorette party. It sounded more crunk than his bachelor's party. Slipping the key into the lock, he quietly crept in and locked the door behind him. Peeking into the living room, he saw the ladies getting busy on the dance floor. Angel's mother was the ringleader. They had two male strippers who they were taking turns dancing with. He even found and sent for Angel's cousin DeElla Favors from Tennessee. It was worth it when he saw the look on her face when she stepped into the house. She was getting crunk on the dance floor with the strippers and had a drink in each hand. I wonder what Faheem and Marvin would say if they walked in on this? Jaz and Kyra were really wildin' out.

"Brace yo'self, fool!" Angel held a bottle of beer pressed to his back as if it was a gun. "What you doin' creepin' around my property? Who sent you?" He went to turn around and she pressed the beer harder into his back. "Uh-uh-nigga. Don't move. You could be packing some heat for all I know." She eased the bottle down onto the floor. "Assume the position." She patted the inside of his thigh, causing him to spread his legs. "Hands on the wall. Now!" He did as he was told.

She began to sensually frisk him, rubbing all across his chest and shoulders. "Damn, you are built. I like what I'm feeling . . . a lot. Are you married?"

"Yes, ma'am, happily."

"Then where's your wedding ring?" She was still massaging his chest and then slid around to his back. "Oooh. Nice strong back. I like that. The ring. Where is it?"

"My wife has it. We're having a phat wedding ceremony to-morrow."

"I see." Her hands were making seductive motions across his abs. "Nice abs."

"What are you looking for, ma'am? I'm not carrying any heat."

"Then what's this?" She slid her soft hands down his boxers and up the length of his dick.

"That's my nightstick, ma'am." He closed his eyes as she stroked him the way he liked to be stroked.

"And who do you plan on using this nightstick on?" She was rubbing the precum over the head.

"I wouldn't ask that question if I was you, ma'am."

"Oh, you're getting smart? Turn around, nigga. And do it slow. Keep your hands in the air."

He did as he was told, dick throbbing, making a huge tent in his sweatpants. He looked down and smiled at his wife. Her see-through blouse was tight over her hard nipples and she had on a short-ass miniskirt that barely covered her ass.

"Keep your hands up while I check out this nightstick." She slid his boxers and sweats down a little over his ass and pulled out his dick. "Oh, shit, mister. I am really liking what I see." She began stroking him with both hands. "This . . . is . . . a . . . big nightstick," she purred. "You're making me want to fuck you." The music in the background stopped and they could hear each other's heavy breathing; then it started back up. He watched her slide down in a crouch position and put him in her mouth with one hand and start to play with her pussy with the other.

"Oh . . . sss . . ." Kaylin groaned as he put one hand on her head, trying to get her to swallow some more of him while he got really turned on as she fingered her pussy. "Damn, Ma . . . you killin' me." When he put the other hand on her head she eased his dick from her throat. "Ahhh . . . shit, that was feeling damn good."

She slowly stood up and slowly headed for the stairs. "Ma, you killin' me! Where you going? Stop playin', Red." He was holding on to his dick as his eyes worked his way from her four-inch stilettos, crept up those long, sexy legs to her ass cheeks hanging out of that skirt. Halfway up the stairs he couldn't take any more and grabbed her around her waist. Yanking the tiny skirt over her ass, he bent her over.

"Baby, my mom . . ." He was already ramming his dick into her hot, juicy pussy. "Oh . . . oh . . . oh . . . damn . . . shit mutha-fuck . . . give me that dick . . . oh, Daddy, long-stroke this . . . shit . . . give me that big fat dick . . . yes . . . good . . . Daddy . . ." He was fuckin' her so good she was talking out of her head. He was holding on to her hips with both hands ramming her with-out mercy. "Oh, shit!" she screamed as she started cumming.

Jaz stuck her head out into the hallway. When she saw Angel bent over, and Kaylin bangin' that pussy, she said, "Ooohkay!" and went back into the party.

Kaylin was still holding on tight, digging deep.

"Angel," Mrs. Smith yelled, sticking her head out into the hallway.

"Ma'am." She tried to stand up real quick. Kaylin was trying to pull his sweats over his ass while shielding her body and lead-ing her up the stairs.

"Is that the baby I hear screaming?"

"No, Mommy," she barely got out.

Mrs. Smith was staring at them suspiciously. Then she finally said, "Okay," and went back into the party.

"See what you made me do?" Kaylin told her. "You almost got us busted, and by your mother!" He pulled his dick back out and tried to bend her over again.

"Kaylin," she giggled. "No. Come on now. We have a bedroom. I got you."

"You better have me. And tell me why you're not down there enjoying your bachelorette party. I went through the trouble of getting y'all some faggot-ass strippers. Why you ain't down there putting money in their G-strings like the rest of them?" he teased as he kissed her neck.

"Because I had to feed and put your nosy daughter to sleep. Then I had to put on sumthin nice just for you. I knew you would be creeping around here before the night was over." She looked behind her and smiled at him.

"Oh, did you? And how did you know that?" He turned her loose so that he could gaze at her luscious ass.

"I knew those strippin' bitches would get you all worked up and we know that only Mami can give you the fix that you need. Nigga, I know my husband." She grinned seductively at him over her shoulder. She entered the bedroom with Kaylin on her ass. He closed the door and locked it.

She slowly took off his sweatsuit jacket and hung it up. Then she watched him as he went over to Jahara's crib in the adjacent bedroom. "How long has my precious Angel been asleep?" he asked, not taking his eyes off her.

"About a half hour. She just went right before you came in," she told him as she admired him admiring his baby. She then left him in Jahara's room and sat on the bed. "Come here. I told you that I'm not through with you. Let me give you what I've been dying to give you before she wakes up." He looked over at her. "Come here. You know you don't have any business here anyways," she teased. "You know it's bad luck to see the bride the night before the wedding. You think we would have it right by now."

He leaned over, grabbed her ass, and kissed her soft lips, her chin, her throat, back to her mouth. "We are already married, remember? So, technically, you aren't even a bride," he teased back.

"Whatever, nigga. I'll be a bride in the next few hours." She wrapped her arms around his neck.

He kissed her softly on the lips. "That was an intense fuck on the stairs. I really liked that shit."

"Me too. But I still want to do a little sumthin more to you. I'm not finished with you yet."

"What do you want to do to Daddy?" He kissed her again, this time playing with her tongue, doing a sensual tango. "Daddy needs a lot, you know he's been stressing over putting this wedding together."

"Nigga, please. You ain't did nothing. Courtney's been doing everything."

Kaylin chuckled. "Oh, so you just gonna blow up my spot like that?"

"It is what it is, negro."

They kissed again. "Well, I'm still stressing, so get back to telling Daddy what you want to do to him." He tasted her neck and hungrily nibbled over to her throat. "'Cause Daddy knows what he wants to do to Mommy."

"And what's that, Daddy?"

"Daddy wants to make love to you right now."

"No, Daddy. We have all the time in the world to make love. Tonight I want you to fuck me. Fuck me long and hard. But first, I want to suck Daddy real nice like and make him bust all in my mouth," she purred, causing his dick to twitch.

"I think he heard that." He stood up, looked down at his hard-on, and then back at Angel. "Yeah, he heard you."

She tugged at his waistband and pulled him closer. She scooted up to the edge of the bed, causing her skirt to rise all the way up. Kaylin looked down and could see a peek of her pussy, causing his dick to get even harder.

"Oooh, Daddy." She made a swift motion, pushing his baggy sweats and boxers down over his ass. She leaned over and grabbed the jar of chocolate cream that she had on the night stand. She opened it and scooped some up with her fingers and began to massage some onto his dick. "Oooh, baby, I can't wait to suck this off." She smiled as she stroked him, stretching him all the way out.

"Now, this is the shit I'm talking about. Look at this," he moaned as he glanced down at her glossed-up lips and pretty fingers wrapped around his dick.

"I'ma make him dance." She stroked him harder and flicked the head with her tongue, causing Kaylin to wiggle his toes. She stroked, and flicked, stroked, flicked, wrapped her lips around the head, teasing it with a hot, juicy mouth. "Mmmmm, you taste good, Daddy."

Kaylin grunted and closed his eyes as she fondled his nuts and sucked him harder, swallowing him deeper, moaning as if she was waiting on this dick all of her life.

He grunted again, not wanting to scream like a bitch. "Suck it, baby," he commanded. His dick was now all the way down her throat, and both of his hands grabbed on to her head as he pumped in and out, a nice thrusting rhythm, fucking her mouth, harder, faster, harder, his climax rising, feeling so good . . . rising, knees buckling, nut cumming. "Shit, oh, shit! Unggghh!" Buckets . . . that's what it felt like to him . . . buckets of cum oozing, shooting from his dick. He got that off, his legs now feeling like rubber.

She moaned and moaned as she felt him squirt down her throat and then slowly eased him out of her mouth, sucking lightly. As his breathing turned from ragged to almost normal, she sucked him to a semierection. Good enough to get her started.

"Damn, Ma. I am so in love with you," he whispered.

She eased him all the way out of her mouth, leaned back on her elbows, propping her legs up on the edge of the bed. He eased down onto his knees, ran two fingers up into her pussy, and heard her gasp. She closed her eyes as his thumb massaged her clit and his fingers worked her pussy. "Ssssss, baby," she purred.

"Whose pussy is this?"

"I love you."

"I ain't asked you that." He slapped her ass.

"Oh God . . . Dad . . . eee . . . yours . . . it's yours," she squealed as he leaned over and lapped her clit, faster, pressing his fingers deeper, faster. "I'm cum . . . ing." Her legs twitched and kicked as she fell backward.

He lifted her blouse and his mouth moved over her breasts, hungrily, as her body calmed from the orgasmic-induced trembles.

She pulled him up and their mouths met, kissing eagerly . . . hungrily. He broke loose, stood up, and damn near ripped off her blouse. "Turn over," he commanded.

Pulling her skirt up over her ass and admiring the view, he stroked himself. Angel glanced back at him, spread her legs wider, and purred, "Fuck me, Daddy, please fuck me."

Kaylin grabbed her hips and thrust hard, only to insert the head of his dick in, and pulled it back out, causing tingling sensations to tickle her pussy and nipples. She bit down on her bottom lip as Kaylin squeezed her ass while she remained doggied up with a juicy, dripping pussy.

"What?" Kaylin slapped her ass as he slid halfway in and held her hips in place.

"Oooooee, baby." She clenched her pussy muscles pulling him in . . . slowly . . . more. "C'mon , baby," she teased. "You know you want this, Daddy." He grunted as her soft, warm walls enveloped him and sucked him all the way in. She threw that pussy at him as he gripped her hips tighter and pumped in and out. "That's it, Daddy!" she squealed. "D-don't it . . . feel . . . soo good? That's it Daddy," she squealed again. "Fuck this pus . . . sy."

"Damn . . . you feel good as fuck!" he groaned, picking up his pace, grinding faster . . . harder.

"My spot," she screamed out as her pussy burst into flames. "Oh . . . Kay . . . I'm cum . . . ing." Her entire body quaked as Kaylin rode both her orgasmic wave and his own.

They remained still, trying to catch up with the rhythm of their normal breathing.

"Mmmmm, this pussy keeps me falling deeper and deeper in

love wit it." Kaylin rose, pulled his boxers and pants up, slid Angel's skirt back over ass.

She grabbed her blouse and handed it to him. He pulled her up and put it on her as she slid her hands behind his neck, pulling him close and melting into those LL Cool J lips. "I . . . love . . . you," she told him in between kisses.

"You ain't gonna have no more niggas busting up in our wedding, are you?"

She slapped him against his head. "That's not funny, Kaylin." She pouted.

"I'm just messing with you, beautiful." He hugged her. "Well . . . I guess this is it until a few hours from now."

"I know." Her stomach fluttered. They stood there hugging and reflecting as she melted farther into his embrace. "These last nine months have been crazy."

"That's putting it mildly." He peeked into the room at Jahara. "But we are more in love, right?"

She smiled. "Yes, baby. That we are."

"I'll meet you later at the altar, Mrs. Santos."

"I'll be there, Mr. Santos, with bells on."

Kaylin drew up the game plan and Courtney Moran made it happen: the ultimate hip-hop, thugged-out fairy-tale wedding.

The wedding was held at the African American History Museum, officiated by, once again, Reverend Run. The one and only Patti Labelle was hired as the star chef along with all of the catering.

The celebrity guest list included; Outkast, Jennifer Lopez, Marc Anthony, Mary J. Blige, Fat Joe, Diddy, the Queen Bee herself, Lil' Kim, Jimmy Henchman, Wyclef Jean, Queen Latifah, Angie Martinez, Juelz Santana, and Styles P.

The clothing color scheme was white on white for everyone. Angel and her bridesmaids were done up lovely by stylist Andre

Leon Talley and dressed by Beyonce's new line: House of DE. All shoes were by Zanotti.

Kaylin and the groomsmen were suited up by Sean John and finished off with Ice Cream sneakers.

Angel, her bridesmaids, Kaylin, and the groomsmen were all iced out by Jacob the Jeweler. They felt that he wasn't guilty and were showing their support.

After the wedding vows were exchanged the married couple took off their shoes and jumped the broom. Then they were serenaded with a song by the Harlem Boys Choir. That led to the cutting of the seven-tier chocolate wedding cake and then a dance by the groom and bride serenaded with a special wedding song written and performed by Jaheim and Keyshia Cole.

The wedding crowd dispersed as everyone stood outside the museum. The bride and groom along with the entire crew were paired up. Faheem and Jaz were to his left and they were flanked by Marvin and Kyra and then Bo and Shanna. To their right, Trae and Tasha, Omar and Kajuan, who rolled stag. They both asked, "Why bring sand to the beach?"

"Okay, people. Move in a little closer," the photographer instructed as he began to snap the camera. The guests were all clapping, laughing, throwing rice, and having a good time, anticipating taking the party to the reception.

"Oh, shit, cuz," DeElla yelled. "What other stars y'all got coming to the after party?"

"It's called a reception, not an after party," one of the guests snapped at her.

"It's whateva the fuck I wanna call it," she shot back.

"DeElla!" Angel shot her a look that said, *Chill.*

"Don't make me get country up in this piece," DeElla screamed.

But all eyes were glued to the shiny, jet-black stretch Navigator that was encased by a regular Navigator truck leading the way and another Navigator behind it. On the right and left of the stretch Navs were two black Mercedes-Benzes.

The motorcade slowed down in front of the wedding crowd and then came to a complete stop. Omar, Bo, and Kajuan all reached for their heat.

Trae and Kaylin looked at one another, no words needed to be said. They knew what was up.

Angel felt Kaylin tense up. "Baby, who is that?" she questioned.

Kaylin didn't hear her. He was giving the eye to his crew. "Yo—"

"We got you, nigga." Kajuan, Bo, and Omar all said it at once.

"Baby." Angel held Kaylin tighter.

Everyone's eyes went to the back door of the stretch Nav as it came open. "Kaylin!" Don Carlos called out. "Angel, you are such a beautiful bride." Don Carlos stepped out, went over to Angel, and gave her a big hug. "Congratulations." He handed her a thick envelope filled with money. "I can't stay and I do offer my sincerest apologies. But may the saints bless you both to live happily ever after." He hugged her again.

"Thank you," she told him.

"I need to borrow your husband for five minutes. Beautiful Angel, is that okay?"

Angel was still speechless.

But DeElla wasn't. "Damn! Who dat is? Mafia nigga passing out money envelopes. I wanna get married. I'll marry one of them niggas in a heartbeat! Sheeit. Thank I won't?"

"DeElla, shut up!" Angel pleaded.

"But I'm sayin—"

"Shut up!" Angel snapped.

Like I said, heey sexy," DeElla seductively called out.

Kaylin leaned down and kissed his wife on the cheek. "I'll be right back, baby, wait right here." He took off toward the Navigator, with Trae on his heels.

Tasha came over and stood next to Angel and they clasped hands.

"This is crazy. This is my fuckin' wedding day," Angel hissed.

"Chill out," Tasha warned. "Chill the fuck out. Ain't that what you told me?"

The fam was now standing as close to the motorcade as they could get, while Kaylin and Trae climbed into the limo.

Don Carlos's bodyguard, Jorge, held the door open until all three of the men climbed inside. He shut the door and stood guard.

Seated in the back of the huge limo was Don Alexjandro.

"Kaylin!" Don Alexjandro reached over and gave him a hug and kiss on the cheek. "Congratulations on your wedding day!" He handed him an envelope. Then he turned to Trae.

"Trae, Trae, Trae." He reached over and embraced him. "How are you feeling?"

"I'm getting there," Trae answered.

"It is so good to see you. You have been in the prayers of us all. I talk about you two often. The both of you were always a huge asset to our organization. Your work will never be forgotten. Good to see you, especially to see you, Trae, doing well."

"Good to see you too, Don Alexjandro."

"Gentlemen. Kaylin. Forgive me for interupting your wedding day. But I must depart the country in a couple of hours. Kaylin and Trae, let me make some brief but very important introductions. This is Don Ramirez. Don Felipe. Don Antonio. Don Adolfo. Don Mario and Don Elias. Gentlemen, this is our man," he said to the other dons seated in the limo. "Everyone . . . this is Kaylin. Kaylin Santos. This man here is responsible for ridding us of that scum Mickey." All of the dons nodded at Kaylin.

The first don, Ramirez Gonzalez, leaned over and kissed Kaylin's hand and placed an envelope in it. "Don Kaylin," he acknowledged. After that simple but important gesture the rest of everything else all became a blur and Kaylin wasn't listening. The rest of the dons followed suit doing the same thing Don Ramirez did. When they all finished everyone clapped and raised their glasses into the air for a toast. Kaylin didn't notice who poured or where the drinks came from. He was still in a daze.

Don Alexjandro handed Kaylin a glass and slapped him on the back. "Drink up."

Kaylin didn't hesitate at throwing the shot back. "May I speak what's on my mind, Don Alexjandro?"

"What's troubling you, Don Kaylin? This should be a happy moment for you." He still had his hand on his back. "You did us a huge favor. And to show you our appreciation we gave you all of Mickey's territory. Do you want more? I can always—"

"No, no, Don Alexjandro. Again, no disrespect and I'm honored. Your generosity never ceases to amaze me. Believe me, I am. Had this been years ago, maybe I would have jumped at the opportunity, but I'm done. I want out. I need out. I was under the impression that you only needed this one favor, which I had no problem with honoring. I don't want Mickey's territory. I just want out," Kaylin gritted.

"Don Kaylin, what is this about? I'm sensing some hostility. Are you in your feelings? Wait. Don't answer that. I think I know why." Alexjandro glared at him. "We have nothing against black people. Mickey disobeyed too many orders and he was bad for business, bringing too much notice to our organization. We have nothing against Mickey's illegitimate son, if that's what you are thinking."

"Don Alexjandro, what beef you and Mickey had was just that. Your beef. You used me to get the job done. I did it. My only and humble request is to be out. No territory, no strings attached. I want nothing but for you to respect my wishes. I speak for Trae as well."

Don Alexjandro looked him over. He seemed to be thinking about what he had just heard.

"I just want out, Don Alexjandro." Kaylin persisted.

"Don Kaylin, I must run this by the heads of all of the other families. Nevertheless, I will get back to you."

"Don Alexjandro, the heads of the other families are right here. Can't I get your blessing now?"

Don Alexjandro let out a chuckle. "Don Kaylin, always the one to never bite his tongue. However, there are other heads of families not present and they all voted to put you into this position. I have to take your request in front of the board. You understand, *si*?"

"I understand. We also have someone in mind to step in for me, if that will make their decision easier." Kaylin said. All eyes were on him. Trae's eyebrow shot up as if to say, *We do?*

"Do you, Don Kaylin? What is his name so that I may present this to the board as well?"

"Who says it's a him?"

Several of the dons gasped. Don Alexjandro's expression didn't change. "I see. I must be going. You will be hearing from me."

"Thank you," Kaylin said.

Don Alexjandro held out his hand. Kaylin grabbed it and they hugged. Trae did the same as they exited the limo.

"What the fuck?" Trae mumbled, trying to play it cool.

"Nigga, you heard the same shit I heard," he said, grabbing Angel's hand and kissing her on the cheek.

"Baby."

"Everything's cool, beautiful. This is our wedding day. Nothing is going to fuck it up." He gave her a gentle kiss on the lips. He placed his lips to her ear. "I just need to get my dick sucked again, just like you hooked a nigga up last night." She mushed him in the face and the photographer snapped, causing everyone to laugh.

Limos and buses were revved up, ready to take everyone to the reception held on the D & D Yacht. As everyone was unloading, ready to get crunk and get their party on, Kaylin had to check and see what all of the commotion was up ahead. He pushed through the crowd with Angel holding on to his hand.

"My water finally broke." Tasha basically jumped up and down in front of Angel. "Finally. My due date was four days ago."

"I'm getting ready to be a daddy again, everybody," Trae yelled. Kaylin and Angel both let out a huge sigh of relief.

Yo, this is Kaylin. It's been real but I'ma about to fall back, do this reception, get my honeymoon on, and chill the fuck out. Y'all thought that me and Angel had drama. That's an understatement. It's time for Wahida to show y'all what's really good with my man, Trae, and his wife, Tasha. So, stay tuned and be on the lookout for *Thug Matrimony*, *Volume II*. Or whatever Wahida is gonna call it. Oh yeah, thugs get married and fall in love too! One!

GREAT BOOKS,
GREAT SAVINGS!

When You Visit Our Website:
www.kensingtonbooks.com
You Can Save Money Off The Retail Price
Of Any Book You Purchase!

- **All Your Favorite Kensington Authors**
- **New Releases & Timeless Classics**
- **Overnight Shipping Available**
- **eBooks Available For Many Titles**
- **All Major Credit Cards Accepted**

Visit Us Today To Start Saving!
www.kensingtonbooks.com

All Orders Are Subject To Availability.
Shipping and Handling Charges Apply.
Offers and Prices Subject To Change Without Notice